REDEMPTION SONGS

REDEMPTION SONGS

LYNDA R. EDWARDS

Palmetto Publishing Group
Charleston, SC

Redemption Songs
Copyright © 2020 by Lynda R. Edwards

First Edition
Printed in the United States

ISBN-13: 978-1-64111-697-8
ISBN-10: 1-64111-697-8

THIS BOOK IS DEDICATED:

To my husband, Tim: I will never take for granted his unwavering love and support. As long as he is with me, all things are possible.

To the children of my heart, Christopher, Ethan, McKenzie, Benjamin, Liam, Austin, and Blake.

To *you*: Thank you for choosing to read this book. I hope you find Jo's story—of love, loss, betrayal, and love again—resonates with you as much as it did with me. Life was never meant to be lived in a straight line. Thank you for taking this journey with me.

TABLE OF CONTENTS

FOREWORD BY,
ANNA RUTH HENRIQUES

Award-winning artist and author of *The Book of Mechtilde*

The 1970s and 1980s in Kingston played out as a tumultuous, violent period in Jamaica's history. The island had recently gained independence from Britain. The class and color divisions were still firmly in place, yet the economy was in free fall. The United States, the new colonizer, was gaining its own foothold using the same tactics it applied to the rest of the developing world, destabilizing the leading government by arming its opposition and encouraging violence while exerting tactical financial control.

Lynda Edwards and I came of age in those times, two cousins moving from childhood through the teen years as close friends sharing a sheltered yet privileged upbringing. I spent many hours of my youth listening to Lynda's stories of the family. Her tales were compelling, a fine mix of the ordinary juxtaposed with intrigue. I chalked up her natural gift at storytelling to the eccentric family we come from, their tales compelling by their absurd truths alone.

But then the novel *Redemption Songs* arrived in my inbox. There was no discussion, just an announcement from Lynda that she'd written this book and a question next. Would I read it and let her know what I thought? Lynda values my frankness. "I know I'll get an honest opinion," she said. *Damn,* I thought, *it's her first novel and I've never known her to write anything. She might not like what I have to say.* Yet I was compelled to read it, so I delved in. To my great surprise, I couldn't put the book down. The narrative leaped off like a horse at a steeplechase, galloping, leaping, taking sudden twists and bounds while I hung on, as it raced toward an unsuspecting and dramatic end.

But it should not have surprised me. I had always known Lynda for her sharp mind, her wit, her astute observation and most memorably, her razor tongue that had me in stitches of laughter at her keen, clever, yet cutting use of language. She could assess character immediately and play it back later with honesty and humor, placing the individual in the larger context of family, society and the politics and economics of the time. It soon became clear as I read along that *Redemption Songs* is a complex distillation of imagination and experience, blended with the author's love of her country, Jamaica.

It is a story that at first seems sensational with requisite subjects of death and drugs. Yet in spite of the illicit nature of business carried out in the book, it is a modern-day mythological tale. For the story holds a greater message, one of taking responsibility of oneself and others, of righting wrongs, of recognizing duty, honor, loyalty, equality and fairness. And of course, there is love. All this made for an entertaining book, but its greater message makes it a worthy read. I then realized that Lynda herself lived her message, proving herself over and over in person as a friend, a cousin, a daughter, an aunt and a sister, qualities that now spilled forth from her into her first remarkable book.

CHAPTER 1

JOSEPHINE

Deep down, I knew something was wrong. His skin turned from a healthy tan to a dry gray and then to a brittle yellow. He lost weight and his energy level plummeted. The warm touch that could always ignite a fire in me had turned cold and frail. Thomas had slowly faded away; I had been powerless to stop it. He was only forty-three when he died and I still could not believe fate had dealt us such a cruel blow. My mind rebelled against the reality that he was no longer with me, rebelled against the notion that I would no longer see him, touch him, feel him, or breathe him in. He was my life and just like that, he died. I could not face my life without him.

I lay there in the realm between sleep and consciousness; I did not want to wake up. I dreaded opening my eyes and looking at the clock because I knew I would lose the battle to go back to sleep. I could see him, in my subconscious, in my mind's eye, holding his arms out to me, begging me to stay with him just a little longer. It was painful to give that image up. I felt the pain of loss start to radiate out of my heart and reverberate throughout my body.

I had no idea how hard it would be to lose the one person put on this earth just for me. Every bone in my body hurt; it was impossible to smile again and just getting up in the morning required more energy than I could summon. Sleep was my only respite because he was always there smiling at me, making love to me, calling me his baby girl. Thomas was alive in my dreams and so was I.

I waited to hear my mother and Aunt Julie outside the door, trying to decide if it was time to come in and wake me up. They had this discussion every morning; it was almost as if they were afraid to come in, afraid of what they would find. For the last six months they had found the same thing: me lying in bed, staring at the ceiling and praying for a few more moments of sleep, a few more moments with the man I loved. They would come in each morning, full of false cheer and a cup of tea, regaling me with all the fun they had planned for the day—another luncheon, card party, tea with my growing number of widowed aunts, or some form of shopping. There was always grocery shopping to do. Even though it was just the three of us living in the apartment (my mother, myself and Paulette, who took care of us), it seemed that the grocery shopping was almost a daily occurrence.

I lay there waiting, feeling the pain of loss wash over me and wondered for the thousandth time how I had reached this point. Married at nineteen and widowed at forty. I had been married for one more year than I had been single, and I did not know how to live without my husband. My mother said it was harder for me because we did not have children. She constantly worried that I was an only child and would be left alone and bereft in the world. Aunt Julie said it was harder because we had not had time to grow apart, but I knew it was because he was my soul mate, my better half, the reason for my being. It had only ever been him and now he was gone.

I marveled at how my mother and aunts handled widowhood. Some thrived, others managed, but all seemed willing to carry on. I did not; I just wanted my husband back. I wanted my life back. I rolled onto my back and looked out the window; the sun was high in the sky. I had lived in the United States for all of my married life, but somehow, I had never seemed to forget the Jamaica of my childhood. The sun, the sea, and the sand—constants in my childhood were now to be constants in my widowhood.

Sleep was becoming harder and harder for me. I had decided two months ago to stop taking the sleeping pills the doctor had prescribed and declined antidepressants. I was determined to feel every emotion, hoping against hope that it kept me close to him. Now I was beginning to question that decision. I had never been one to feel any emotion on a very deep level; now every emotion felt magnified, and the weight of it seemed to crush me. They were coming; I could hear the footsteps coming up the hallway. I just lay there, trying to figure out what my reaction would be, what excuse I would try to use today in the hopes of just being left alone. The door opened and only Paulette walked in with the obligatory cup of tea.

"Good mawning, Jo, time to get up. I have your tea." My name was Josephine, but my family had always called me Jo. Nicknames were common in Jamaica and because my name was so long and cumbersome, I was called Jo for as long as I could remember.

"Morning, Miss P. Are you alone?"

Paulette chuckled. "Your mother and aunt are out for the morning. It seems your cousin Beth has had yet another life-altering crisis, and a family committee has been convened to deal with it." The sarcasm in Paulette's voice was unmistakable. My cousin Beth—every family had one—was the one member of the family who had to be constantly cared for because no decision she ever made was the right one, so she was incapable of handling the consequences of her decisions. Almost every week, there was another crisis, no doubt brought on by the no-good drunk she was married to. However, today I was grateful for her meltdown; it gave me the respite I needed to do some thinking. I had to figure out what to do with the rest of my life.

"How long you think I have, Miss P?" I was cautiously optimistic.

"Probably most of the day, but I have been told not to let you stay in this room and to make sure you eat."

Paulette always knew what I wanted or needed and was willing to try to help me, first as my nanny and now as my trusted gatekeeper, but we were both limited by the powerful forces of nature who were my mother and aunts. Don't get me wrong; their hearts were in the right place. Technically, they had all been through what I was going through. I was a young widow with no children, no siblings and few people I could truly count on if I needed to. I had the rest of my life to look forward to and my compass was gone. I was adrift in the Caribbean Sea. No family committee could help me with that.

I stretched to wake up my tired body. I never seemed to feel rested anymore. Thomas used to like watching me stretch in the morning as I woke up. He said I reminded him of a contented cat. The way I stretched, with a seductive smile on my lips was always enough to get him to stay in bed with me just a little bit longer. I moved the hair out of my face; another feature Thomas had loved. It was long and thick, and he enjoyed sinking his hands into the soft strands he said felt like silk. To me, it had always been an annoyance. It was hard to manage and was constantly falling onto my face, so I pulled it into a loose bun on top of my head and reluctantly crawled out of bed.

The apartment we lived in was in the heart of the city of Kingston, on the top floor of a high-rise. The wraparound balcony offered stunning views of the Blue Mountains, the backdrop to the city. On a clear day, you could see down to the harbor, but most days, it was a wonderful perch for me to watch the hustle and bustle of the city as life moved on without my participation. It never ceased to amaze me how vibrant the colors were on my little island. The sun seemed to illuminate everything it touched; you could see every shade of green in the trees and bushes, which were everywhere you looked. Flowers of every color bloomed wild in open lots or cultivated garden beds. Even the sky seemed to be a more animated color of blue, with fluffy white clouds floating lazily along. I took the cup of tea and stood looking down at the scene below, wondering how and if I would ever fit into it.

It was time to take stock. My husband had left me financially comfortable; the American dollar went a long way in Jamaica if you were careful. I could continue to write articles for the magazines I freelanced for if I wanted to and my current living situation was working. Our house in the United States had been shuttered for months now. I could not bear the thought of going back there and having to go through our lives, deciding what to keep and what to throw away. I was not ready to face that yet. Maybe later, but not now.

Several hours went by as I sat watching the city go about its business. Everyone below seemed to have somewhere to go, something they had to be doing. The hustle and bustle of Kingston had always excited me; it was a city that never seemed to stop and I loved that. Now I just felt completely disconnected from everything I had once known. I was no closer to finding the answers I needed. I heard the front door open and knew my period of reflection, such as it was, had come to an end. I looked over and Beth's son Timothy walked toward me. It was heartbreaking to see a young boy look like he had the weight of the world on his shoulders.

"Hey, kiddo, what's going on?" I asked gently and reached for his hand.

"Dad's being unreasonable and Mum is trying to reason with him." He smiled at me ruefully. I smiled back at him.

"Some marriages can be very hard," I replied, never sure what to say to him in situations like this.

"Yours wasn't; I never saw you and Uncle Thomas fight, I never heard you say anything bad about each other."

"We sometimes argued, not very often. We never fought, that is true and no, we did not say anything bad about each other. There was nothing bad to say. Your uncle always had my back and was a good man; I would not have married him if he wasn't."

"I miss him," Tim said as he wearily put his head on my shoulder.

"I know. I miss him too." I didn't know what else to say. Thomas would have known what to say to Timmy, but I did not, so I just held his hand.

"What are you doing out here?" he asked, already bored with sitting around pondering life's woes. The optimism of youth wasn't missing in this one.

"Just sitting here and watching."

He thought that was funny. "Mum says that is all you do, sit around and watch life pass you by."

"Interesting insight, coming from your mother." I regretted saying it the minute the words left my mouth, but Beth knew how to push my buttons. She should be trying to figure out the mess that was her life, not criticizing how I was living or not living mine. But it seemed everyone had an opinion on how I should be living my life.

I tried to change the subject. "Well, it is not often I get to spend time with my favorite cousin." Due to Beth's petty jealousies and insecurities constantly getting in the way. Thomas and I had always had a special bond with Timmy and we had tried to spend as much time with him as his mother would allow. Beth is a firm believer in using any weapon available to her, including her son. What she was too wrapped up in herself to realize is that it hurt Timmy more than it hurt Thomas or me. Maybe she did realize it and didn't care. When someone is that selfish and self-involved, it is hard to understand their motivations. My mother and aunts wanted her to divorce her husband, but I didn't. Strangely enough, they were perfectly suited for each other and deserved the hell of a life they had created together. The only casualty was this darling boy, who did not deserve to get caught in their dysfunction. As Thomas used to say, there are always innocent bystanders that will get hurt in any conflict.

"He is going to have dinner with us tonight," my Aunt Julie announced as she entered. "Time to wash up for dinner, darling." Her smile was gentle as we both watched Tim disappear into the apartment.

"Your cousin seems determined to live her own version of *Dante's Inferno* and take us all along for the ride." Aunt Julie's smile was no longer gentle. She had never been a fan of Beth's and resented the soft spot my mother seemed to have for her favorite niece. Aunt Julie could never understand why my mother coddled Beth as much as she did and felt it had turned out to be a disservice to Beth in the long run.

"Have you been out here all day?" Julie asked.

"Yes, just trying to figure things out. I answered some emails; one of the magazines I write for wants me to do an article about the true Jamaica, an insider's guide to living like a Jamaican. I am trying to decide if I want to do it."

"Living like a Jamaican, eh? Would that be the privileged version or the impoverished reality they want?" While Jamaica was famous around the world for its music, cuisine and a laid-back lifestyle envied by most, we were equally known for the tribalism that warring political parties had created over the years and the disturbing violence that came along with it. No matter which political party ruled Jamaica,

7

their motto seemed to be "Keep them poor, keep them hungry, keep them ignorant and we keep our power." It seemed to be working well for the politicians, but not so well for the rest of the populace.

"I haven't decided if I want to do it yet," I replied quietly.

"If it gets you out of this apartment, I say go for it." Aunt Julie was never one for mincing words. I quietly looked down at my hands folded in my lap. I never knew how to respond to comments like that. It's not that I didn't want to do something; I didn't know what I wanted to do. Isn't that what being lost was?

"Well, I suggest you get ready for dinner too. Your mother will be back with Beth soon." Oh God, dinner with Beth, I knew that was something I did *not* want to do.

CHAPTER 2

LONG NIGHTS

It had finally arrived: the night I had been dreading since my life had turned upside down. I could not sleep and I was in a panic. If I could not sleep, I could not dream and if I could not dream, I could not be with Thomas. The one respite from this overwhelming grief was sleep and now it was eluding me. I was trapped! If I left my bedroom, someone would hear me and run to keep me company, forcing me to talk. I looked around in desperation; there had to be a way out. A breath of fresh air, *yes, that would be perfect*. Escape into the night air so I could breathe. A door next to my bed opened out onto a small patio the size of a postage stamp. It could hold a chair and little else, but it was outside and for some reason, that is where I needed to be now.

I opened the door and stepped out, breathing deeply. The moon was high in the sky and the stars shone brightly as only they could shine on my island, twinkling like diamonds against an ink-black sky. I closed my eyes and took a deep breath. I looked around and wondered why I had never come out here before; it was very quiet and peaceful, high above the activity on the street below. I looked down and was surprised to see so many people out and about at this time of night. I focused on the people below and stared to watch their lives unfold.

The four women standing in front of the large gate were dressed very provocatively and I finally realized they were prostitutes. Two men standing off to the side seemed to be their security guards and the men coming and going were their customers. I had never seen this kind of real-life drama before and was quite fascinated. The men came and went, but the women always came back, handing something to the bodyguards upon their return. It took me a few minutes to figure out that it was money they were handing over. It dawned on me that they were not bodyguards but pimps. It was an interesting insight into human nature. The women talked, joked, and smiled among themselves, but you could see the change in their demeanor when their customers arrived. The relaxed chatter ended and they were all business while trying to entice the men to hire them. The pimps were all business all the time, overseeing the women, always within menacing earshot as prices were negotiated and giving discreet nods to the women when an agreement was satisfactory to them. A couple of times, I saw them step in to run someone off who was not a customer but one of the many beggars hanging around trying to get a much-needed handout. You could tell the pimps were violent men and I wondered what happened to the women if they tried to defy them in any way. I settled in to watch and before I knew it, the sun was coming up.

Watching had been my nightly ritual for nearly a week now. As sleep eluded me and I became more anxious, I would slip out onto the tiny balcony and watch the show below. I had given the women names. The smallest one—and I assumed the youngest—I had named Tiny. She was about five-feet-two and looked young. I couldn't guess how old she was under all the makeup. Then there was

Mother, who seemed to me to be the oldest and more experienced of the group; she also appeared to be the leader and stepped in when negotiations were not going well. Finally, you had Precious and Dancer. Precious always seemed to be smiling, happy, and jovial. I wished I could see her eyes to see if they matched her smile. Dancer, well, her name was obvious. She never stopped dancing and seemed to be the most popular with the customers. The pimps I nicknamed Frick and Frack. Frack was far more vicious than Frick and I had watched him slap the girls around a couple of times, except for Mother. Neither of them seemed to mess with Mother. I watched and waited anxiously for her to step in and stop Frack's attack on the girls, which she did every time.

Something is fascinating about watching human degradation. My upbringing had conditioned me to find this nightly soap opera abhorrent, but I found it intriguing. More and more, I found myself curious about who these people were. All my life, I had been taught to stay away from people like these. They were the sad souls who lived in the shadows, not in the bright Jamaican sun. What was the Jamaican saying? "Cockroach don't belong in fowl fight." The injustices that these women faced, the hardship—just watching them fight and scrape for every scrap gnawed at my sensibilities, but common sense warned me that they probably would not appreciate my opinion of their lives.

What would I say? "I have been watching you for the last week and your life sucks. How bad is it that you have to sell yourself for money?" I didn't think they would appreciate those observations and questions. More importantly, I didn't think they would appreciate my pity. I resented everyone who approached me with pity instead of understanding. Why would they be any different? Of course, this was all rational for what I was feeling: fear. Fear of these people who might think it best to rob me, try to take advantage of me in some way, or even kill me. If I was completely honest with myself, it was fear that kept me away, nothing more than that.

CHAPTER 3

A SNOWBALL IN HELL

Hurricane Beth swept through with all the lightning and thunder of a category five storm. I arrived to find my mother and Aunt Julie bent over her as Paulette rushed off to get an ice pack and antiseptic. Battered and bruised from a run-in with her husband, her hysterics could be heard throughout the apartment.

"What the hell happened?" Aunt Julie demanded.

Still sobbing, Beth managed to choke out, "It was my fault, Aunt Julie. I pushed him to this with my constant demands." She dissolved into tears.

"Seriously, Beth? You are blaming yourself for your coward of a husband beating you to a pulp?" I could not believe what my idiot cousin was saying.

Beth shot me a look and I understood immediately what this was all about. She had come to get from my mother and aunt what her husband had denied her.

"What did you ask for?" my mother asked anxiously. In my mind's eye, I could see her reaching for her checkbook.

"I need a new car and I just kept pushing and nagging him..." She trailed off as the waterworks started again.

"Where is Timmy? Has he had to see you like this?" I didn't want him seeing his mother in this condition.

Beth did not acknowledge my question. "No, dear, Tim is sailing this week and won't be back until next weekend." Aunt Julie was quick to answer me and I knew she was grateful for small mercies.

Her husband arrived, looking wildly around to see who could be a possible threat to his control over Beth. Peter was a short man with a round shape. I could never understand why Beth found him attractive. My father, Aunt Julie and my uncles were tall people with slim but agile builds; all of us were lithe and moved with grace and elegance, while Peter Clark seemed to shuffle along. More than once Thomas and I had commented on how grateful we were that Timmy took after Beth in height and features instead of the slug he had for a father. I could see him relax and smirk when he realized that it was just women and none of my male uncles or cousins had been summoned yet. He quickly realized this was a situation he could deal with and assumed his most commanding voice.

"Beth, why do you always run home to your family every time we have a little misunderstanding?"

"Misunderstanding? Look at what you have done to her!" Aunt Julie's anger and resentment were evident. Beth was already getting up to run into his outstretched arms. I stepped in between them and faced her husband.

"What kind of coward lifts his hand to a woman in anger? You don't even have the right to call yourself a man; you are lower than the dirt you walk on." Everyone was shocked into silence by my outburst.

I turned to Beth. "How can you possibly blame yourself for him hitting you? Don't you have any pride, Beth? Don't you have any consideration for yourself and your family having to see you like this? You can't seriously be going back to him?"

Her husband found his voice. "Shut up, bitch! You're just jealous because she has a real man in her bed, while you lie in yours pining away for a ghost."

I could not help myself. A right cross and then a left hook followed by a round kick and he was lying on the floor gasping for air as all hell broke loose. Beth swore at me as she ran to him. The look on my mother's face told me that she blamed me for sending Beth right back into his arms. I thought it best if I left the room.

The night only got worse. Frack was particularly vicious tonight, continually picking on Precious. I turned away. I don't understand why men think they have the right to treat women as their punching bags. Maybe it was best if I forgo the show tonight and take a walk. I was angry at everyone. Angry at Beth for being pathetic and weak, angry at my mother for always taking Beth's side instead of forcing her to face reality—there was no point in being mad at her husband because you can't blame a dog for being a dog. But most of all, I was mad at Thomas for leaving me to deal with this crap. That thought led to an overwhelming sadness enveloping me. I could not breathe.

I took the elevator to the ground floor and waved to the security guard as I scurried through the gate. I could see him stand in alarm, obviously wanting to ask me what I was doing walking around at this hour of the night, but I did not want anyone to stop me. I didn't know where I was going, but my subconscious did. I took off in the direction of my nightly show. It was a ten-minute walk. I rounded the bend in the road and stopped dead in my tracks as I saw Frack pinning Precious against a tree as he raped her, right there in front of everyone. All but Frick looked away. The pity the ladies felt for Precious was painfully evident on their faces. Again, anger took over and before I realized it, Frack was on the ground, grabbing his groin in pain as my kickboxing skills were put to good use.

Breathing hard, I looked around at the shocked faces staring back at me. Having never seen anything like this before or even imagined that something like this could happen, disbelief made everyone motionless. No one knew if the crazy white woman standing in front of them was real or a ghost. *I must look like the White Witch of Rose Hall;* I thought as Tiny made a sign of the cross to protect herself.

That was until they heard the police sirens. The sound seemed to mobilize everyone and they took off in all directions, except, of course, for Frack, who could not move even though he very much wanted to. I stepped out of the road as two squad cars surrounded us. I was surprised to hear a familiar voice. "Jo, what the hell?" I turned to look at my cousin Simon, the police commissioner.

I was suddenly very tired. "Simon, what are you doing here?"

"I think the more important question is, what are *you* doing here?" he asked. When I did not answer, he volunteered, "The security guard called your mother when you bolted through the gate and she called me. What are you doing out here at this hour? It is not safe for you to be out here." He looked around at the tableau in front of him. Except for Frack writhing in pain on the ground, no one moved.

As if on cue, Frack groaned in agony and it was obvious he felt it was safer for me to be out there than him. "I decided to go for a walk," I said as I turned toward the apartment building and headed back to face the music.

My mother and Aunt were apoplectic. They feared my grief had finally caused a break with reality, so they were busy convening a family meeting to decide how to handle this latest development. I sat quietly and watched all the excitement, wishing I could wake up to find out I'd had a bad dream.

Simon arrived and took a seat beside me. "You mind telling me what that was all about?" Simon was a good man and I had always been fond of him. His quiet, gentle nature belied a man who was as tough as nails, but fair and decent as well. His job was seen as beneath him by the rest of my family, but his sense of duty and purpose was stronger than my family's disapproval.

"I haven't been able to sleep at night, so I have been going out on my little balcony and watching the people on the street." I was not sure how much to say.

"You mean watching the whores, pimps, and street hustlers? They are the only ones out there at that hour of night." There was no fooling Simon.

"I am sure if they could find something else to do to put food in their mouths, they would," I snapped at Simon; no one had the right to judge these people.

"I'll give you that. Go on." I told him everything—how long I had been watching them, the names I had given them and my observations about them.

"Frick and Frack are the pimps and the protection, but they abuse them terribly, which is not fair because they would not be able to earn a penny without those girls, but the girls could certainly earn without them. They should work for the girls, not the other way around!" I was angry at the unfairness of it.

"You don't know how the system works. These women are discarded by society and deemed worthless. These men take advantage of that, but they do provide valuable protection. You don't want to know how many prostitutes we fish out of the harbor or find in gutters with needles in their arms. It is men that run the sex trade, always have and always will." Simon's acceptance of these circumstances shocked me.

"How can you be so cavalier about it?" I asked. "Suppose it was one of your sisters!"

"It wouldn't be one of my sisters," he replied flatly.

"Simon, would it be too outrageous for me to ask if the police could provide protection?"

He laughed at this suggestion. "You do know that prostitution is illegal, right?"

"So are drugs, but the politicians and lawmakers in this country make too much money off of the trade to enforce any laws. Ganja has surpassed beautiful beaches as the reason tourists come to the island."

Simon did not answer me and looked away. "I am not asking you to protect the act of prostitution; I am asking you to protect citizens from being robbed, raped, and murdered."

"Why does this mean so much to you?" It was my turn to look away. How do I explain that it was time for someone to get a break, time for the cycle to cease, time for someone to be happy since I never would be again? How could I explain that helping them made my life not feel so hopeless and unfulfilled?

"They will never go for it, Jo. They don't trust the police, and I can't ensure that my guys won't take advantage of the situation either."

"Let me talk to them! Let me give these women the option and see if they will go for it. I will ask if they know any policemen they can trust and then I will talk to those officers myself. If they tell me to go to hell, I will drop the whole thing, I promise."

I could tell that Simon would agree to this because he believed a snowball had a better chance of surviving in hell than I did of pulling this off. "Okay, but you have to explain what you are doing to your mother and Aunt Julie and get their blessing first. Once they sign off on it, I will help you if I can."

Another snowball in hell that had to survive.

CHAPTER 4

THE WHORE'S CO-OP

It had taken me two days to calm my mother and aunt down, then convince them I wasn't' losing my mind. They made it clear that they did not approve of my new project but decided it was best to concede this battle for the sake of winning the war. It was going to be a lot harder to convince the ladies of my good intentions. I was not sure what my intentions were; this could be over long before it ever really got started if the women decided I was just a crazy white woman who had no right to involve herself in their lives.

My best course of action would be to convince Mother. Once I had her blessing, I think she could sell my plan to the other women. I just had to figure out exactly what my plan was.

I rounded the bend and saw Mother and the two women at their usual spot. Frick and Frack were gone and the women were more nervous and furtive than before. All but Mother backed away as I approached. She watched me suspiciously as I walked over to the women. It was obvious they were not happy to see me.

"Good evening," I said to Mother and nodded in the direction of the other two women. No one moved and no one said a word. All eyes were on me.

"My name is Josephine—everyone calls me Jo—and I live in the apartment complex over there." I pointed nervously to the imposing building in whose shadow they stood. Their eyes followed my finger and then turned back to me; no one said a word.

"I watch you every night from my balcony…"

"From your balcony, you watch us? Why?" Mother's voice was hoarse and deep; the sound of it startled me.

"I can't sleep at night, so…so I watch you." My explanation sounded silly, even to my own ears.

"Why a little lily-white princess like you caan' sleep at night?" Mother asked. Her tone was harsh but curious. "You tink because you caan' sleep at night, you have the right to come down here and mash-up we business? Police pass by here every hour now and we caan' do no business, is that because of you?" Mother took a step toward me.

"I thought they could offer you some protection; my cousin is the police commissioner and I…" I was beginning to understand the meaning of "Cockroach don't belong in fowl fight." I had only managed to make things worse for them, much worse. Because of police protection, no customers were approaching them.

"I'm very sorry; I guess I did not think this through."

"Think what through? Why would a lily-white princess even bother with the likes of us? Why you involve yourself in what you don't know about?" And there it was: in trying to make myself feel better, I had done a lot of damage. The force of this revelation unbalanced me and I sat on the curb. I had no idea what to do now.

"I am so sorry; I saw Beth abused and then Precious and I don't understand why men like that are allowed to live while my Thomas died. He was such a good man; he loved me, protected me and has always believed in me. He was everything to me, then fate took him and left men like Frick and Frack and Beth's worthless husband. I don't understand..." I looked at Mother, who had moved closer to me, her eyes compassionate but still distrustful. Precious and Dancer looked at me like I had confirmed their suspicion that I was, in fact, crazy. They wanted nothing to do with me.

"You husband dead?" she asked. I managed an affirmative nod.

"How long ago?" she asked.

"Six months ago." My voice was soft and I knew I sounded defeated.

Mother sat down next to me. "I remember what it was like was six months after my husband died. You feeling like your insides are outside your body, you can't get warm, colors don't look so bright and everything seems to move in slow motion." I looked at her, slightly stunned. I had never been able to put into words as eloquently as she just had how I was feeling.

"You were married?" I could have kicked myself the minute the words came out of my mouth.

Mother laughed. "Yes, I was married for a long time and had children, too, but my husband was murdered. I had two children to take care of and whoring was the only way I could earn enough money to take care of them."

I looked at Mother, really looked at her. I saw the story of love, loss, tragedy and circumstance written all over her face. This woman had lived a tough life but had never given up because she had to live for her children. She did what she had to do and never questioned why. I felt embarrassed by my self-pity and the extent to which I had indulged it. This woman had never had a moment in her life to feel self-pity, much less lose herself to it

"I'm lost." I looked into her eyes and could tell she understood what I meant. This whore sitting on a street curb in the middle of the night was the first person to understand what I was feeling.

"I know, but I can't help you," Mother said bluntly and stood up. "We can't stay here because we not making any money because of what you did, so we have to find another corner and we have to find a way to take care of ourselves. You can't help me with dat and I can't help you. You need to go back to your balcony, little lily-white princess and get on wid' your life and we have to get on wid' ours."

Before I knew it, I was on my feet. "I can help you."

Mother looked at me. "I think you have helped enough," she said curtly.

"You know, the most selfish thing you can do is help someone in need and the most generous thing someone in need can do is accept the help," I said softly.

Mother moved closer to me and spoke gently. "Which one is you and which one is me?"

I looked away; I honestly did not know.

"How you think you can help, little lily-white princess?"

"I don't know. Tell me about yourself." For the next two hours, I listened to stories only too familiar in the lives of women in third-world countries. Born into a cycle of poverty that they never could break, stories of abuse by parents who were supposed to protect their children, stories of abandonment, rejection, lack of opportunities, leading to a lack of self-worth and a feeling that they were no better than their circumstances. It was the worst humanity had to offer and something I had never experienced in my own life. I could sympa-thize, but I could not empathize. I realized that was my limitation, not theirs. Compared to these women, my life was blessed. I had a roof over my head, food to eat, money in the bank and all the comforts in life I could ever want, but I was weak and self-indulgent. These women had nothing and they were strong and self-reliant. I realized I could learn a lot from them and maybe, just maybe, they could teach me how to join the world of the living again.

Slowly a plan of action came together. I asked Simon to have the police keep their distance but still keep watch. I also kept my distance because customers were put off by a crazy white woman standing under the tree watching them. Mother laughed that I was better protection than Frick and Frack and far less vicious. It took time for trust to build, but when the women realized I was serious about finding a solution for them, progress was quick.

It turned out that the best business model for a whore was a co-op. They needed to make money, yes, but they also required child-care during the days and nights as well as medical care for themselves and their children and some form of money management because traditional banking institutions were not available to them. It turned out that if you are not a productive member of society, then you don't really exist in society, so we had to get creative.

The first step was to find a place of business and that is where I was able to help. Right in the heart of the working girls' business area was an abandoned hotel. The infrastructure was sound, but the building had been abandoned for years and tracking down the owner of the building took some effort. He was an old man who lived alone, but was willing to accept some comfort, cooking and housekeeping services in exchange for "reopening" the hotel and putting all the utilities in his name. Once I had negotiated that agreement, we moved on to the next phase of the operation.

The first floor of the hotel was perfect for "working." The front desk would check-in the customers and direct them to the rooms they would use to conduct their business on the first floor. The second and third floors were perfect for living quarters. With "families" living there and adding some legitimacy, the landlord was more comfortable with this arrangement. All but forgotten by Jamaican society, he still felt the need to show some degree of decorum.

We got to work setting up the hotel for business and living. I was amazed at how industrious these women turned out to be. All the furniture came from the garbage. The women knew exactly which neighborhoods to go to score great furniture tossed out into the street. I soon learned that they were carpenters, seamstresses and interior decorators who could do a lot with very little. I also learned how scorned and shunned these women were by society.

Like most societies grown out of colonial rule, Jamaica was more class conscious than color conscious. Class was determined by the cars you drove, the house you lived in, whether or not your children went to private or public schools as well as who your family and friends were.

In the 1970s, Jamaican politicians tried to capitalize on the black power movement by attempting to change this colonial class dynamic by making it about color. Joshua Patterson's socialist rhetoric advocated for a redistribution of the island's wealth, but because he, himself was a member of Jamaica's elite ruling class, with an Anglo-Saxon mother, this reform failed. Dire consequences to the island's economy were still being felt fifty years later. His rhetoric had shone a spotlight on the small white population of Jamaica, whose roots were deeply entrenched and nurtured the financial survival of the island. This economic power was resented by those who felt they would never share in it, much less benefit from it.

But Benji had shared in it and benefited from it. Benji not only worked for my father as his driver, but my father also considered him a friend and confidant. Benji's wife, Edna, worked in the secretarial pool of my father's office and they had been married two weeks after my father and mother were married. My father cut his honeymoon short to be Benji's best man at his wedding to Edna, much to my mother's dismay. Benji and Edna had a nice car to drive and owned their own home. Their children had gone to one of the best public schools Jamaica had to offer. Both had gone on to university and also worked for my father in senior positions. Benji attributed his success to my father's support and was loyal to my father, as much in life as now in his death. So, it was with great anxiety and opposition that Benji was recruited to drive the whores of the Working Women's Association of Jamaica around to the affluent neighborhoods of Jamaica looking for cast-off furniture.

After subjecting me to an hour of sermonizing on the impropriety of my association with these women and the shame it caused not only me but also my family and his family, Benji recognized my tilted head, my arms defensively crossed in front of me and the steel in my eyes as my father's resolve and understood I would not be dissuaded. He spent the next few days slumped down in the driver's seat of his small truck, hurrying the girls along and praying no one would recognize him. His payment was sitting me down again and lecturing me on how improper my behavior was and what an embarrassment I was to his good friend, my father. I thanked him for his support and left him to his righteous indignation. *Whatever got the job done*, I thought to myself.

Once word of the "whores' co-op" got out, the good, the bad, and the ugly surfaced. The good turned out to be women who needed work at the co-op. Mother, Precious and Dancer were able to recruit some interesting characters. Mary turned out to be a teacher who'd developed a nasty drug habit and had suffered mercilessly at the hands of her various pimps. She had been able to get clean but not break the cycle of whoring, so Mother arranged for her to teach the children of the working women in exchange for room, board and a modest stipend. It did not take long for her to blossom under the dignity of getting her self-respect back and returning to something she had loved to do. It turns out drug addiction would never be a problem for her again and she would see 90 percent of her students go on to earn tertiary degrees.

Aggie had been in the business since the age of twelve. No one knew how old she was, but judging by her looks, life had not been kind to her. In her case, looks were deceiving because she turned out to be a genius with scheduling and organization and had the first floor running like a *Fortune* 500 business in no time. She found other "old whores" who would cook, clean and babysit for room and board and a chance at some kind of retirement plan. Two weeks of marketing on the streets to old customers was all it took to put the girls back in business.

The bad came in the form of not being able to use traditional banking institutions. It took some time for a solution to present itself and it came from the most unexpected of places.

My husband's best friend was a man by the name of Michael Fremlin. I never really understood why Thomas liked him so much. He was sarcastic, rude, offensive—and those were his good traits. Thomas had loved his sense of humor and always told me he had a heart of gold; he just hid it well.

Michael took me to dinner once a month. I think it was his way of keeping Thomas's memory alive for himself. I had always found these dinners to be tedious and uncomfortable because, frankly, the only thing we had ever had in common was Thomas, but Michael was a financial genius and I soon realized he had valuable knowledge that would benefit the co-op. While I had learned to be on time during my years with Thomas, Michael was always on "Jamaica time," and I realized I would be sitting by myself for at least the next half hour. I ordered a drink and remembered when and where Michael had brought Thomas into my life.

We were on summer break; I was heading into my final year of high school in the fall and looking forward to my seventeenth birthday. During school holidays, Kingston was hopping with parties every weekend and I had begged Simon to take me to one at Morgan's Harbor. I loved to dance and tried not to miss any opportunity to do so. I was swaying to the music, standing next to Simon, when he was joined by an old friend, Michael and his American friend from the University of Central Florida, where they both attended school. I noticed Thomas Blakely right away. He was tall and lean with dark-blond hair. He had delicate features that clearly showed off his Viking ancestry. I knew right away that his chest would be rock solid if I rested my head against it and that his arms would make me feel welcome and warm if he wrapped me in them. I was immediately attracted to him, as he was to me. He asked me to dance and I was surprised at how well he moved to Caribbean music. He was a quick study, agile on his feet and I thought he was beautiful. We dated through the summer, but he promised to be back for Christmas break. I thought that would be the last of it. After a tearful goodbye at the airport, I realized I could not wait to see him again at Christmas.

True to his word, he was back with Michael for the Christmas holidays. I was busy applying to universities in Miami and Tampa when Michael suggested that I consider the University of Central Florida in Orlando.

"Why would I consider that one?" I teased.

"Because I am there and we could be together all the time." Thomas was dead serious, so without another thought, I applied and was accepted. For the first year, I was under eighteen, so I had to live in the dorms. As my second year approached, Thomas and I rented a house with friends, but we still maintained separate bedrooms. Thomas wanted to make sure we were friends before we were lovers.

The night of my eighteenth birthday was fast approaching. I knew I was in love with Thomas and I knew he loved me too. He had been hounding me about what I wanted for my birthday. I finally worked up the courage to tell him.

"I want you," I said softly.

"You have me. What do you want?" It took a moment for him to realize what I was saying. "Are you sure? Are you ready?" he asked, hope in his eyes. He had been so patient and had waited so long.

"Yes. I have never wanted anything in my life more than I want you," I said and kissed him shyly. I left everything to Thomas and he did not disappoint. He took me to Cocoa Beach outside of Orlando. He instinctively knew that I would be more at ease in surroundings I knew and trusted. Having been around the ocean all my life, he knew it was my happy place. He picked a small inn right on the beach. We could see the dunes and the waves crashing into them from the balcony. As sunset approached, he took me in his arms and we watched the sun sink into the ocean. He kissed me with all the longing and tenderness he had been keeping at bay for the last year. I was lost. He took his time and allowed my desire to build to dizzying heights. Many years later, he had admitted that he had used every ounce of self-control he had because he wanted our first time to be perfect. We made love through the night and I knew he was the man I would spend the rest of my life loving. I woke up in his arms and realized that I had been right. Being in the circle of his arms made me feel welcome and warm.

"Marry me!" he whispered in my ear.

"What?" I turned around to face him as he continued to hold me.

"Marry me! I graduate in April; I have a good job lined up. We can buy a house. You can fix it up any way you want, finish school and we can have the most amazing life together." He had it all planned out.

"Yes, yes! A thousand times, yes," I said as I kissed him. I did not think that making love could get any more beautiful than it had the night before, but Thomas took me in his arms and showed me all the passion and love that would be ours for all of our time together.

For the Christmas holidays, we returned to Jamaica together. Thomas had invited my parents out to dinner and just after dessert was served, he asked my father for my hand in marriage. My mother squealed in delight; she loved Thomas, but my father was not as enthusiastic.

"Josephine is still a young girl, too young to know what she wants and too young to make a commit for the rest of her life," my father responded. I was livid and about to tell him off when Thomas took my hand to stop me.

"I love your daughter more than anything and I want to make her happy. I am prepared to spend the rest of my life doing just that. I intend to make her my wife and I would rather do it with your blessing." Thomas's voice was quiet but firm.

"Jack," my mother said. "He loves her." She held up her hands as if that explained everything.

"Where will you live? How will you provide for her? She is not exactly low maintenance," my father cautioned.

I could tell Thomas was losing patience. His mouth tightened, but he kept his cool. He objected to my father's characterization of me because that was not the woman he loved. We worked at being true partners to each other and Thomas was offended by my father's portrayal of me. This dinner would be the start of a tense relationship between Thomas and my father. "We will live in Orlando; we are going to buy a house. Jo will finish school and we will start our life there."

My father scoffed at that statement. "If my daughter lives in the United States, she will be your responsibility financially. I am not going to pay for a married woman to finish an education abroad."

I could feel the tension in Thomas's body as he physically recoiled from my father. "Josephine will be my wife and my responsibility; I am not asking you for a damn thing."

"Daddy, please. I love Thomas and we want to be together." Thomas's proposal could not have gone worse.

"Come to my office tomorrow and we will discuss this in more detail. I will give you my answer then." My father's dismissive tone pissed Thomas off. He had asked for the bill, paid it, and we had left. Thomas did not say a word about what had transpired while I was flush with indignation.

The next day Thomas went to meet my father as I waited with my mother. I was still mad as hell and let my mother have it. She said nothing in defense of my father and advised that we wait to see what the outcome of the meeting was. Thomas and my father arrived for cocktails and I could sense the tension between them. Thomas came directly to my side, kissed me and squeezed my hand comfortingly. I could tell he was depleted from his time with my father. Honestly, my father did not look much better.

"Jo, I want you to be at least nineteen when you get married. I will agree for you to marry Thomas if you take the next year to make sure this is what you want and that you can build a satisfactory life for yourself in Orlando. If it works out, we will set the wedding for December twenty-first of next year." My father had spoken.

I kissed Thomas joyfully as my mother hugged my father. My father did not look happy and Thomas did not look like he had just won, but my mother and I were thrilled and started wedding plans as my father and Thomas sat silently, listening to us and drinking heavily for the rest of the night.

The next year was a whirlwind, and before I knew it, Thomas and I were standing in front of three hundred people, exchanging marriage vows and promising to love each other forever. The wedding was a circus, but Thomas and I had agreed to keep it about the two of us. On our honeymoon, we had a second ceremony just for us, where we reaffirmed our commitment to each other in an intimate and meaningful way. Thomas never told me what he and my father had discussed and for some unknown reason, I did not want to know, so I never asked him about it.

I was reluctantly snapped out of my reverie as Michael took his seat across from me, apologizing for being late.

I had tried to be very discreet in my dealings with the co-op. After all, my cousin was the police commissioner and my family had a reputation to uphold, but I also lived on a small island with a very small "high" society whose main currency was gossip. While Simon had opted to look the other way, Michael was not as supportive when I explained to him what I needed.

"You are doing *what?*" Heads turned in the restaurant to look at us. The incredulous look on Michael's face was enough to make me think that this may have been a bad idea.

"These women have been subjugated their entire lives, taken advantage of, abused. They have an opportunity to take charge of their lives, break the cycle of poverty and give their children a better life, but I need your help." I tried to explain.

"My help? Are you kidding me? If Thomas were alive, this would kill him!" He instantly knew he had gone too far with that comment. I decided to take full advantage of his discomfort.

"Michael, we live in a matriarchal society. Women are the backbone of this island and they keep the economy running while raising the next generation, mostly on their own. It does not matter which strata of society they come from; women run things, but these women need help and I don't know how to help them. You do."

"Why do you think I can help them?"

"Because you are a financial wizard. These women are not a part of traditional society; they have no papers. They can't even open bank accounts. They have no clue how to handle their finances. I was hoping you would be able to advise them."

"Seriously, you are asking me to give free financial advice to a bunch of whores?"

"No, I am asking you to give free financial advice to a group of women who need to find a way to take care of themselves and their children because they don't have anyone else to help them."

Michael thought about this for a second. "How do they run this 'business'?"

"Well, it is pretty simple. Cash in and cash out. The ladies have bartered for the rent, so there's no money exchanging hands there. The landlord covers the utilities. They give him cash for that because they are in his name. They buy food, clothes, school supplies and then divide up what is left. Right now, any extra money they have, they hide it in their pillows."

"Jesus, I can't believe I am about to say this." Michael shook his head and took the plunge. "They need to start a not-for-profit company with a board of directors. The first thing they should do is take out a loan and buy the building. Then set up a school, salaries where they pay all the necessary taxes and a retirement plan. Put all the money back into the company and, well, don't make a profit."

"How are they going to set up a company and get a loan? They don't even have birth certificates. Michael, these women don't even exist."

"But you do. You will have to start this process for them. Jo, this is Jamaica. If you can't find their birth certificate, buy them one. If you want this to work, you are going to have to put some skin in the game; put your money where your mouth is. Pick your cliché. You want to legitimize the invisible? Then you need to make them visible first."

Reality was starting to set in. Just how involved did I want to get with the Working Women of Jamaica? *That is an excellent name for the co-op*, I thought to myself. I did not think this through. Thomas would have. He would have taken my enthusiasm for this idea, sat me down and walked me through it before I committed. But he was not here and I had leaped before I had fully looked. Michael could see realization was beginning to set in.

"You still think this is a good idea? Something *you* should get involved with? What will your family say, Jo? This is not exactly how uptown ladies of Kingston spend their days." He was right. There would be consequences for me.

The first thing Thomas did when we got married was move me back to the States with him. He loved my family and they loved him, but he quickly realized that for our marriage to work, we needed to be away from their influence and he was right. For twenty-one years, we had made all the decisions about how we lived our lives. It was an independence I cherished and I was not going to give it up. At least not willingly.

"I have a favor to ask."

"Another one?" Michael was reaching his limit with this conversation and my next question could very well push him over the edge.

"Will you be on the board of directors with me?" I saw Michael choke on his drink. As he turned beet red, I plunged in. "If my family knew you were involved, they would not object to my involvement and you know it. You brought Thomas into my life; at our wedding, you said you had introduced him to his most expensive souvenir. You know Thomas would have loved this. Please, Michael, for Thomas, for me." It was the biggest weapon in my arsenal, and I had used it.

"Let me get this straight." He was not going down without a fight; it was the Michael way. "You want *me* to be on the board of directors of a whorehouse because you think Thomas would have loved the idea?" Now he was mad. "The only thing Thomas loved was *you* and if he thought this put you in any danger, he would have torpedoed it and you know it. I know you are going through something—the whole island knows you are going through something—but you are sadly mistaken if you think you are dragging me down into your crazy pit." His response was not what I had expected.

"Going through something?" I asked, controlling my anger.

"Yes, everyone is talking about you, the withering widow. You left for twenty-one years. Now you come back all battered and broken, what did you expect? You thought the sun would warm you like Thomas did and bring you back to life? The waves would soothe your soul and the sand would dry your tears? You miss Thomas; we get it. We all miss Thomas, but he died, Jo, not you." I could almost hear Thomas's voice.

Michael looked like I had hit him; he was more shocked at his outburst than I was. I knew it was not him speaking; I knew it was Thomas speaking through him, pushing me to move forward. For the first time, I thought about Thomas and how he would feel if he saw me now. I was ashamed. I was not honoring the love we shared. I was wallowing in the loss of it. My selfishness surprised me. I was not the only one who had lost a good man. I sighed and looked at Michael. "You are right; I need to honor Thomas and join the land of the living. I am doing this, Michael, with or without your help." The conviction in my voice strengthened me. Hell, yes, I was doing this.

Michael, clearly shocked by his words and my response to them, looked at me for a long time. "Fine, it will be with my help. I will get the necessary paperwork together, but you have to talk these 'ladies' into it and make sure they have birth certificates and passports. They have to come out of the shadows for this to work."

As I drove away, leaving a stunned Michael standing alone, I could hear Thomas in my head. "Just keep swimming, just keep swimming." Timmy loved it when Thomas read him, Finding Nemo, on the few nights he would be allowed to sleep over when we visited Jamaica. He would lie between Thomas and me and shout, "Just keep swimming, just keep swimming!" with Thomas as he read it. Everyone had just kept on swimming—except me.

CHAPTER 5

GENERATIONS OF MISTRUST

Selling the ladies on this new proposal was not as easy as I thought it would be. Even with the mutual trust we were building; it was not enough to erase those last shadows of doubt. This crazy white lady wanted them to do *what*? Even as I tried to explain it, I felt the generations of slavery and colonial oppression bringing the wall of mistrust between black and white crashing down.

The one person I thought would be the hardest to convince, the landlord, jumped at this opportunity. Being a "Jamaica white" himself (someone who looked white), he was enjoying the perks of good food, proper care and most of all, good company. In exchange for a small "rent" to cover the expenses of the property and keep him in rum, he would finance the mortgage himself. Upon his death, he would consider the mortgage paid in full. Then the building and property would belong to the Working Women of Jamaica. I am sure this was due, in no small measure, to the affections of Tiny. The old man had developed a genuine liking for her and her for him.

It was a shock to me that the ladies did not see this for the gift that it was. They sat stone-faced and quiet as I explained the good fortune this agreement would be for them. They did not share my excitement. One by one, they started to look away. I was angry and frustrated by their reaction.

"Help me understand." I could not contain my anger. "You are off the streets in a safe place for not only you but your children and you don't see this as a good opportunity?"

The women were defiant, their mouths set in thin lines. Finally, Precious spoke up. "Miss Jo, you want us to hand over our money and our bodies to Backra to pay for something him get fe free, so that one day it *may* be ours. Den on top'a dat, you want to tek way we likkle money and put it inna bank? When we draw pardner, we nuh haffe pay a bank to do dat." The ladies' current form of banking and saving consisted of them giving Mother a portion of their money each week. At the end of the week, one person collected the pot and so it went until all the women had received their savings. Then they started the process again. I stared at them, dumbfounded. I did not know where to start.

"Precious, this place is not free for Backra or anyone. There are taxes to be paid on the property, utilities, and upkeep that cost money." Something she said nagged at me. "Why do you think Backra got this property for free?" Backra was the name used to describe a slave master. It was a derogatory term, in my opinion and I had always found it offensive.

It was Dancer's turn to speak. "Me know this Backra long time, him neva work a day in his life, yet him always have money to keep this place and keep a bottle of rum in him hand. If him have money, why we have to give him the likkle we have fe someting him get fe free? See how life nuh fair to black people."

I was speechless. *What the hell had I gotten myself into?* I looked to Mother for support, but she was stubbornly quiet and would not meet my eyes. She stood off to the side, arms crossed in front of her,

37

with her head down. She was not willing to offer one shred of support. Before I said something I would regret, I decided a quick retreat was the best course of action. So, I jumped in my car and drove to the sea wall surrounding Kingston's harbor. My favorite place to sit and think. I hadn't been there in years, but now I felt drawn to it.

"What a set of ungrateful and ignorant people!" I thought, rife with indignation.

The more I replayed the conversation with the women in my head, the angrier I got. I knew what it meant to be a white person in Jamaica. You realized early in life that you would always be a stranger in your own country, subject to "Hey, whitey, where in foreign you come from?" Having to prove I was a born and bred Jamaican in Jamaica was almost a daily occurrence. Not long after I returned to Jamaica, Miss P. and I were out shopping. I hadn't noticed the young girl in the school uniform following us as we browsed the outdoor market, but Miss P. had and turned to confront her.

"What you want, young lady?" Miss P. had asked, as she clutched her purse to her chest.

The girl must have been about nine or ten and wore the uniform of the all-age school next to the market. "How de white lady know to speak like me?"

Miss P. was shocked by the question. "But what de teaching dese young people inna school dese days, eh? What is the motto of Jamaica, young lady?"

The girl turned to look at Miss P. "Out of many, one people," she answered automatically.

I had asked her what that meant to her. She thought for a minute before answering me. "It mean if you are born ya, then you are a Jamaican."

I nodded. "I was born here."

Her eyes grew wide, and her mouth opened in a big *O*. "I didn't know white people born inna Jamaica."

Miss P. could not contain herself. "What a level of ignorance, eh. You don't see Indian people, Chinese people, all color of people walking around Jamaica? You don't know white people born in Jamaica?" She was shouting at the poor girl, who looked at me again before scurrying off, with her head down after being chastised by Miss P. I wanted to go after her, but I had been distracted by the argument that had ensued between Miss P. and the market vendor we were buying produce from.

"What you mean de banana is four hundred dollars a bunch? Last week, it was two hundred dollars?" Miss P. asked indignantly. As the vendor shot furtive glances at me from under hooded eyes, the answer dawned on Miss P. "Now me understand, because de white woman is with me, the price gone up. Go way wid you bad-minded self," Miss P. admonished as we walked away from the squawking vendor, who was trying to amend her prices.

While Miss P. had been offended by the vendor's actions, I was not surprised and had been willing to pay the price. Miss P. would not allow me to, so we went home without the produce. Miss P. said she did not need it right away and would return the following day to buy it, without me. My grandfather called this inflation of pricing, the "colonial tax," imposed on us by forebearers who had not foreseen the lasting societal consequences of their empiric dreams. Remembering the incident, I thought about how I had handled it— realizing I hadn't handled it at all but allowed Miss P. to take control of a situation that she instinctively knew made me uncomfortable. I expected these women to give me their unconditional acceptance and gratitude, not the distrust and resentment that I had experienced. I expected them to spare my feelings at the expense of their own.

I was so engrossed in my thoughts; I did not hear the car pull up next to me—not a smart thing to do in an isolated part of Jamaica. My cousin Simon knocked on my window, startling me out of my reverie.

"What are you doing out here by yourself? Don't get me wrong; I am glad to see you out of your apartment." Seeing my face, he immediately asked what was wrong.

"Simon, why are Jamaicans so damn backward in their thinking?" I asked despondently.

Simon smiled. "Backward as opposed to open-minded and enlightened Americans, you mean?" Simon loved to tease me about my American citizenship, a gift from Thomas.

I was not in the mood. "I may carry an American passport, but I will always be a Jamaican by birth."

"Yes, but a Jamaican with options. The majority of Jamaicans don't have the same options."

I looked at Simon. "Is that why they hate us?"

"Who is 'they,' Jo? No one hates us; the average Jamaican is too busy trying to survive to think twice about us and how we live our lives. They see us in our big cars, our big houses, living our big lives and we are just images in the tableau of *their* lives."

I thought about this for a minute. I was proud of being Jamaican, but in my heart of hearts, I was resentful of being an anomaly, a white person born and raised on an island identified by the whole world as black. An island that had given the world a culture of pride complete with a reggae music soundtrack, one that I could never be a part of. That culture was born out of a yearned freedom from oppression— oppression I was associated with because of the circumstances of my birth and the color of my skin. Something nagged at my conscience. Yes, I was trying to improve a horrible situation for them, but what had I done to build their trust in me? Their faith that I would keep my word to them? To date, all I had done was bulldoze through their lives to ease the pain in my own.

"They will never see me as anything but a crazy white woman trying to take what little they have. How do you overcome generations of mistrust to prove that your intentions are good?"

"What exactly are your intentions?" Simon had asked the very question I had been wrestling with. I watched the waves crashing against the break wall for a long time without answering.

A storm was coming in; I could see it in the distance, coming in fast and hard against the sky, turning it from blue to pewter in a matter of minutes. The waves had gone from a lazy roll to a rolling boil and they matched my mood.

"Maybe in saving them, they will turn around and save me? Maybe they are the lifeline I have been looking for, the one that will drag me back from the dark abyss I seem to be hovering around. Maybe if I take them out of the shadows, I will find my way back to the light." My voice cracked as I put my greatest fear into words. I was losing myself to my dreams and if I continued like I this, there would be a day, soon, when I would not come back from my longing for Thomas and the life I had made with him, now gone forever.

I could see that Simon understood what I was saying. "Then you have to make them see past the color of your skin and where you live. Find your commonality with these women and work outward from that intersection."

Simon knew what he was talking about; he had done the same thing in getting a black police force to follow a white man's vision of justice in Jamaica and how it was to be meted out. When Simon had become the police commissioner, his first order of business was to root out decades of corruption in a police force that was seen as an oppressor instead of a protector of the Jamaican people. His life was threatened many times and his constabulary force had come to respect his vision, many protecting it and him with their own lives. He was a hero in Jamaica and when they spoke of him, they never mentioned the color of his skin or the circumstances of his birth. He was making Jamaica better for all Jamaicans and they recognized his intentions and loved him for it. I thought about what Simon had said as I watched the wind kick the waves over the break wall.

"Jo, go home. This storm is picking up and I would feel better if you were safe at home." Simon's voice was authoritative.

"I will, Simon, thank you. I have to make one stop first."

"Okay." He said as he smiled and patted my shoulder. "You are the best of us, Jo. That is why Thomas chose you."

I laughed at this. "Right, Simon. This from the man who gave him an award for, and I quote, 'Best easygoing husband with honors for living the farthest away from the in-laws.' You know Mummy never forgave you for that one."

Simon smiled. "One of many things your mother has never forgiven me for. You know, when you married Thomas, you were a timid little girl afraid of doing anything without your parents' permission or input. You blossomed under the independence your marriage gave you. You need to find that again, grab it and hold onto it. Don't let being back here stifle that. You are not one to live your life with every decision about it made by committee."

Simon was right; I was a strong, intelligent woman and I could not let the complacency of life in Jamaica take that away from me. I smiled back at Simon and put the car in reverse. There was somewhere I needed to be before this storm hit.

Mother was the key. If I could convince her that we were doing the right thing for everyone, then she would open the door and the others would walk right in. The trick was trying to figure out what to say to her. I found her in the little office off the front desk. She eyed me suspiciously as I knocked on the door and asked if I could come in.

"I didn't think I would see you again."

I was surprised by that. "Why would you think that?" An unwelcome question crossed my mind: Did Mother want me out of the picture now?

Mother looked up and shrugged her shoulders. "I dunno, you looked mad when you left."

"Not mad, a little surprised, definitely confused, but not mad. Everyone is entitled to their opinions." Her eyebrows went up at that comment.

"Look, Mother," I started hesitantly, "it is not my intention to make anyone's life harder than it is. What I am proposing will give everyone a future in a home that will belong to you for as long as you want it. By forming a company, you will be able to pay salaries, get retirement benefits, educate your children and have a life after whoring. You will not be living off the scraps from the table; this will give you a seat at the table, a say in your future and the future of your children. You don't have to steal what you need; you will be able to earn it and no one can say you don't deserve it, or it does not belong to you, ever again."

She wasn't listening to my pitch. "Why, Miss Josephine? Why you want to do this? What is in it for you?"

I took a deep breath. "First, please stop calling me Miss Josephine; my friends call me Jo. I would be honored if you would do the same. To answer your question, I need this probably more you do. I am lost, Mother, so lost and I need to find my way back home. I don't know how to; I don't even know where home is anymore. The easiest way to run away from your problems is to run toward someone else's, so I was hoping, I am asking—if I run toward yours, will you run toward mine and maybe you can find a way home for me and I can find you a home in return? Like you, I want to feel safe and secure enough to sleep through the night." I could not look at her. The fear of her showing me the door was more than I could stand.

"So, you save me, and I save you? Just like that?" she asked. I could hear the skepticism in her voice. Maybe I was another responsibility she did not want.

"Yes, just like that. A friend helping a friend find their way," I answered quietly.

I could feel Mother studying me as she contemplated what I had said. I lifted my eyes to look at her and held her gaze. "Tell me again what you want to do." And just like that, the Working Women of Jamaica's co-op was born.

CHAPTER 6

SAINT ELIZABETH

The work began to legitimize the Working Women of Jamaica Co-op; to my great surprise, all the women except Mother had their birth certificates. In a postcolonial society, you may not know who your father was, but you always knew who your mother was and mothers made sure their children, especially their daughters, had their birth certificates.

Michael had them all come down to his office, where he dutifully, if not enthusiastically, made copies of all the birth certificates, had them apply for passports and collected the necessary fees. In a surprising act of generosity, he was not charging them for the services of securing their passports or setting up the co-op. I decided not to look a gift horse in the mouth.

Mother, on the other hand, was not happy about this part of the process. She claimed she did not know where her birth certificate was, did not know her legal name and did not even know what her birthdate was. Michael found this all very suspicious. So, I decided to handle this matter myself.

"Fine. Pick a name and birthdate and I will 'buy' a birth certificate for you. We need it to get a passport and then we will set you up as chairman of the board."

Mother was having none of it. "Jo, don't you tink you should run this ting? You know more about business than I do."

I was beginning to get frustrated. "Mother, I am not going to have a seat on the board. This whole deal is for you and the girls; I am not going to do anything more than consult and give advice. That is the way you wanted it, remember?" That, indeed, had been the only condition Mother had stipulated if we were to move forward with the co-op. It would belong to her and the girls wholly and solely. I had willingly agreed.

"Pick a name and birthdate, Mother. That is all I need you to do."

"To get a passport, you need a picture. A picture that will be on file with the government, right?" Mother was nervous about this, but I was too busy with the final result to pick up on this right away.

"Yeah, so what? We need a birth certificate first and we can buy that. I need you to pick a name and birthdate. You can be anyone you want to be." I smiled at her as I said that, hoping to end this particular conversation.

Mother was chewing on her lower lip and I could tell something was weighing on her mind. Just as I was about to ask her what was going on, her cell phone rang. She looked at the number and walked out of the room. I turned back to the articles of incorporation I was reviewing.

It was not long before a distraught Mother ran back into the room. I was sitting in a chair by the window in the room she lived in at the hotel. She ran in and started throwing clothes into an overnight bag and then started frantically searching for her wallet.

"Mother, what happened? What happened? Why you so upset?" I had never seen Mother this flustered before.

"Me haffe, me haffe!" She could not even speak.

"You have to what? What do you have to do?"

"I have to go to my children; they need me."

"Your children?" I asked. "Where are your children? I thought they were here with you?" It was almost impossible to keep track of the children who had moved into the hotel and who belonged to whom. I naturally assumed hers were here too.

"No, my children are..." She looked at me hesitantly. "My children are not here."

"I can see that. Where are they?"

"I have to go!" Mother was nearly out the door.

"Go where?" I ran after her. "For God's sake, Mother, slow down. Where are you going? Let me take you." I grabbed my purse and car keys and ran after her. Catching up with her, I was able to get her into the car.

"Where are we going?" I asked as I started the car.

Mother looked at me and quietly replied, "Saint Elizabeth."

"Saint Elizabeth? Why are your children in Saint Elizabeth?" I asked as I pulled out of the parking lot. It was a four-hour drive, and I had a captive audience.

"Mother, you need to start talking now," I said as I drove into oncoming traffic.

She talked for the next two hours straight. "I was married once; I had a home on Princess Street and a husband who loved me and took good care of me. We had two children, a girl who is sixteen now and a boy who is fourteen. They were young when their father was killed, murdered in front of me. I could not stay at my house, so I took them and ran. Ran away from the man that killed their father. I ran as far as I could run and found myself in Saint Elizabeth. I stayed there until the likkle money I had saved started to run out. I put the children in boarding school and I came back to Kingston. I had to make money to keep them in school. I could not do that in Saint Elizabeth, so I came back." Her voice trailed off; this was painful for her.

She told me how she had found accommodation for her children in two prestigious schools on the South Coast and I was again surprised. I knew those schools; you got in based on recommendations or scholarships, or if you had gone to them yourself. It suddenly dawned on me. Mother could be well-spoken when she chose to be.

"Mother, did you go to the girls' school?" I asked.

Mother looked at me and then out the window. Very quietly, she said yes.

"What?" I looked at her closely. "How the hell do you go from that school to a street corner in Kingston?"

Mother started to cry and I would not get anything more out of her for another hour. It was apparent she needed to have a good cry. Whatever had upset her could wait. We had a long drive. I concentrated on the road as she cried softly next to me, waiting for her to speak.

"The headmistress call and say I must come to pick up my children."

"Why?" I asked. "Do you owe the school money?"

"No. Every penny I earn I send to dat school. I don't owe any money."

"Then, why?" I asked. Again, knowing a school like that in Jamaica, they were not going to put out children whose parents paid well and on time, especially full-time boarders.

"I don't know. I don't know." Mother started to cry again. It was close to 4:00 p.m. when we drove into the schoolyard. I followed behind as Mother went into the administrative office and asked for the headmistress. She was waiting for Mother and she did not look happy.

"You have come for your children? I will call down and have them brought up." Mother started to speak, but the headmistress held up her hand to stop her.

"The decision has been made; they cannot stay here any longer." Mother looked like the headmistress had punched her in the stomach.

"My name is Josephine Myers. What seems to be the problem here?" I used my most uptown Kingston voice. The name had the desired effect and stopped the headmistress in her tracks. I pushed the advantage.

"It is my understanding that no money is owed on the accounts of…of the…" I realized I did not know the children's names. I did not know their mother's name, either. "Of the children you are trying to kick out unfairly." I finished with a flourish.

The headmistress was confused. "It has come to my knowledge that Ms. Baker," (okay, we were getting somewhere; Mother was Ms. Baker,) "Ms. Baker does not live up to the standards that we require for our students."

"Excuse me? What does that mean?" I asked, fearing I knew the answer.

"It has come to my attention that Ms. Baker, well, Ms. Baker, has a job that is not in keeping with the standards of our school." The headmistress was uncomfortable with this conversation.

"And what, exactly, do you think her job is?" I asked, ready to do battle.

"It has come to my attention, well, that, she is a lady of the evening and I cannot have that here, Ms. Myers. Surely you can understand that." The headmistress was pleading with me not to let this get more uncomfortable for her.

"I see. And how was this brought to your attention? Did you see Ms. Baker plying this trade?" I asked.

Again, the headmistress looked like she wanted to crawl under the desk. "Well, no. Not me, but one of our faculty says he saw her in Kingston when he was visiting. Well, visiting someone." It dawned on the headmistress that this admission might not look good for her or her expertise in choosing faculty members.

I pressed the advantage. "Your faculty member must be mistaken." I made sure to emphasize the scorn in my voice as I said *faculty member*. "Ms. Baker is a valued member of my family's staff and has been for many years. She has been my assistant since my return to Jamaica. I suggest you call said *faculty member* in here so we can get to the bottom of this." Mother looked at me nervously as I silently prayed this woman would not call my bluff. "Of course, if he is mistaken, I will be asking for his immediate dismissal and an inquiry by the board of directors as to why such a person was hired to teach here. If I am not mistaken, my Aunt Julie is the current chairman of the school's board." Message sent.

Message received. "That will not be necessary, Ms. Myers. This is a case of mistaken identity and a glaring error on my part: listening to gossip." She scuttled behind her desk.

"I agree you have made a mistake. Potentially a fatal one for your continued stay as headmistress of this school." *Be careful*, I cautioned myself. *You don't want to make her your enemy, but your champion.* "One I am willing to overlook if you are willing to withdraw your expulsion of her children. I understand you were only doing what you thought was best for the school." I softened my tone and smiled at her as she cowered behind her desk.

"Now, if you would be so kind as to fetch the children, we would like to visit with them and with your permission, we would like to sign them out for the weekend and take them to my father's home in Alligator Pond. I will leave money on account for them. Anytime they wish to visit, with your leave, of course, I would be grateful if you would arrange transportation for them." I reached into my purse and pulled out a wad of money and handed it to her. "I think this should suffice," I said.

"Of course, of course, Ms. Myers. I will fetch the children immediately." She was all business now. "Please have them back by two o'clock on Sunday afternoon; they must return in time for chapel. I'm sure you understand." She was all smiles and graciousness.

"I do, madam, and I thank you again for your consideration." I smiled as I stood and shook her hand. I gestured to Mother; it would probably be best if we waited for the children outside and away from prying eyes.

Mother's children were beautiful, tall, and statuesque, their dark mocha skin as clear and fresh as only youth can make it. They were polite children, but I noticed the same cautiousness in them that Mother had, so I held back and watched as they greeted their mother, whom they clearly adored. I nodded as they were introduced to me and said it was a pleasure to meet them both. We jumped into the car and I drove as they filled their mother in on life at school. I could tell it had been a while since they had seen each other and they needed time to catch up.

I decided to spend the weekend at my father's beach house. By the time we left Saint Elizabeth, it would have been well after midnight when we got back to Kingston and I did not relish driving through Kingston at that hour of the night. I had called ahead and asked the housekeeper to make the arrangements for us to stay and prepare dinner. Going to the beach house was not an easy thing for me to do. I had not been back since my father had died many years ago. I tried to tell myself that it made sense to spend the night there. I had always hated going there. It was my father's favorite place in the whole world.

Thomas had always said I hated it as much as my father loved it. My relationship with my father had always been complicated. I suspect it was because I was not a boy named Joseph, the name he had picked out for me before he had the disappointment of knowing his only heir would be a girl. I was a dutiful daughter, if not a loving one. In Thomas, I had found the love, support and encouragement that I did not know I was missing from my father.

It was my father's family the money came from. They had been in Jamaica for eight generations. The family story was that our first ancestor was the second son of an English lord who did not inherit a title or lands, so he came to the Caribbean to find his fortune. Who knows? It could easily have been a lowly shipman who had enough of the sea and decided to settle down at the next port he disembarked at. The English lord ancestor was never identified, so it was always suspect, but a story my father held hard and fast to.

They had gone from being ship merchants and traders to land-owners. Then to having a say in the future of a tiny island in the Caribbean. My grandfather had the uncanny ability of anticipating the island's needs and filling them before anyone had the faintest idea of what he was up to. This ability led to the purchase of bauxite mines that allowed for the acquisition of aluminum factories. Sugar factories opened up export opportunities, which required investment in shipping companies and the port services they needed. Companies were purchased or started to support the myriad of opportunities he foresaw for Jamaica's development. He passed this gift onto the eldest of his three sons—Jack, my father—and the fortune grew, as did the family. His oldest child was my Aunt Julie, who had never married. She was by far the most intelligent of my grandfather's four children, but by being born a girl, she had taken herself out of the hierarchy my family clung to. The three sons had children. My father was the only nonprolific one of the family. Thomas and I had thought we had all the time in the world to have children. My father's fortune had come to me upon his death, not to my mother. My grandfather felt that the men in the family had to be given the necessary opportunities to provide for their families, but if the women got married, then their husbands were responsible for them, so he did his utmost to make sure those husbands never benefited from his hard work—a tradition my father enthusiastically supported until fate played the cruel joke on him of giving him a girl as his sole heir. My mother said this tradition is why Julie never married, but I think it was more because she could never find an equal, especially in the men she was forced to meet.

My mother had the use of his property and fortune until the day of her death, but all the assets and the bulk of the money belonged to me. Thomas was furious when he found this out after my father's death. He loved my mother and felt it was grossly unfair to her and what she had had to put up with all the years she had devotedly loved a man who loved himself more than he could ever love anyone else.

My father had fallen in love with the land in Alligator Pond before he was old enough to buy it, so he gave the money to his mother, who bought four acres of beach property in her name until he was old enough to have it transferred to his. He had built a cottage on the cliff overlooking the beach. Steps led from a huge veranda down to the beach, which was nothing more than a cove, so he called the property Hidden Cove and escaped to it as much as time would allow him. Begrudgingly he dragged my mother and me along, but only when she complained that he was not spending enough time with us—more precisely, her, as I was always her excuse.

Ironically we had both stayed away from the property since his death. To my knowledge, only my cousin Simon stayed there regularly. It was with very mixed feelings that I looked at the sea below me as I stood on the veranda of the house, on the land he had loved so much. I listened to Mother talk excitedly with her children as I let the emotions wash over me. Mother was a different person around her children. She was soft, thoughtful, open, but mostly loving. The way she straightened Andre's shirt or moved a lock of hair out of Ella's eyes—her touch was gentle and kind. I marveled at how life made us all play different roles for different people and circumstances. The saying "Life is but a stage, and we are all actors on upon it" popped into my head. It seemed fitting as I watched her with her children.

After dinner, Mother took her children for a walk around the property. I heard their voices disappear into the night and sat on the veranda looking at the sea. The sea had always had an unexplained draw for me. Thomas said I was seduced by it and our lovemaking was always more passionate when we were by the sea. I was lost in my thoughts and I did not hear Ella come in.

"Miss Josephine, I wanted to thank you for what you did for us today," she said softly. While she spoke with a Jamaican accent, she did not speak patois at all.

"Ella, I did nothing. I am not sure what it was all about, but it turned out to be a mistake." I was stuttering and unsure of what to say.

Ella looked me in the eye. "I know what my mama does to make a living and keep us in school. I have known for a long time." Her voice was still soft but firm.

"Oh." I did not know what to say, so I said nothing.

"It was only a matter of time before someone at school found out. Jamaica is a small island," she said and it occurred to me that no matter what strata of Jamaican society you were in, you were still subject to the malicious gossip known as Jamaican chat.

I looked at her; she was not judgmental at all, considering the school she attended. *Surprising,* I thought. Her love for her mother was first and foremost in any thought she had of her mother. Something, I could not have related to until I met Thomas and understood the concept of unconditional love.

"Your mother is a good woman; she has had a hard life, but she is working hard to make sure you and Andre don't have to go through what she has gone through. It is one of the things I admire most about her. She is selfless and loves you both more than anything." I felt the need to defend her mother.

"She does and yes, she has had a hard life, but I am glad she has a friend like you. She deserves that and again, I thank you for what you did today." She continued to look me in the eye. She did not look down; she looked at me as an equal and for some reason, I was humbled by her direct gaze.

Taking a chance, I said, "Ella, what is your mother's name? I only ever call her Mother, and I am embarrassed to say I don't know her real name."

Ella looked at me for a long time before she answered, "She was married to my father, so her married name is Sally Brown." Ella's words were carefully measured and I thanked her for the information. She turned to leave the room and then looked back. "Her maiden name is Rollins. Her father is John Rollins, John 'Biscuit' Rollins." She watched me as that news sank in. It took me a minute, but I knew who Biscuit Rollins was. My mouth fell open as I raised my eyes to look at Ella.

From the look on my face, she realized that I had recognized the name. "Good night, Miss Josephine. Enjoy the rest of your evening." She left the room as soundlessly as she had entered, leaving me to digest this news.

"Dear God, what have I gotten myself into?" I thought as I turned once more toward the comfort of my sea view.

CHAPTER 7

THE PLOT THICKENS

I was dreaming and did not want to wake up. Thomas was making love to me. I could feel the passion awake in my body. I could feel his hands on my waist, picking me up and putting me down on top of him. I could feel myself move against him and the pleasure mounted, but something was wrong! Something was knocking at my consciousness. I could feel the sunlight against my eyelids and Thomas began to fade. *No, no, no!* My unconscious screamed. If the knocking would go away.

Just like that, I was awake, my body ached with loss and a sob escaped my lips. The knocking continued at the door. I was drowning in the pain of my loss.

"Jo? Josephine, wake up. Do you want to come down to the beach with us?" Mother was knocking. I could hear the worry seeping into her voice.

"I'm awake; I'm awake! Just catching up on some work." My voice was hoarse and broken.

"Oh, okay." She sounded uncertain.

"Go, have a good time with your children, Mother. I am fine. I have to finish up an article I am writing. It is quiet here, so it is easy to write." I looked at the notebook lying next to me. I wasn't lying; I had been up most of the night writing down what I could remember about the life of John Rollins.

My dream had disturbed me; it brought up the feelings of loss and longing that hurt so much I couldn't move. I let the pain wash over me as the tears cleared the sleep from my eyes. I looked at the notebook lying next to me. "Run away from your problems by running toward someone else's." I grabbed the notebook and got out of bed.

Not much was known about John Rollins's life as a child. He was educated in the United States and came from Jamaican parentage or had married a Jamaican. It was unclear how he had ended up in Jamaica, but it was well known that he was an educated man. His nickname was the Professor Don. At the height of his power, he was the most successful drug dealer in the Caribbean, South and Central America as well as the United States. He had opened transshipment ports between South America, Jamaica and the United States. Hard drugs came into Jamaica from Panama and Venezuela. He got them to the United States in exchange for cash and weapons that Central and South American countries used to consolidate their power. He was a hero to poor Jamaicans because he put them to work, even farmers who grew ganja for him to export. He built schools in the communities that protected him, set up hospitals and took care of his neighborhoods. He was Jamaica's version of Robin Hood. Because he controlled the guns, it was not long before the various political parties in Jamaica came calling and he became the fighting force of Jamaica's most prominent political party—one my family had supported since its inception.

In an ironic turn of events, the same political party turned on him when the United States offered aid packages in exchange for him. He died in prison awaiting extradition to the United States.

Rumor had it that he was killed because he could name names and it was too much of a threat to the power structure for him to go to the United States and start talking. The people reacted to his death by making sure it was twelve years before that party was ever in power again. He was so popular in Jamaica, he was given the equivalent of a state funeral, with his body given a police escort as his casket was paraded through the very streets he protected. I was living in the States during this time, so I only heard snippets about this during my visits and overheard my uncles discussing how badly the party had handled the "Biscuit Fiasco." His son, John John, had taken over the family business and the political party, now back in power thanks to John John's support, was not making that mistake again. The current prime minister was caught up in a fight with the United States to protect John John.

An informant working with the DEA had managed to wiretap John John discussing his crimes. Now, that powerful arm of the United States government was demanding his extradition. The prime minister was fighting it because wiretapping was illegal in Jamaica and the wiretap had been of a telephone conversation John John Rollins had made in Jamaica. Thomas had thought it strange that the government would get involved in protecting a Jamaican drug dealer. I had lost all interest in following the story when Thomas got sick.

It was nearly one o'clock in the afternoon, so I showered and dressed and was sitting on the veranda deep in my thoughts as Mother and the children came up from their morning spent at the beach.

"There you are," Mother said. "I thought you were going to sleep the morning away."

"I thought about it." I smiled as I looked at her. "That is how I get through being down here, sleeping, or getting lost in a good book." I showed her the book I was not reading as proof of what I was saying.

"You don't like it down here?" Ella asked as she looked out at the sparkling sea. When the sun hit it just right, it looked like a million diamonds were dancing on top of the waves. I followed her gaze. The diamonds were dancing in their full glory. "I think it is the most beautiful place on earth." She sighed as her transfixed gaze stared at the sea.

"My father would have agreed with you, Ella. Unfortunately, I have never shared his love for this place. I was always happiest when leaving." She turned her gaze to look at me, and again, I felt like she could see through to my soul. This girl could unnerve me and for the life of me, I could not understand why. I felt like I knew her, but I couldn't understand why I identified with her. Maybe it was from a past life if you believed in that kind of thing. All I knew was that there was a familiarity about Ella that I felt but could not explain.

"I'm glad you like it down here. I have arranged for you and your brother to come down here whenever you want." She jumped up and down, clapping her hands as she ran to hug me.

"Thank you, thank you, Miss Josephine. It does get lonely at school over the holidays. This house will be the perfect place to come to." She was very excited at the prospect.

"You don't come to Kingston for the holidays?" I asked and could see Mother getting uncomfortable.

"Children, go and change for lunch. You said you were hungry, remember? I am sure Jo has not eaten anything, so let's hurry and feed her." I noticed that Mother's English was perfect when she was around her children; all traces of patois gone from her speech. It was also not lost on me that she did not want to discuss why the children were never brought to Kingston. I sat down as she hustled the children into the house and tried to figure out where to go from here.

It is evident that Mother did not want her connection to the notorious John Rollins known, but her brother was now in charge, so why would she not be under his protection? Of all the secrets she was hiding, this was the most perplexing. She was staying away from her family for a reason, hiding out in the shadows and keeping her children as far from her as possible. Why? I knew I could not ask her and for some reason, I did not want to involve anyone in my research. Deep in my bones, I knew I had to keep hiding her, even if I did not understand why. However, this led to an even more pressing problem in seeing our plans to fruition. I had wanted Mother to run the Working Women of Jamaica—she was the best person to do it—but it would mean bringing her out of the shadows and I knew we could not do that. So, who would take the reins?

I watched her during lunch and tried to figure out what I was going to do. The first thing I decided to do was to find out what she was hiding from and why. Once I had that information, I was hoping everything else would fall into place. I decided to go to the newspaper archives. Everything that was ever written about anyone in Jamaica would be there and it was all computerized now. I figured I could do my research without arousing any suspicion. I bided my time. I could not wait to leave this place, but I could see Mother was enjoying these moments with her children, so I gave them their space and filled my time with reading and missing Thomas. Same old. I was excited about the Working Women of Jamaica and now it had hit a roadblock that I was not sure we could overcome to move forward. I was angry and frustrated, but not at Mother, which surprised me. After all, she was the roadblock, but I felt protective of her and her children. It took another sleepless night to realize that in my spoiled, selfish-little-girl self, I was afraid of losing my distraction, my new reason for waking up in the morning.

I was dressed and ready when everyone came out for breakfast on Sunday morning. It was the same sense of excitement I felt when it was time to leave this place. I was ready to go but stopped myself when I saw Mother's face. She knew this would probably be the last time she would see her children for a long while and she wanted to prolong the goodbye for as long as possible. I respected that; it was something I understood completely. I gently reminded her that we had to have the children back by 2:00 p.m. and then left them to enjoy the rest of their time together.

The headmistress was waiting for us when we returned with the children. I gave her the name and telephone number of the house-keeper at the beach house and asked her to make the arrangements anytime the children wanted to go down there. She was all sweet-ness and charm and I knew the children would be safe in her keep-ing moving forward. I watched as Mother kissed and hugged her children goodbye. I could relate to the pain she was feeling, but at least she had the chance to see them again. Thomas was gone from me forever. I realized I was jealous of Mother; she had two fantastic reasons for getting up in the morning. I was not sure what I had to hold on to. The children came over to say goodbye with hugs and kisses. Ella held me for a moment longer. Her gaze said so much: *"Be careful with the information I have given you. Take care of my mother."* This girl had an ancient soul and I found myself not only respecting her but feeling very protective of her and her brother.

The drive back to Kingston was quiet; both of us lost in our thoughts. It was not until we were driving into Kingston that Mother spoke, "I have no words to thank you enough for what you have done for my children and me." I noticed, in her language, she was still showing me her true self. This trust in me tugged at my heart.

"You don't need to thank someone for doing the right thing, Mother. I know you have things to hide and I will keep your secrets, but we have to figure out who is going to run the association. You can't do it and I can't do it. The Association is the right thing to do, but we can't blow up both our lives to make it work." I was deflecting. She understood and appreciated it. We needed to concentrate on the problem at hand and how to solve it.

"You're right. Let me think about it. We will come up with something. We have so far; this is no different." She followed my lead and was all business. I dropped her off with the promise that we would meet in the next couple of days. I explained that I had obligations the following day and would not be available until Wednesday. She understood and said we would meet then to discuss how to move forward. I drove off, knowing exactly where I would be at 9:00 a.m. tomorrow.

CHAPTER 8

THE TIES THAT BIND

I found a little corner at the back of the small, dark room they kept the computers in. I could pull up what I wanted to look for by putting in keywords, then everything on the topic would come up. I started with John Biscuit Rollins and filled in the gaps. He had been born in Jamaica, but his mother had migrated to the United States with him when he was a baby. He had spent summer holidays in Jamaica, but no one knew where. His mother's family had lived in the neighborhood he ultimately returned to live in. No one knew how his life of crime had started, but his good deeds were documented right along with the crimes he had been accused of but never convicted of. His death had been documented in detail. I had no idea it had been so gruesome. There had been a fire in his prison cell. No one could explain who had started the fire or why no effort had been made to rescue him before he burnt to death, but it was clear the people who supported him held the government responsible. The ensuing riots and their fall from grace bore this out. While there was no mention of a daughter, there were pictures of him with John John.

I decided to search for the name Sally Rollins Brown and found a picture of Mother on her wedding day. Standing next to her was John Rollins and John John Rollins! *Jackpot.* She had married a man by the name of Marvin "Gaye" Brown. He got the nickname because he was always singing Marvin Gaye songs. I typed his name into the browser and gasped as I read about his death. He had been shot in his bed as he slept next to his wife, accused of being the informant who had supplied the DEA with the wiretap that had been the start of John John's legal troubles. My heart broke for Mother. It was clear why she was in hiding and why she had sent her children to the other side of the island, away from her. I am sure John John was still looking for her and her children. To men like John John, killing her husband would not be enough and he wouldn't care less about killing his sister, niece or nephew if it silenced a threat to his authority. I pushed the chair away from the computer; I was shaking. Again, I asked myself what the hell I had gotten myself into. It was not long before I found out.

———

As with everything in Jamaica, your business was always known. No matter what you said or did, someone was always listening, always watching. Being away from Jamaica for so long, I had forgotten that golden rule. Mother and I were in her office, it was late at night and we were discussing potential candidates to run the association when three masked men with guns burst in and confronted us.

We were both startled, but Mother recovered her composure much faster than I did. I had never been held at gunpoint before. "We nuh have no money in here. It gone to the bank dis morning." She was quiet and deliberate when she spoke.

"We nuh come fe money, we come fe di white woman." This shocked Mother. No one kidnapped, much less killed, white people in Jamaica. That was a guaranteed death sentence and the authorities would not stop until they found the culprits. Being white had certain unspoken but clearly understood privileges.

Mother and I looked at each other. We were not expecting that. Two of the men moved toward me to forcibly grab me as Mother stepped in their way. The third man hit her, clearly dazing her. Not a sound came out of my mouth, even though it was open to scream. Before I could think, we were both in a car, Mother slumped against me and crushed by the girth of the two men on either side of us. A hood was put over my head. I must have fainted because when I awoke, I was in a small windowless room with Mother lying next to me on the floor.

I no longer had the hood on, but my head ached terribly and I had trouble focusing. I had no idea if I had been knocked out or if the adrenaline coursing through my body was affecting my vision. I know that I tingled all over as if I was waking from a nightmare. I shook Mother, but she just groaned; she did not wake up. At least she was alive. I said a silent prayer of thanks for that. I slowly stood to my feet. My legs felt like rubber and I grabbed the wall to stop myself from falling. I looked around the small room as I steadied myself. A single naked bulb in a socket above me provided the only light in the room. There was a door to my left and I slowly moved toward it. I did not expect the door to open as I turned the handle.

I was almost relieved when it didn't. At least I knew what I was dealing with in this room; on the other side, I was not sure what terrible fate awaited me. For the life of me, I could not think of anyone who would want to hurt me. Why would someone think they could kidnap me and get away with it? The minute my mother and Aunt Julie realized I was missing, there would be hell to pay and no stone on this island would be unturned looking for me. I took some comfort in that, but only a small measure because I had no idea why I was here or where here was. I tried the door again but it held fast. As I turned to look around the room, the door opened and light flooded in, blinding me. A large woman entered the room; standing behind her were too large men with guns. The room was too small for them to follow the woman, so she stepped in alone as they waited by the door.

"Good, you are awake." She looked me up and down, trying to see if there was any permanent damage. I had no idea who she was. She grabbed my arm and dragged me out of the room. The two men followed us as we entered a long hallway. I was trying to keep up, my legs were still not working right and I felt like I was going to fall with each step. Finally, we walked into a room where several men were eating and I looked around. I stopped dead in my tracks when I saw the man at the head of the table, eating an entire chicken with his hands. He looked up. There I was, face to face with John John Rollins. He motioned for the man next to him to move and I was unceremoniously pushed into the seat he had vacated. John John wiped his hands and looked at me with no emotion whatsoever on his face.

"Are you hungry?" I looked at him, clearly shocked. I was not here for a social visit. He laughed when he saw the expression on my face. "Girlie, bring some water for her. I don't want her to faint again." I was finally able to look away from him when the glass of water was put down in front of me. I realized I was very thirsty and drank the entire glass, motioning to Girlie to fill it again for me. "Please," I croaked at her. I looked back at John John. There was no question that I was scared, but I managed to haul my natural arrogance out of hiding and leveled my gaze at him.

"Man, I know that look." He laughed, and everyone else around the table laughed with him. I continued to stare at him. "Your father had that same look." People always told me I had a lot of my father's expressions. I was too frightened to focus on how he would know my father well enough to recognize his "look."

"Do you know who I am?" he asked.

I nodded that I did. "Yes, but I have no idea why I am here." My voice was much stronger than I felt. There was something familiar about John John that I couldn't place. It was the same feeling I had when I looked at Ella. The thought of Mother's daughter reminded me that I needed to be careful. I was here because of Mother; I understood that even if I didn't understand why.

"You should learn to clear your browser history." He looked at me as he let those words sink in. Browser history? It had been four days since I had paid a visit to the newspaper's archives. I had been too shocked at what I had found there. I had not cleared the browser history after my search. I mentally kicked myself as I remembered that I had run out without doing something I had always done in the States when using a public computer. *How stupid*, I thought. I had to be very careful; I was praying he did not realize that he held his sister in the same small room I had just left. He watched me closely, and I tried not to let my thoughts change the expression on my face. Luckily, growing up with my mother and aunts, I had a lot of practice in not allowing my thoughts to show on my face.

"Why you looking into my family? Specifically, my sister?" I was at a loss for words and took a long drink of water. I had no idea how to answer his question; anything I said could implicate Mother and, more importantly, her children. I was stuck. Then providentially, an idea flew into my head.

"I am a writer and a newspaper I work for has asked me to write an article about you and how you came to be, well, you. I was doing some research for my story." While not exactly true, it was close enough to be plausible.

This answer amused him. "An article about me? I would think the Americans know more about me than they want to know." It was then that I noticed he was not speaking to me in patois; it was more like my own uptown Kingston accent. *Interesting*, I thought. Then I remembered he was the son of the Professor Don; of course, he would have had the best education money could buy. So had his sister. I had to get out of there and more importantly, I had to get out of there safely *with Mother*.

"Why do you think I am writing for an American magazine?" I asked.

He looked slightly uncomfortable. "I know who you are. You moved back to Jamaica nearly a year ago, after your husband died in America. Now you are back with your family and from what you say, still writing for American magazines." Anybody could have gathered this information from a cursory internet search or listening to general gossip about me in Kingston. I relaxed a little.

"Well, I guess this saves me some time in trying to track you down for an interview." He looked at me as nervous laughter erupted around us. He raised his hand and the laughter stopped as quickly as it had started. He looked around the room and asked everyone to leave, instructing that the table be cleared as they departed. I guess he didn't want me around any of the cutlery. When the room was empty, he sat back, folded his arms across his chest and started twiddling his thumbs. He leaned his chair back and balanced it on its hind legs. My gaze was fixed on his face.

"I have been watching you and I am curious about something." He looked at me to see if I was paying attention. How could I not? "I know you took those women off the streets, found that hotel and set up a business for them. But why would an uptown white woman be interested in a bunch of whores and how they live?" It was my turn to look uncomfortable. I had no idea how to answer him.

"I would think you would understand that better than most." He raised his eyebrows in question but said nothing. "Your father was the resident Robin Hood; he took care of his own. I felt the need to do the same thing." He laughed at this.

"Whores are your people?" I had to be more careful.

"People in need are people in need. I saw a need I could fill, so I did." I figured the less I said, the better.

He thought about what I said and his next words frightened me so much, I froze. "What does that have to do with me, with my father and with my sister?" He was no fool and I may have made a critical mistake with my flippant answer.

"Why would you think they are connected? As I said, I am doing an article." He cut me off.

"Yes, an article about me. You said that. What does that have to do with my sister and who she married?" I could see the wheels turning in his mind and I was petrified. "I have not seen my sister since her husband died. Her husband caused a lot of problems for me, but you already know that, don't you?" His gaze never left on my face.

"I only know what I read in the newspaper. I assume you blamed him for turning you over to the American authorities?" It was now tit for tat. He would find out what I knew as I would find out what he knew. Hopefully, I would win the knowledge game first.

"I did, at the time. Did you know my sister watched him die? I did not realize she would be there. I figured the Americans had hidden her and the children away long before, well, long before he died." He watched me carefully to see what my reaction would be.

Inwardly I wanted to vomit; my fear was almost overwhelming. "Are you sure it was Marvin who betrayed you?" I sensed he was trying to unburden himself.

"At the time, I was convinced, no one was closer to me than my sister and Marvin. The fact that she was there did not make sense to me. If he betrayed me, the Americans would have made sure they were all safely in hiding. Marvin would have insisted on it before giving them anything. But there he was, lying in bed next to my sister."

"If you had doubts, why did you kill him?" I leaned in to hear his answer.

"I had been told by someone I trusted that it was him. I had no reason to doubt him and by the time we were at the house, there was no turning back." There was genuine sadness in his voice.

"Why are you telling me this?" As much as I wanted to hear what he was saying, I could be signing my death certificate by listening to his confession.

"I think you know where my sister is." There it was, he had won. Checkmate!

"Even if I did, why would I tell you? You know who I am. Why would I help you kill your sister? I am an American citizen; you can't hide behind any government, let alone a tiny Jamaican government, against the wrath of the United States if you hurt me in any way. My family alone would make sure you never saw the light of day again, much less what the American government would do to you." He laughed at that. He laughed at me and my confidence crumbled.

"I have no intention of killing my sister. I am at a time in my life when I want my family around me. She may never forgive me and I can live with that, but I need her to know that I love her, that I am truly sorry. She and her children have nothing to fear from me. If anything, I want to make sure they are cared for when I go away."

"Go away?" I asked.

"I'm not going to be burned alive in a prison cell like my father. The Jamaican government will cave to the Americans and hand me over. They have no choice, but they also have no choice but to kill me. If I tell the Americans what I know, what my father knew, Jamaica would never recover from the repercussions of doing that."

"The sins of the father," I said.

He looked at me. "The sins of the fathers." I knew what he meant. The sadness in his eyes moved me and I took his hand in mine. No one was more surprised than Mother when she walked in to see us. It turns out Mother was an expert on picking locks and had heard the entire conversation.

The three of us stood there awkwardly; I did not realize I was still holding John John's hand until Mother's eyes went from our faces to our hands and back up to our faces.

"John John," she said quietly.

"Sally," John John replied softly.

John John positioned himself behind me while Sally stared daggers at him. I am not sure what protection John John thought I could offer him, but he made sure to look Sally squarely in the eye from behind me. For what seemed like an eternity, they circled each other, never taking their eyes off each other. I tugged at John John's hand, which I was surprised to realize I was still holding.

"Sally, I am so sorry."

"Save it, John John; I can never forgive you. I *told* you it was not Marvin who betrayed you."

"I know, Sally. I know that now." John John tried to placate her rising anger.

But she would not be silenced. "I would never have lied to you about that, not even to protect the man I loved. Why didn't you believe me? We have never lied to each other. We promised each other, growing up the way we did, that we would never lie to each other. You know what hurts the most, John John?" She was jabbing her finger at him. "You never believed me. That hurt more than losing Marvin, hurt more than the life you forced me to live after Marvin. The fact that you did not believe me caused me more pain than anything else." She wasn't crying, but she was furious.

"One thing I wish for you, John John. I wish you feel pain like that the rest of your miserable life." She was exhausted and fell into the chair. I let go of John John's hand and ran to her, putting my arm around as much to protect her as comfort her. I looked at John John, who was crying openly. His hand was covering his face as he sobbed loudly. Sally and I looked at each other. Neither of us expected sobbing from a hardened killer.

Sally got up and crossed over to stand over him. She looked at him for a long time. Then she wrapped the sobbing man in her arms.

"I am so sorry, Sally, so sorry. I am too ashamed to even ask for your forgiveness." He sobbed as she held him.

"I don't forgive you, John John; I don't know if I ever can. But I never stopped loving you. You are my baby brother; I will never stop loving you." She rocked him as she spoke, and it was sometime before he quieted and I noticed he moved to hug her back. They stayed like that for what seemed like an eternity. I watched and I waited. I was not sure what to do. I had never witnessed anything like this before, so I just stared. The sadness of it all moved me to tears. I grieved silently for the time lost between this brother and sister, for the lies and deceit that had come between them. It was then I noticed Girlie standing at the door. She could not see John John and Sally; she just looked at me sitting by myself. She looked uncertain and confused.

"Miss, your ride is here."

"Thank you, Girlie," I said automatically. *Wait. What? My ride was here?* Who the hell was my ride, and how did they know to pick me up here? I looked at Sally and John John, who was standing up but made every effort to avoid eye contact with me. I turned as I saw Simon come through the door looking like the weight of the world was upon him. I sat there, my mouth open, looking from Simon to Sally to John John, my head on a swivel, finally settling on Simon as he quietly said, "Hi, Jo." I felt like someone had just punched me in the stomach.

CHAPTER 9

THE SINS OF THE FATHERS

We stood there for a long time, just looking at each other. I was the odd man out. It was clear that Simon knew John John and Sally and had for a very long time. I could sense the history between them, but I didn't know what to think. I couldn't think; my mind was spinning and would not settle on any thought long enough to process it.

It was Simon who broke the silence. "Sally, it is good to see you."

Sally shot him a look. "You recognized me, didn't you? The night you came for Jo." She thought that it had been Simon who told John John where she was.

Now it was John John's turn to look surprised and turned his gaze toward Simon, who seemed very uncomfortable. "You knew where she was? You knew I was looking for her and why? You couldn't tell me?" John John and Sally looked at each other in surprise and then turned back to Simon.

"I have always known where she was, but I figured when she was ready, she would reach out. She has always known where to find any of us." Simon's words made no sense to me. How did we know these people?

"I found Jo; I had no idea she knew Sally or even where to find her. It was pure coincidence," John John said as the realization of what he said dawned on all of them. All of a sudden, all eyes were on me.

"Don't look at me; I have no idea what is going on right now." Those were the truest words I had ever spoken in my life.

All of us just stood there, looking at each other. No one wanted to speak first and no one wanted to let me in on the secret. "John John and Sally are brother and sister. John Rollins was their father. I see the connection there. I know how I know Mother…I mean, Sally… and"—I laughed sarcastically—"I know how I know John John. The question is, how do you all"—my finger jabbed pointedly at each of them—"know each other?"

Again, the sheepish looks were exchanged between them and my anger grew. "Simon, I swear I will kill you myself if you don't start talking." My voice was low, but my tone unmistakable. I was angry and getting angrier by the minute. My temper was legendary and everyone who knew me knew it was not something to be trifled with.

"She 'ave a tempa like Uncle John," Simon said to the others, who nodded as if they understood what he was referring to. I emitted a low growl and ran at Simon, who stepped out the way just as Sally stepped in to grab my upraised arm.

"Come, Josephine, behave yourself. You never raise your hand to family." I looked at her and my jaw dropped with surprise. I sank into the chair next to me. Again, my mind started to spin. I had heard that mantra all my life, from my grandfather, my father and my Aunt Julie. When my temper had gotten the better of me, I had heard those words. "Behave yourself; you never raise your hand to family." How did Sally know to say that to me? I was exhausted, spent and the thoughts tumbling through my mind confused me. God, I wish Thomas was here.

Simon started to talk. I tried to focus on his words, but it was not easy. "Jo, our grandpa is grandpa to John John and Sally." I leveled a blank stare at him, so he rushed on. "Grandpa had four children with our grandmother, but he also had one son with a woman he fell madly in love with. She worked in one of the factories and was a rare beauty. Grandpa told me she was the love of his life. At that time in Jamaica, he could not leave Grandma and marry her, so when she found out she was pregnant, she left Jamaica and went to live in the United States. Grandpa never saw her again. He told me on his deathbed that she was the only regret in life he ever had. She gave birth to a boy, a boy named John Rollins." He paused as he allowed that to sink in. John Rollins is, was, my uncle.

John John took up the story from there. "Daddy knew who his father was and spent the summers in Jamaica with him. Grandpa made sure he was well taken care of and educated at the best schools. Our father had everything he needed and he loved his father very much. Against Grandpa's wishes, he joined the military and was in Panama during the height of America's war on drugs. He learned a lot but became disillusioned with America and how they destroyed the economies of countries, who relied on the drug trade, then just left them to fend for themselves. A lot of these countries never recovered and the poor get poorer. After he left the military, he came back to Jamaica."

Simon picked it up again. "During that time, Jamaica was having economic problems, caused, in no small measure, by the United States' war on drugs and the corruption in the government this war created. It was causing incredible hardship for all Jamaicans, including us. John came to our grandfather and his brothers with the idea that saved us from misfortune. He would use Jamaica as a transshipment point for hard drugs going into the United States from Central and South America in exchange for hard currency and guns. He had all the connections he needed because of his time in the military. He knew that the minute the US government cut the head off one snake, two more heads grew in its place. So, he used his connections and knowledge to create a network of suppliers and distributed the drugs successfully, but he needed the family's warehouses and port connections. The political connections he gathered on his own with one specific party. It was the one that we supported and Grandpa introduced John to whom he needed to know.

"For the plan to work, we had to separate as a family. John ran the illegal side of things and your father ran the legitimate businesses. John excelled at what he did. Soon he was making so much money; no one knew what to do with it. It was Aunt Julie who came up with the 'Robin Hood' idea. John started to channel the money back into the communities in exchange for protection. It was the best way to 'clean' the money. It worked for a long time, until government officials got greedy, one in particular."

John John continued from there. "My father made sure this man rose steadily throughout the party. He wanted to be prime minister. But Daddy did not feel he was ready and was concerned that he was so integral to the running of the drug business that if the US government wanted to turn anyone, it would be him that they would compromise easily because his greed came before his honor. Daddy backed his opponent, who became prime minister." *I know this story*, I thought, but I did not interrupt him.

"This man turned on our father. He went to the DEA and told them everything he knew. He then had Daddy arrested and was going to have him extradited to the United States. Daddy told him that if he did that, he would never see the Jamaican sun again. This man did not know about our father's connection to the Myers family, so he confided in your father that he was going to have Daddy killed before the Americans could find out what he knew. The United States would owe him and with their support, he would become prime minister of Jamaica. It didn't happen and the people were so mad at Daddy's death. They never let that party back into power." Until now. The man they were talking about was the current prime minister of Jamaica, the same one who was fighting John John's extradition.

Sally continued, "Your father went to Grandpa to tell him what was going to happen to Daddy, but he was too late. By the time Grandpa got to the prison, he was dead. Grandpa came to our house, picked up John John, my mother and me and put us on a plane to America that very night. We stayed there until Grandpa came back to get us and John John took over for Daddy. Grandpa never recovered from our father's death and he died shortly after that."

Oh my God, I thought; I remembered this time in my life like it was yesterday. Grandpa got sick almost overnight. He started losing weight; he wouldn't eat, no matter what delicacies were put in front of him. He took to his bed. I remember having to be very quiet when we went to visit. I remember the feeling of sadness that enveloped the once happy home and the smell of death that grew stronger every time I visited. I remember the day he died, my father had come to school to get me and I remember him hugging me and turning my face away when Grandpa's body was brought out of his room. It was the only act of kindness and compassion that I can ever remember my father showing me. I had mourned my beloved grandfather openly and loudly. I looked at Sally and John John; they had grieved for him as well but in secret and in utter silence. It did not seem fair.

They had also lost a father they adored, a man who had loved and protected them against incredible odds. A man who had let them know who they truly were. Whereas I had been raised by a man who had lied to me my entire life, a man who had withheld family members from me. Cousins, I could have grown up knowing. The family who always preached that family was everything and nothing else mattered, had lied. To the men in my family, there was one thing that mattered more than family and it was money. I was angry and hurt. Angry at the unfairness of it and hurt that no one thought to tell me. They had allowed me to live my life based on lies. Every happy moment, every gift from my family, every experience, was now tainted. I could not reconcile this dark history with the bright light I had lived my life in. Had this drug money paid for my education? Had this tainted money made it possible for me to meet Thomas? Love Thomas? Marry Thomas? My thoughts threatened to overwhelm me and it was Sally who rescued me.

"Jo, we were, are happy, with our lives. Except for some bumps in the road." She shot a dark look at John John, who looked away. "We had loving parents, a loving grandfather who shared everything he had with us, including our history. We understood the role we played and we accepted it. I, we"—she pointed at John John—"have no regrets and no malice or ill will toward you or Simon or any of our cousins."

"Then you are a better person than I am!" I shouted at her. "I have no history; my whole life has been based on lies, one piled on top of the other. I lived my life in the sunlight and you lived yours in the shadows. How do you not feel as betrayed as I do?" Her words confounded me.

"Because you are looking at this the wrong way, Jo. It was I who lived my life in the sunlight; I knew who I was, who I belonged to, who loved me and why. You were the one living in the shadows and now it is time to come into the sunlight."

The realization hit me so hard, it took my breath away. I had no claim to the resentment I was feeling. The hypocrisy of it made me cringe. My family were drug dealers and gunrunners. The realization knocked me backward; I was the beneficiary of the two worst plagues known to humanity. Everything good about us was a puff of smoke curling up to the sky. I started to cry as I explained this epiphany to my cousins.

John John was the first one to react. "You are wrong, Jo. We did what we had to survive, and in doing so, we helped a lot of people."

"We also hurt a lot of people. All those people now hooked on drugs we supplied. How can you possibly justify this? All the bad we have done will never validate the little good we may have accomplished. I can't believe you just said that."

I stopped short as something my father said came back to me with such force, it was as if he shouted it at me. "People will always try to escape their lives—alcohol, ganja, drugs, it doesn't matter. People will find a way to get high if they want to and there will always be people standing by to make money off of it." We had been discussing the opioid crisis in America and how it was fueled by drug companies lying to doctors and patients about the potency of the drugs they made. My father had been very nonchalant about my anger and justified this behavior as being the addict's problem because he thought them weak. He had attributed none of the blame to the drug companies' deceptive practices. I had felt him heartless when he said this, but now it took on a different meaning. Was this how he vindicated our family's drug dealings? By telling himself that he was taking from the weak to give good people, with higher aspirations, a chance at a better life?

"I've had enough for one night. I want to go home." I was not sure where that was anymore. I looked at John John and Sally. "You have a lot to discuss and I need time to myself. Tomorrow I am going back to the States, to the home I shared with Thomas. I need time and space to process all of this."

Simon was alarmed. "Do you think that is a good idea? You need to be around family now; this is a lot to take in."

I looked at him long and hard. "Family is the last thing I need right now, Simon. Frankly, I don't even know what that means. The only family I can count on as being real and true is the one I had with Thomas and he is gone, so I have no definition of my family right now." Sally came and kissed me on the cheek. John John just looked at me. Simon moved aside to let me pass. We said not one word to each other the entire way home. He stayed and spoke with Aunt Julie as I walked past them both, walked to my room and closed the door. I was determined to pack my clothes and leave them all behind. I would go home to the only life that had ever made me happy. I would go back to living with a ghost because right now, he felt more real to me than the generations before that had called Jamaica home.

I heard a knock on the door and Aunt Julie asked to come in. She did not wait for me to answer; she closed the door behind her, sat on the chair and watched me pack for a long time without saying a word. I did not look at her or speak to her, but her watching me was beginning to unnerve me and shake my resolve.

"I hear you have had an eventful night." She was calm and composed. It was as if she had asked me how I was enjoying the warm weather. I just looked at her and shook my head.

"I'm leaving, Aunt Julie; I am going home." She said nothing, so I continued, "Back to the States to what I know is real and true and, and mine." I stammered.

"I understand, I just never took you for a coward." Again, I looked at her; I was speechless. "I know you, Josephine, I know what you are capable of, even if you don't know yet. Now is the time to stand up and take your rightful place in this family." I looked at her as if she had lost her mind. What the hell was she talking about?

"Name one woman in this family who has ever had the power to control their fate. The men have always placed themselves at the head of it and done a wonderful job of fucking it all up, based on what I learned tonight." I was now throwing clothes into a suitcase.

"You have a lot to learn, little girl. The men may be the head of this family, but the neck turns the head and men have not been in charge for a long time. I have always known where Sally was and how she was living." She had my attention now. "I was the one who took Ella and Andre to school and enrolled them. I have been paying their school fees all this time."

"But Sally has been killing herself, on her back, I might add. Where has all the money gone?" I asked incredulously.

"In an investment account set up for each child. They will get it at the age of twenty-five along with other money, just like you did."

"You let Sally suffer, let her think the lives of her children and her life were in danger all this time? Why? To what sick end?" I was angry again, not for me but for Sally and the life she had been forced to live for no apparent reason.

"It was the right thing to do at the time. John had died, Grandpa had died, John John had gotten himself caught talking about his— our—business, had Marvin killed in error, as it would turn out. At the time, I thought it was the safest place for her. In hindsight, maybe I was mistaken."

"You think?" I shouted at her.

"Those were hard times for this family. Difficult decisions had to be made. No one stepped up, so I did. Your father never ran this family, Jo, Uncle John did. Your grandfather listened to every word he said. He always said John had his gift of foresight and while he did things I did not agree with, the truth is he saved us; he saved the family when we were all but lost."

"He saved our wealth, Aunt Julie; he did not save this family. It is more fractured and broken than I can ever remember. There is an entire side of my family I know nothing about, cousins who should have grown up with us, but because of the color of their skin, they were not allowed a seat at the table. How is that fair?"

"It was not your grandfather's choice. When John came back to Jamaica, your grandfather welcomed him! He did have a seat at our table. Every Sunday, like the rest of us. He was accepted and loved by us all. He was our brother. But because of the color of John's skin, he could go places and do things that we never could because of the color of ours. He saw the only opportunity to save us and he took it, knowing he would lose his seat at our table not only for himself but for his children and grandchildren."

"Why? Why would he make a sacrifice like that for us?" I could not fully comprehend what she was saying.

"Because to us, family is everything and that included John."

I started to cry. The weight of losing Thomas was crushing. Add that to the loss of my family and I could not stand. Once again, I found myself on my knees.

"The time has come for you to step up, Jo, to take your place among us. Fate has given you a unique opportunity to unite this family once and for all. It was your Uncle John's dream and you are in a position to now make it happen. It is a big responsibility and not without risk, so I will understand if you want to run away from it. That is your choice, but I sincerely hope that you do not. I know you have the character to stand and fight and that is what we all need to do now. More than ever, we need to fight for the survival of our family." I could feel her standing over me, looking down at me. I had no idea how to respond to her. For the millionth time, I wished Thomas was here, but he was not. He was gone and I was left here with a family I no longer knew.

I was battered but not broken. I thought of Sally and all she had endured. Her children, especially Ella, whom I had felt a strong connection to that I could now explain. To Timmy, whom I loved with all my heart. Sally had done the unspeakable to make sure her children survived, so had Uncle John, so had my grandfather. We would protect our children above all else; it was something we instinctively knew how to do. I was a member of this family, for better or for worse; I loved them. They were all a part of me, my past, my present and my future. Fate had brought Sally and me together. My destiny was clear and the path I had to take lay like a beacon in front of me. I stood up, dried my tears and turned to Aunt Julie. "What do you need me to do?" She smiled at me, not in the least surprised by my response.

"Get some sleep; tomorrow will be another busy day." I unpacked my clothes, put away my suitcase and fell into bed. A night of deep, restorative sleep came over me, the first in a long, long time. I did not wake up until Aunt Julie knocked on my door the next morning.

CHAPTER 10

THE PLAN

Coffee in hand, Aunt Julie and I set out on our journey. She insisted on driving. I was not happy about that. Aunt Julie was taught to drive by one of her brothers. At the time, he was twelve years old, so he was not equipped to teach her how to drive, but no one else volunteered, so he was it. She drove at one speed, sixty miles an hour, whether it was on a quiet street or a crowded highway. She and the brake were not friends. She visited it sporadically, instead taking her foot off the gas to slow down. Every stop sign was a suggestion; most of them in her opinion, not necessary. So she slowly rolled through them, expecting everyone else to move out of her way. Thomas had tried valiantly to reteach her how to drive, but finally gave up and refused to go anywhere if she was behind the wheel. I was not as forceful.

It did not take me long to figure out where we were going. The drive from Kingston, on the southeastern end to Alligator Pond on the southwest side of the island, was incredible, offering every vista of Jamaica's magnificent topography. Navigating the traffic of Kingston to get to the highway required deep concentration from both Aunt Julie and myself; it was not uncommon to have drivers cutting in front of you from both the left and the right, even though you were on a single-lane road. Everyone in Kingston seemed to be in a hurry to get where they were going. The rule of the road tended to be survival of the fittest. Once you got to the highway by Caymanas, things evened out a bit until you got to May Pen, which was a town aspiring to be a city with a never-ending bottleneck of traffic at the town square. Once we cleared that, the drive to Mandeville, through the interior of the island, was gorgeous, with roadside vendors selling everything from bananas by the hand to Otaheite apples, guineps, oranges, roasted corn and breadfruit, to name a few of the island delicacies. The road from Mandeville going down Spur Tree Hill offered the most magnificent views of Jamaica's southern coastline. Traffic always slowed down on this descent because of the big trucks carrying red aluminum soil. Getting behind one of the vehicles was guaranteed to add an hour to the trip, but the view of the mountains dappled green, gray and brown with the backdrop of the endless shades of blue coastline was worth the inconvenience.

I decided to sit back, try to enjoy the drive and find out more about my family. Aunt Julie was only too happy to oblige. She had been fond of John, and in him, had found an ally she did not have in her other brothers. John's mother was a woman by the name of Lillian, who had come to work for my grandfather in the secretarial pool. She was not only beautiful, but she was smart. She soon rose in the ranks to become my grandfather's secretary, his eyes and ears in the businesses he ran and his official voice in many cases. Aunt Julie came to know her as a child when she visited her father at work. Lillian was the one with the hidden candies and quick smile. As Aunt Julie got older, she relied on Lillian to be her champion. Even when Lillian left the island to move to the United States, her influence on my grandfather never waned and Aunt Julie utilized her as often as she could. Lillian, was first and foremost, a feminist. She was in love with my grandfather but commanded his respect when women of that generation did not. She was not afraid to voice her opinion and demand to be heard and then respected. Lillian was the love of my grandfather's life. Aunt Julie said he was never the same after she left.

The women in my family were bred to further their family's ambitions. Without even realizing it, we were being groomed to marry well, set up the perfect home, then create an environment in which the men in their lives were comfortable and could concentrate on excelling in business. The women handled any issues with the household and the children. We were taught to put on the perfect dinner parties with the right people seated together so business deals would be finalized over after-dinner drinks. Husbands came home to a well-organized house, where their every need was anticipated and filled before they could express it. The home was where they came to relax and recharge. They did not want or need to know how it functioned. My grandmother loved my grandfather wholly and blindly, as she had been taught to do, but she never challenged him intellectually or sexually. Lillian filled that roll in my grandfather's life and he loved her for it.

When Aunt Julie was seventeen and had finished high school, her mother had wanted her to go to England to finishing school as the generations before had done, but Lillian had seen that Julie had more to offer and had her father's head for business, so it was she who had stepped in and asked, actually demanded, that Julie be sent to her to study business at a university in the States. The compromise was that she did a fine arts degree along with her business degree, but Lillian had won out. Aunt Julie had lived with Lillian and John for four years as she completed her studies. Julie came to understand why her father had loved Lillian as much as he had because Julie came to admire her quiet dignity and enjoy her uncompromising will when it came to those she loved—Julie was one of those precious few. Julie lived as fiercely as Lillian had and was not afraid to voice her opinion to her brothers, earning their respect in many circumstances in which she was right. Being raised how they were, her brothers never admitted they were wrong, but in taking her advice, they tipped their hat to her intellect.

Aunt Julie once told me that if she had met a man like Thomas, she would have married, but men who were comfortable in their manhood enough to love a woman and make her a true partner in his life instead of a participant were nonexistent in Jamaica during her lifetime. Instead, she took the lessons Lillian had taught her and protected her family with the ferocity of a lioness. As we were pulling into the beach house, I asked Aunt Julie what happened to Lillian.

She sighed as she turned off the car and sat silently for a long time. "She died not long after your grandfather died. I think it may have been of a broken heart. She never did accept that Daddy would never be with her. He provided for her, he loved her desperately, but he was not strong enough to give up his family for her. John came to understand that, but Lillian never did; she was a proud woman and rightly so. At your grandfather's funeral, she took her place and stood with the family, next to John. No one dared say anything to her, especially your grandmother. She stayed by the gravesite for a long time, long after everyone had left. She told that grave everything she had ever wanted my grandfather to know, especially how much she had loved him and still did. How grateful she was for John and the life he had given them, but mostly how much she had missed him because he was the love of her life.

"John and I stood with her and listened to her talk for hours. We both knew that while she could live apart from him, she was not strong enough to live without him. Within six months, she was dead. John and I grieved for her, but we could not be sad because she was finally with the man she loved and that is where she always wanted to be." Aunt Julie wiped a tear from the corner of her eye. "She was a remarkable woman. I always aspired to be like her. I loved her, maybe more than I loved my mother because she fought for me until she had given me the strength and confidence to fight for myself." Her voice trailed off as she turned to look out the window, trying to compose herself. We both noticed Simon standing at the door waiting for us.

I was surprised to see John John and Sally when I walked into the house. While the Jamaican government had not officially arrested John John, he did not venture far from the community that protected him. It was not outside of the realm of possibility for the DEA to scoop him up under the rendition program, making him disappear forever. It was then I noticed the armed guards posted discreetly around the perimeter of the house. Not sure what to make of this new normal, I sat as Aunt Julie closed the door to the outside world and motioned for all of us to sit down.

"Now that fate has brought us all together, it is time we utilize this gift and correct the mistakes of the past and right all the wrongs." She had our attention, as we all stared at her.

"John knew this day would come and he has given us the tools we will need to see his vision for Jamaica come true. There is a cave at the top of the hill behind us. You can only find it if you know where to look. In that cave, are recorded conversations, documentation and proof of all illegal activities in drug dealing, arms sales and murders committed by Jamaican government officials, US government officials, several Latin American government officials along with their drug czars and kingpins. There is enough there to implicate and convict a lot of important and influential people. The time has come to start using it." Aunt Julie paused as this sunk in with us.

"Is that why Daddy was killed? Did they know about what he had collected?" Sally asked.

"No. Your father was killed because he was a threat to too many people. The contents of the cave would have been enough to bring the Jamaican government to its knees. He loved Jamaica too much to plunge it into chaos, but at some point, he had planned to put a stop to the illegal drug trade and the corruption it bred. They just killed him before he could put his plan in motion."

"When men are confronted with the consequences of their misdeeds, they will choose to atone for them instead of facing them," John said very quietly. Sally and Simon sat back in their chairs, stunned.

"What does that mean, John John?" I asked.

"It was something John used to say; it was a realization he had come to very early in his life and it was his grand plan," Aunt Julie said.

"I don't understand," I said.

"John knew if he turned over everything he had to the Americans, governments not only in Jamaica but in many Latin countries would crumble, plunging them into chaos, they would never recover from." Again, it was Aunt Julie who spoke.

"Like Haiti?" I asked.

"Exactly. The power vacuum that would be created would lead to violence, corruption and poverty so intense that it would affect generations to come," she explained. Now I was beginning to understand. Rome would fall, but it would not only be Rome; it would be every empire in history that would fall, all at the same time, like dominos.

We sat in silence as Aunt Julie let us think about this. It was apparent she had a plan; she and John had put one in place many years ago and she was anxious to start implementing it.

"Only Jo will know the location of that cave." I nodded but said nothing. "Then you will go to meet with the DEA agent in charge of John John's case; his name is Robert Manning. You will negotiate John John's transfer to their custody, on the condition that he is protected from harm. If anything—and I mean, anything—happens to him, they will get nothing more from us."

"What, no, what? I am going to jail, Aunt Julie?" John John was not happy with this news.

Aunt Julie was angry with John John, but it was anger born from fear for him. Sally and I could see that and we both took his hand. "Yes, you damn fool. You got yourself wiretapped, remember that? I am not going to let you die like your father did. The only way to keep you safe is to send you to the Americans."

John John was having none of it. "Why do I have to go to jail? Why can't we use everything we have to negotiate *not* going to jail?" John John could not see the big picture. He felt that prison was a fate worse than death. Sally and I understood why Aunt Julie was doing this; she would rather visit an American jail than a Jamaican gravesite.

"John John, if you are killed, everything would be lost. I can't fulfill John's wish if I am worried about you being killed by someone every minute of every day. You are not going to jail, you idiot. You are a cooperating witness; they cannot charge you with anything unless they can prove you have committed a crime. In America, you are innocent until proven guilty. If you are with the Americans, you will be safe until it is time to come home."

"And when will that be?" John John asked. He was beginning to realize the danger he was in. While John John knew he lived a dangerous lifestyle and that his life could be forfeit at any moment, he had never really had to face his own mortality. Now he was beginning to understand that he was worth more dead than alive, to a lot of people, while the only people who would give him up to save his life were the people sitting in this room with him.

Aunt Julie looked at him, tears in her eyes. She shook her head; she had no idea if or when John John would ever come home. The pain of that weighed heavily on her. We were beginning to realize how hard the decisions that we had to make would be for all of us, especially John John.

"What's the plan, Aunt Julie?" John John asked, bravely looking her in the eye. He would do his part.

Over the next twenty-four hours, Aunt Julie laid out the entire plan. It was terrifying, but if it worked, it would change the course of not only the family's history but the history of Jamaica and possibly the world.

"Jo, you will negotiate turning John John over to the DEA. You will negotiate where he will stay and how he will be protected, in exchange for the information we will be providing. I want him as far away from harm as possible, but it has to be in the United States and he is treated as a cooperating witness only. All American citizens are innocent until proven guilty."

"Aunt Julie, they will never agree to that. He is not a US citizen," I argued.

"Oh, yes, he is." Aunt Julie handed me John John's birth certificate and Social Security card, proof he was a card-carrying member of Uncle Sam's republic, as was Sally.

Sally and John John had no idea that they had been born in the United States and spent the first six months of their lives under the care of their mother and grandfather. The news surprised us all.

"Then you will tell the DEA that you will be the person giving them everything they need to put people behind bars. It will be done in stages so that the damage will be minimal and honest people can replace the corrupt ones. We will start with the Jamaican prime minister and his contact in the US government. By bringing those two down, we will start dismantling the pyramid, block by block." Again, she paused to let this sink in.

"How are we going to do that?" I asked.

"I have dossiers on both men; you will hand these over to the DEA once our terms and conditions are agreed to by the Yanks. It will contain everything they need to put both men behind bars for good." Of course she did—piece of cake. "One more thing. It is only a matter of time before the US legalizes marijuana. We, meaning the family, want the only license to export cannabis to the United States from Jamaica."

Is that all? I thought.

Simon chimed in. "Aunt Julie, ganja is not even legal in Jamaica. How do you want a legitimate company to export an illegal product?"

"By the time this all comes to pass, it will be legal in Jamaica," Aunt Julie said, which was news to all of us. "Canada has legalized the recreational use of marijuana and Jamaica, through a joint venture between the government and our company, will export the first shipment of cannabis to Canada within the next two months. Eventually, that company will belong solely to the family."

She looked at all of us, one by one. She knew this was a lot for us to digest, but she was in a hurry. She knew things we did not know—that was obvious—and she was in a big hurry to see the plan that she and John had worked on for thirty years come to pass. The pieces had finally fallen into place and she was not wasting any more time.

"Jo will fly to Washington tomorrow; you have a meeting with Robert Manning. He is the man in charge of putting John John behind bars. Here are the dossiers you will be taking with you. Read them and know everything in them. Under no circumstances do you hand them over until you have the deal we discussed in place, but you will need to know enough to make the deal happen." The dossiers were at least two hundred pages each and I was leaving tomorrow morning.

"Go to bed, Aunt Julie." Sally took charge; we had been at this for two days straight, sleeping and eating as needed. "John John and Jo, take the US dossier. Simon and I will take the Jamaican one. Study them; we will prepare Jo for her meeting. I don't think I need to tell you how important it is that you know this information inside out. We cannot afford to get even one detail wrong." Sally started handing out papers and giving us our assignments.

Aunt Julie watched us as we took our directives and started to work. Slowly and quietly, she stood up and left the room. She knew we would do what we had to in order to succeed. We were a family who believed in the principle that a house divided would fall. We were no longer a house divided, so we would never fall. We had a common belief in each other and were committed to the plan Aunt Julie had outlined. We worked together throughout the night, fully understanding the consequences of what would happen if we failed. We would not fail each other. Generations came together that night to bind us in their love and collectively give us the strength we would need to accomplish Uncle John's dream.

CHAPTER 11

THE MEETING

Robert Manning was a tall man; his hair was beginning to gray at the temples. He wore a button-down shirt with jeans and seemed entirely unaware of how ruggedly handsome he was.

He is nothing like Thomas, I thought and was surprised that I had made that comparison.

As I waited for him to turn his attention to me, I studied him. He had a melancholy about him but also a strength of character that begged me to trust him. I wondered if all government agents were taught to foster that appeal for trust or if it was something he had organically. I was scared and out of my comfort zone, but on the outside, I was calm and confident as I assessed him through hooded eyes. For now, he was the enemy.

In reading the information in the dossiers, Simon, Sally, John John, and I had decided to modify Aunt Julie's plan slightly. We would give the US government information on illegalities in their own country as well as Latin American governments. As for our own government's misdeeds, we decided to keep this to ourselves and use it for leverage to better our own country. If I could convince the United States to stay out of Jamaica's business, then we could clean up our mess without any interference from Big Brother. The long-term goal was to stamp out the corruption and greed that was permeating the political parties, thus paving the way for a government of people dedicated to the uplifting of Jamaica and Jamaicans as a whole and not based on their political affiliations. Simon had the perfect person in mind to lead this utopian government, while I worked on my end, he would work on his end to achieve the removal of the current prime minister and install the man we thought was better suited for the job, all the while trying not to get John John killed in the process.

Aunt Julie wanted the PM removed. The sooner, the better. She had waited a long enough to exact revenge and it was now or never for her. I was nervous; this was a new Aunt Julie and I did not know this side of her. She was smart, cunning and dangerous. It was the dangerous side of her that worried me. I was shocked to find out just how ruthless my aunt was. I had to reconcile this Aunt Julie with the Aunt Julie I knew who would catch a little lizard to release it back into the garden while my mother screamed bloody murder and demanded its immediate death.

I put all thoughts of Aunt Julie out of my mind as I waited for Robert Manning to look in my direction. I had been shown into his office and offered a seat across from him, but it had been several minutes and he had yet to acknowledge my presence. He was engrossed in whatever it was that he was writing. I sat quietly, watching and waiting.

At last, he put his papers away and addressed me. "Mrs. Bradley, to what do I owe the pleasure of this visit?" I was surprised by his question. Aunt Julie had somehow set up a meeting with this man without letting him know what it was about. Again, I was in awe of her.

"My name is Josephine Myers-Bradley." If he recognized the name, he did not show it, and there was no change in his expression.

He was now waiting as I had been. It was hard to read his eyes and it unnerved me slightly. "I believe you are familiar with my cousin, John John Rollins." My words surprised him; I could see that I had his full attention now.

"Your cousin?" he asked.

"My cousin," I replied. "His father was my uncle, my grandfather's son."

"I see." I was not sure what about this news threw him, the fact that his investigations had not found this connection or that the relationship existed at all. He stood up, walked around his desk and took the chair next to mine. He leaned in to look at me intently.

"I am here on my cousin's behalf." I felt silly, like a child trying to play intriguing games with an adult who saw me as an amusement. I was beginning to doubt myself and my abilities to pull this off. So much counted on how this meeting went, I was suddenly nervous and afraid. My lower lip trembled and I turned away from his intent stare. I could see he thought me to be a beguiling child who had innocently come to plead her cousin's case.

"John John wants to be extradited to the United States. He is willing to provide the proof you need to bring down a major drug ring operating in the United States with connections to most of the large drug suppliers in Latin America, in exchange for certain conditions your government will need to agree to."

He was not expecting this. "We cannot extradite a foreign national without the permission of the country he is a national of. So far, the Jamaican government has not cooperated with our request."

"I am sure you are familiar with the circumstances of my Uncle's death." He said nothing but I could tell from his expression that he was. "The man responsible for my Uncle's death is now the prime minister of Jamaica. He will not turn John John over to you for the same reason that he would not turn over my uncle before him." I could tell that Robert understood what I was implying and had suspected as much.

"I have a solution. John John is a US citizen; here is a copy of his birth certificate." Robert made no move to hide his surprise at this news. He took the document from me and put it on the table between the two of us after examining it closely. "We can arrange to turn John John over to you before anyone in the Jamaican government knows he is gone. But for this to happen, we need to agree." Robert motioned for me to stop talking by putting his finger to his lips. Without another word, he got up, picked up John John's birth certificate and grabbed the jacket that was hanging on the back of his chair. He put it inside his coat tucked away in a pocket. He grabbed my hand; together we left the building, not a word spoken between us.

He did not let go of my hand while we were in the building, not while we walked past security, not while he hailed a cab and we got in. Not until he had opened the door to a small apartment away from prying eyes and ears. It had not occurred to me to ask him why he was doing this or where we were going. I had just allowed this man to take my hand and lead me into God knows what, without even asking a question. *What the hell was wrong with me?* There was no way I could pull this off. As we entered the cramped passageway of the apartment, he took my coat and removed his. Again, not speaking, he grabbed my hand and led me into the small kitchen. There was a breakfast bar separating the tiny kitchen from the small living room. Standing at either end of the bar, we stared at each other. I finally found my voice.

"Please tell me what the hell just happened? Where are we?" I did not take my eyes off him.

He ran his hand through his hair and took a deep breath. "Josie? May I call you Josie?" No one had ever called me Josie, but right now, I needed answers. He was waiting for my affirmative nod before he continued to speak, so I nodded curtly. "I am not sure how much you know about your cousin or his business."

"I know everything," I interrupted.

He looked at me and spoke quietly but deliberately. "Then you know that he is involved with a lot of people in this country who would like to see him dead instead of in our custody. I am not sure I can protect him here. I am assuming that is what you want. Protection for him?" He was a lot more intuitive than I had given him credit for.

I took a deep breath; this was not the response I had expected from Robert Manning or the US government. I thought he would have been falling head over heels to offer me anything I wanted to get their hands on John John and secure a win for the war on drugs. The fact that he did not trust his own government to protect John John gave me pause. I took a deep breath as doubt flooded my body. Was Uncle Sam big and strong enough to do what I needed? What my family needed?

"Josie, why are you here? What do you want?" I was not sure how to answer those questions now. I walked to the window that dominated the small living room. It overlooked a river, the Potomac, I thought. I was not sure; I had never been to Washington before. I could feel his eyes on me.

"More than anything, I want my cousin protected from harm. I was sent here by my family to secure his protection." As I watched him, I could read nothing in his eyes, but I instinctively knew he would not make me any promises he could not keep. "In exchange for his protection, we are prepared to give you everything you need to convict the principals involved in the United States, Panama and

Venezuela. In short, I will give you everything you need to destroy one of the major networks supplying narcotics into the United States."

"What about Jamaica?" I had not expected this question so quickly.

I took a deep breath. "I give you my word that we will handle Jamaica. We will destroy the network from within and Jamaica will no longer be a gateway for supplying illegal drugs into this country or any other. I, we, only ask that you give us the autonomy to handle this ourselves and view us as a true and equal partner in our mutual fight."

He looked at me intently as he moved to stand in front of the window next to me. I desperately wanted to know what he was thinking. "What do you have to bargain with?"

Silently I opened my handbag and handed him the first dossier. In it were all the names of the principals involved with accepting drugs shipped from Jamaica into the United States. The dossier outlined dates, times and manifests of how and when the drugs came in. The names of the people who accepted them, the names of officials who enabled them and accounts of how payments were collected and distributed. I knew Aunt Julie had told me not to hand it over until a deal was made, but I felt it was the only way to prove to Robert that what I was saying was true and that we could be partners in ridding both our countries of the scourge of illegal drugs. Robert sat down on the couch and looked it over. Suddenly I felt exhausted. The toll this was taking on me was beginning to show.

"Robert, I am exhausted. Is there somewhere I could lie down?" I asked. He looked up at me and moved quickly to my side, taking my arm and guiding me into a small bedroom. He sat me down on the bed and took off my shoes. He moved the covers and motioned for me to lie down. I could sense he stood over me, watching me, but I did not know for how long. As soon as my head hit the pillow, I was asleep.

I have no idea how long I slept. When I awoke, it took me a moment to remember where I was and why. I felt the weight of the responsibility I had dragging at my limbs and I lay motionless. There was no movement outside the closed door that I could hear. I blinked the sleep of out my eyes and noticed the bathroom through the door next to me. I got up, stumbled to the bathroom and was surprised to see my toiletry bag on the tiny ledge above the sink.

I had gone directly from the airport to Robert's office and had left my overnight bag with his assistant. In the rush to leave his office, I had forgotten it. I wondered how it had ended up here? I washed my face and brushed my teeth. Trying to straighten my crumpled clothes, I walked barefoot into the kitchen. Robert was sitting on the couch; he had read through the dossier and was going through it again, making notes as he turned pages. He had not heard me and did not see me in the kitchen. I took a moment to watch him. He was in his early forties. I remembered from his holding my hand that his grip was firm and the way he looked at me, his gaze penetrating. He was a man of honor, but he was also empathetic. His actions had shown me that. I felt drawn to him and that immediately made me wary of him. I noticed the wonderful smells coming from the stove and realized that I was starving. I moved over to see what it was and Robert noticed me. He immediately put aside his work and came to the kitchen.

"You must be hungry; you slept for most of the afternoon and evening," he said softly.

It was then I noticed the lights of the city illuminating the Washington skyline. It was beautiful; I walked over to the window for a better look. "What time is it?" I asked softly. I was entirely captivated by the magnificent view.

"After nine o'clock. Your Aunt Julie called your cell phone several times; I finally had to answer it. I apologize for going into your purse, but she sounded worried when I did answer. I explained to her that you were fine, we were working together and you had gone to take a nap. She asked me to have you call her as soon as you awoke. I'm not sure she believed me. I think she feels I have you locked up in some dungeon below my office."

I smiled as he said that. I can only imagine what Aunt Julie thought. He relaxed a little when he saw me smile. "I took the liberty of asking my assistant to bring your suitcase to my apartment. That is why your things are here." I could tell he was nervous that he had overstepped our fragile boundaries.

"Your apartment? You brought me to your apartment? How did you explain that to your assistant?"

It was his turn to smile, and it was beautiful. "I said you were an old girlfriend and I could not wait to get you back to my place. You see, you were the one that got away. She reads a lot of romance novels; I knew she would find that explanation enchanting." Now I understood why he held my hand throughout our rushed departure from his office. Despite my shock at his boldness, I laughed out loud; it had been a long time since I had been anyone's girlfriend.

"Josie, what are the conditions you mentioned earlier? The conditions we have to meet to get the information you are offering?"

I was still trying to get used to the name Josie, but it was time to put my game face on. I mentally went over the conditions that Aunt Julie had outlined to me and plunged ahead. "John John is a cooperating witness. He is not your prisoner and you cannot charge him with a crime."

"We have him on a wiretap," he said quickly, but I was ready with a response to that.

"There is no way for you to authenticate that you have John John on wiretap. Furthermore, you cannot prove that John John committed a crime on American soil. That is the only way you can charge him under DEA statutes. Wiretapping is inadmissible in Jamaica. Even if he allegedly committed a crime in Jamaica, we are a sovereign nation and not under your jurisdiction. The only way you can charge John John with a crime is if you have evidence of the crime being committed on American soil. You have no such evidence and as a US citizen, he is innocent until proven guilty. Ergo, he is a cooperating witness and not subject to arrest, just protection."

Robert continued to look at me. "I had no idea you were a lawyer."

"I am not a lawyer, but that does not mean that I don't know the law. Robert, we, I, have the information you need. I am willing to provide you with that information to secure convictions and destroy a plague that is ravishing your—I mean, our—country. I am an American. I love this country. My citizenship was a gift from my husband and I cherish it daily."

"But you are also a Jamaican by birth and born into a powerful and corrupt family that you seem intent on protecting, no matter the cost." Robert had accurately described my dilemma.

"Yes, I am split between two countries, but I am trying to do what's right for both. Everything I am doing is out of love, love for the country of my birth and the country of my heart, but most of all, for love I have for my family. I will sacrifice everything for them." There, I had said it—the pledge of allegiance that I had fought against my entire life. As a family, we had lied to each other, betrayed each other and disliked each other, but when threatened by an outside force, we closed ranks and protected our own. Family first and forever is what I had been taught all my life to believe.

Robert nodded as if he had expected to hear that. The dossier I had provided him was very compelling and was the first phase in destroying the drug cartel Uncle John had built. We would start at the end, destroying it from there, moving back to the beginning. It was the best way to catch the principals unaware and achieve our goals without shaking the family to its core. We had secrets we wanted to keep buried.

Robert looked at me intently and I met his gaze challengingly. Neither one of us spoke for a long time. "I am assuming you have a plan on how you want to proceed," he said.

"The first thing is to get John John to safety; you will protect him as you dismantle the US side of things. My family will take care of dismantling the Jamaican side."

He stopped me there. "You are asking me to trust that your family has enough power and control in Jamaica to take down a corrupt government and replace it with what, exactly?"

"I am asking you to respect the autonomy of Jamaican sovereignty. I am asking you to respect that we are partners, working together to achieve a common goal. It is going to require trust, Robert, if not between our two countries, then between you and me."

Again, he stopped and fixed his gaze on me. I did not flinch. I believed in what we were doing. I let the power of my conviction burn fiercely in my eyes as he gauged my commitment.

"Fine, I accept your terms. John John will not be charged with a crime unless we can prove that he committed one stateside. In exchange, we will keep him safe as an asset for as long as he is needed to eradicate your family's drug ring." I felt a twinge of guilt as he referred to it as "my family's" drug ring, but I was so grateful to achieve this first part of the plan that I decided to ignore it.

My eyes welled up with tears, but neither of us looked away or moved. "I will call Aunt Julie now; she will be delighted to hear that." He nodded and I left the room to make the call.

As expected, Aunt Julie had a hundred questions, but I had no details yet. It would take three days of Robert and me holed up in the apartment, with frequent calls to Aunt Julie and Simon to work out the details of John John's extraction. We decided that Simon would take John John from the beach house by boat to a fishing trawler waiting out at sea. On the trawler would be a Navy SEAL team that Robert knew, had worked with and trusted. They would keep John John with them until indictments had been handed down and arrests made for all the people listed in the first dossier. I would meet John John stateside, make sure he was secure and safe, then return to Jamaica to collect more dossiers to hand over. There were several cogs in the wheel, which had to be in perpetual motion for our plan to succeed. We were all aware that the entire plan could fall apart at any given time.

On the third night of being holed up in that tiny apartment, Robert and I had had enough and decided to go out to dinner. He had been the perfect gentleman, sleeping on the couch, not that I ever saw him sleep. For three days straight, we had worked side by side, working out the details of John John's extraction and the terms and conditions under which he would be detained by Robert and how our mutual arrangement would work. He never once asked what we planned to do in Jamaica, but when I told him that one more condition of our cooperation would be that our family business had the sole license to export cannabis to the United States, he wanted to know why.

I thought long and hard about how to answer this question without implicating anyone; then, I decided to tell the truth. "Uncle John used the profits from the drug trade to help the people in Jamaica; he used it to build hospitals, schools and houses so poor people would have a home to be proud of, in which to feel safe. He used that money to give Jamaicans a hand up so they could make their lives better, their children's lives better. Politicians weren't doing it; they only came around when they wanted votes to secure their power. So, Uncle John found another way to help them. Now that ganja is going to be legalized, we are still going to use the profits to help those in need."

Robert sat back in his chair, his fingers in an inverted *L* on his face as he listened carefully to me. He thought about what I had said for a long time. By now, I was used to these long silences as he carefully considered something I had said. He was not a man to make snap decisions based on emotion; he thought things through and took the time to look at all the angles. It had not taken me long to understand this about him. He hadn't asked me any additional questions but had miraculously made it happen. By the end of that day, I had a signed document with everything we had agreed to in black and white with the seal of the US government on it. I informed him that nothing more would happen until a copy of it was in Simon's hands. He was not surprised to hear that condition.

FedEx had just picked up the package to deliver to Simon in Jamaica. We left the apartment shortly after that. As soon as Simon received the package, Robert would go to meet up with the Seal team. I would wait for his return with John John at a hotel close to the base. It would be our last night together in his little apartment. It had been a busy three days and I was emotionally exhausted. I had not thought of Thomas in all that time. The realization of that made me stop dead in my tracks.

"What's wrong?" Robert asked as he saw my stricken face.

"I…" I was not sure what to say to Robert. "Nothing. Nothing's wrong." I smiled shakily at him. I could tell that he didn't believe me, so I walked faster, slightly ahead of him. He made no effort to catch up and match my steps.

"How long were you married for?"

I spun on my heel and nearly fell as I turned to face him. He grabbed my arm to steady me. The warmth of his hand stayed the harsh retort on my tongue.

"Twenty-one years." He nodded as I said that and we walked on in silence, both lost in our thoughts.

"I can tell you miss him," he said quietly. I looked at him but said nothing. "You call out for him in your sleep. Thomas, right?"

I was shocked but could only nod. I didn't realize that I called out for Thomas in my sleep. I looked away as he gently took my hand. I didn't pull it away as we walked silently to the restaurant.

The restaurant was small and dark, there was no overwhelming music and the few patrons there spoke quietly to each other. The atmosphere settled my frazzled nerves. Robert ordered for me and I let him. The food was excellent and I calmed down as we ate silently.

"You have never asked me how I came to be involved in all of this. Why is that?" I asked.

"I figured when you were ready to tell me, you would." He turned to his plate.

"What do you know about me, Robert?" I asked warily.

It was a long time before he looked up, but when he did, he held my gaze. "I know you are a member of a very powerful and influential family in Jamaica. I know your father ran the family businesses; you are his only child. I know you married before finishing college and left Jamaica. I know you are an American citizen and that you lived in Florida until your husband died of cancer. I know you have no children. I know you are related to the biggest drug dealer in the Caribbean. One you are determined to keep alive, even if it means burning down the house your family built to do it." He recited his findings like he was describing the ingredients for the meal we were eating.

"My family is everything to me," I said defensively.

"And yet, you walked away from them for over twenty years. You didn't even know what the family business was until, what? A week or so ago?" he said.

Had it only been that short of a time? It felt like an eternity. Wait, how did he know all of this? He read the question in my eyes.

"Your Aunt Julie is very talkative," he answered. I knew this was a lie, but I did not respond to him. My Aunt Julie was the keeper of family secrets; she would never share this information with anyone, let alone someone like Robert with the position he held. I made a mental note to warn Aunt Julie and Simon to find the person who had supplied Robert with this information. A source close to Robert might come in handy in the future. I surprised myself at this thought. How quickly I had adapted to a life of intrigue, betrayal and the endless cycle of secrets my family seemed to be trapped in. We finished our meal in silence. I did not owe this man an explanation about my life or how I chose to live it. He paid the bill and we walked back to the apartment in silence.

"We need to leave the apartment early tomorrow. I will drop you off at the hotel, get you settled and then I will go to the base. As soon as Simon gives you the go-ahead, you will text me and I will go pick up John John." He was very matter-of-fact. I nodded that I understood. "Get some sleep," he said. I looked at him, wanting more, expecting more, but unsure of what *more* was. I turned abruptly and slammed the door to the bedroom behind me.

He was ready to go when I came out the next morning. He looked like he had not slept, but I said nothing, neither did he. We drove silently to the hotel. In the distance, I could see the military base where the operation would be secreted while it destroyed everything Uncle John had built. I stayed in the car as he checked me in. Not a word was spoken between us as he led me to the hotel room. I waited outside as he took my bag inside, checked the room and made sure everything was in order. He opened the door and motioned for me to enter. As I did, he closed the door and spun me around, trapping me between the door and his body. His eyes bore into mine. I felt like he was searing me into his brain.

We said nothing, just stared into each other's eyes. Then he was gone, out the door before I could say a word. I slumped to the floor and listened as his footsteps faded down the hallway. I had no idea why I felt his sudden absence so acutely.

Simon called and said that the package was safely in hand. I texted Robert that the plan was in motion. I did not hear back from him, not that I expected to. The way we had left things between us felt awkward and messy. I was not sure what to make of it. Unfortunately, it was a waiting game for me at this point. The last thing I wanted was time on my hands. Sally, Simon, and I had agreed not to contact each other until John John was safe. My only connection to Jamaica was Aunt Julie and I certainly did not want to confide in her what had happened between Robert and me. Truthfully, I was not able to articulate what had happened, not even to myself. I put it down to missing Thomas; he had been my sounding board for everything related to my family. With him gone, I felt so utterly alone. It had just been the two of us for so many years; I did not feel comfortable confiding my innermost thoughts and feelings to anyone but him. For the next two days and in my solitude, I retreated into my memories of him and hid there, waiting for the phone to ring.

CHAPTER 12

ROBERT

Robert was angry with himself as he left Josie. He was definitely attracted to her, but he also felt protective and instinctively knew she would not welcome any romantic attention from him or anyone while she was coming to terms with the loss of her husband.

He had noticed Josephine the moment she walked into his office. She was tall and slim with long strawberry-blond hair. The first thing that struck him about her was how beautiful she was; she had a natural confidence that seemed to be in conflict with the turmoil in her eyes. He had been curious about the meeting with her; all he had been told was that he would be meeting with someone who could provide him with crucial information regarding a case he was working on. The mysterious caller had not mentioned the case but insisted he could not afford to pass up the opportunity, so he had agreed to the meeting with some hesitation. He had not expected an elegant and attractive woman to walk through his door, then turn the most important case of his career upside down.

He paused before starting his car and thought about the nights she had stayed in his apartment. As she slept, he went over the dossiers and marveled at the detail he found in them. Names, dates, times of meetings and drug deals were all meticulously logged. Many came with audio recordings and pictures. It was a prosecutor's dream. Late into the night, he made notes and cataloged everything, so no crucial detail was missed.

Even with the bedroom door closed, he could hear her cry out and it concerned him enough to look in on her. Cautiously opening the door, a thin stream of light illuminated her anxious face as she called out for her dead husband. Slowly, he moved toward her; he smoothed the hair away from her face and noticed that she calmed at his touch. He knelt beside her and held her hand as the night terrors passed and she settled back into sleep. More than once, he had to remind himself that she came from a family that ran the largest drug cartel in the Caribbean.

For some reason, he could not reconcile the woman whose hand he held as she slept, to the cold, calculating violence that he associated with her cousin. During the time they had spent together, he was constantly distracted by how the setting sun kissed the red highlights in her hair as she stood in front of the window and the way her hips moved when she walked. Her vulnerability, coupled with the resilience she was beginning to discover in herself, was intriguing. The way she had outmaneuvered him in their negotiations had earned his respect.

There was an undeniable chemistry between them that he knew she did not want to feel, much less acknowledge. She was not ready for love. The shock of losing her husband was still with her; couple that with the surprise of finding out about her family and he marveled at the well of strength in her that she was tapping into. He had never been so conflicted in his life. He started the car and sped off. The thought of failing and never seeing her again wounded him to the core. He had to stop thinking about her and get his head in the game.

CHAPTER 13

THE EXTRACTION

As it turned out, it was probably best that I did not know what was happening. John John had a drug boat hiding in a cave on my father's property. Simon was not aware of the boat and was livid with John John when he saw where it was hidden. John John had tried to explain that it was there with permission from my father, but Simon knew nothing about this arrangement, which only added insult to injury in Simon's mind. Simon loved boats and this one was a beauty. He tried to put out of his mind what it was used for and took a moment to admire the craftsmanship. It was a high-speed recreational boat modified with extra horsepower; it glided across the water. The color of the boat and low profile made it difficult to detect with the naked eye. Nothing the Jamaican Coast Guard had could catch this boat, Simon was sure of that. He only had to make it to the international watermark, which was twenty-four miles off the coast of Jamaica. He estimated this boat maxed out at seventy miles per hour, so it would take less than twenty minutes at full speed to reach the American fishing trawler. While he did not expect to take it to full speed for twenty minutes, he secretly planned to push it to its limit, just for the rush it would give him.

Simon punched the coordinates into the navigation system and advised John John that it would be lights-out until they spotted the trawler. Turning on their running lights would be the signal to the trawler that it was them. John John did not like the idea of traveling that far out to sea without lights, but Simon had explained that this was the prearranged plan with Robert, and Simon knew the sea in this area better than he knew his name. He reminded John John that he had been fishing in the area since he was a boy and knew what he was doing. John John had never liked the sea and had a healthy respect for the dangers it could deliver to invaders who had no right being on it or in it. His greatest fear was drowning, so he planned to endure the next twenty minutes of his life instead of enjoying it. In his mind, he had more significant dangers ahead of him to contend with than the risks the sea presented. It would be the first time he would ever face adversity without his family by his side. Being away from his source of strength, including his island home, weighed heavily on him.

Simon was an unwilling participant in this venture. He loved his job as a police commissioner and worked hard to maintain his integrity and the standards it demanded of him. In his mind, turning John John over the United States was in pursuit of a greater good, not only for law enforcement but in the hopes of stamping out the greed and corruption that drug trafficking trapped small governments in. That being said, realizing that he was piloting a drug-smuggling boat pricked at his conscience.

It was a beautiful night, the moon hung high in the sky, and the sea was so calm it looked like the moon was dropping shimmering diamonds onto the sea's glistening surface. It was the perfect night to be at sea. Unfortunately, Simon was not the only one who thought so. Simon had just pushed the boat to its maximum speed and was enjoying every moment of it while John John had wedged himself between the deck chair and the instrument panel and was holding on for dear life. Neither one of them saw the coast guard cutter closing in on them until it was too late. Sirens started to wail, and Simon was so startled, he slowed the boat down, giving the cutter crucial seconds to catch up with them.

Realizing his mistake, he gunned the boat, creating a massive wake, causing the cutter to pitch ferociously, forcing it to slow down. Pressing his advantage, he turned the boat in the direction of the trawler lights he saw off in the distance. He estimated it would take him five minutes to reach the trawler and the cutter seven minutes. He took off in the direction of the trawler running parallel to it. When he was directly across from the trawler, he grabbed John John, and they both jumped into the water as the boat took off at full speed. John John was too terrified to do anything but hang on to Simon with both hands as they bobbed like lost corks at sea. Luckily for them, Robert had been tracking the speedboat with his binoculars and saw both men go into the water. He directed the trawler captain to head over to Simon and John John just as soon as the cutter sped past them in full pursuit of the now-empty boat. He also instructed the lights to be turned off on the trawler in the hopes that the cutter had not seen them as well. While they dragged a very subdued John John out of the water, Simon was roaring mad, hitting anything that was in front of him, narrowly missing Robert's face.

"What the hell? I thought you had taken care of the coast guard?" Robert asked an angrily pacing Simon.

"I did. I checked the schedule myself. No one was supposed to be in this area tonight." Simon was running on adrenaline and could not stay still.

"Then why the hell is that cutter out here?" one of the SEAL team members shouted at Simon. As Simon turned on him angrily, they heard a shout from the control deck.

"The cutter is turning around; it's headed our way!"

"There is no way the people on that cutter can board us, and under no circumstances can they find me on this boat with John John!" Both Simon and John John looked at Robert with panic-stricken faces.

Robert shouted at the team to take up defensive positions and yelled at the captain to gun the engines and head out deeper into international waters. To everyone's surprise, the cutter continued to pursue them, even though they had no jurisdiction. Robert instructed Simon to take a shaken John John below deck.

"You don't think...." John Johns's voice trailed off as he looked at Simon.

"I do think," Simon answered. "I just don't know how."

The PM must have anticipated a move like this on John John's part and had put precautions in place. Was it just dumb luck, or had the PM known it was happening tonight? The thought unsettled them. The decision has been made to hand John John over to the Americans, but was it the right one? Would they lose the tenuous power the family held in Jamaica? Were all their plans in jeopardy? It was a sobering thought, and both men fell silent as they contemplated how this had happened.

It was not long before they heard automatic gunfire coming from the deck above them and heard the pings of bullets hitting the hull of the trawler. Neither could believe the PM would start an international incident over John John, but the gunfire proved he was not going down without a fight, and we had all underestimated him.

To their surprise, the trawler had more under the hood than they imagined, and it was not long before the gunfire faded into the night sky. Two SEALs rushed into the cabin with another one between them; he had been shot. Simon helped the man to the bunk and started yelling for a first-aid kit. John John saw one on the wall and instantly brought it to Simon. If there was one thing John John and Simon knew how to handle, it was gunshot wounds, so they muscled the larger men out of the way and went to work on the injured SEAL team member. They worked quickly and efficiently and were able to stabilize him. They removed the bullet and gave him a shot of morphine. They waited until his breathing was a steady rhythm and then decided to go topside and get some air. Simon came up first and saw the other team members moving around the deck; their automatic rifles close at hand. It was when John John came up that all hell broke loose. One of the team members let loose a long string of obscenities and launched himself at John John, getting in some solid blows before Robert and Simon pulled him off John John. Simon took up a defensive position over the fallen John John and launched a string of obscenities back at the SEAL.

"What the fuck is your problem?" Simon screamed at him.

"My fucking problem is pulling third-world assholes like you out of the fire. Why am I here babysitting a fucking drug dealer and putting members of my team at risk?" He was the team captain clearly not happy that one of his team members was hurt protecting Simon and especially John John. Both Simon and John John could understand his anger and even sympathized with the source of it.

"He will be fine; we need to get him to a hospital soon. We patched him up with what we have, but he needs antibiotics and a doctor to look at the wound. Honestly, we don't know if we missed anything," Simon explained quietly.

"We will be in Key West within the hour; we need to sit tight and wait it out. Major, why don't you go down there and check on him?" Robert stepped in and quickly defused the situation. The major shot one more dirty look at John John and went below.

"I guess formal introductions are in order; I am Robert Manning. I am in charge of the case against John. Your cousin, right?" His question was directed at Simon.

"Yes," Simon answered carefully. "My first cousin. Our fathers are half brothers." Robert nodded as he looked at both of them.

"Any idea what happened out there?" Robert asked.

"I have my suspicions, but nothing I can prove yet, at least not until I get back to Jamaica." It was then Simon realized he had no passport on him. He had planned to deliver John John and return the boat to its hiding place. No one would have known he had left the island. Now he was on a fishing trawler bound for the United States with no passport and no way of getting home.

Robert had already thought of this. "Don't worry; I have a private airplane leaving Key West for Montego Bay as soon as you land. You will be on that plane, just not on the manifest. The manifest will show two tourists landed on their way to a private villa in Ocho Rios. I trust you can find your way home from Montego Bay?" Robert asked.

Simon nodded.

"Good, then no one will suspect your involvement in John John's disappearance," Robert said. Robert sat back and regarded Simon and John John for a few minutes.

"Josephine assures me you can handle the situation in Jamaica and clean it up. You will understand that after tonight's events, I have my doubts," Robert said.

Simon nodded and looked at John John. "We can handle it. It won't be pretty now, but we will do what we need to." John John seemed to understand what Simon was saying, but Robert had to take his words at face value.

"Do you think it is safe for Josie to return to Jamaica during your cleanup process?" Robert had asked the question casually enough, but Simon and John John had recognized the underlying protectiveness in his voice. It was something they lived with every day, trying to keep the women they loved safe. Simon and John John stole a single glance at each other.

"Jo will stay with John John until she is confident he is safe and you are fulfilling your end of the bargain. She will be your only contact with our family. She is an American citizen and has the freedom to travel back and forth as she wants, so no one will suspect the reason for her visits is John John or to bring you any information from us. As an American citizen, she is always under the protection of your government, isn't she?" Simon asked, making sure to emphasize her name.

It was hard not to miss the relieved look in Robert's eyes as he nodded curtly. Simon and John John wondered what had happened between their cousin and this DEA agent. John John silently assured Simon with a quick nod of his head, that he would get to the bottom of it. Their arrival into Key West was bittersweet for Simon, John John, and Robert. While the SEAL team secured their gear and took their injured man to the nearby military base for treatment, Robert outlined what would happen next. A six-member protective squad, made up of the same SEAL members who had just rescued them, was assigned to John John. They would fly with Robert and John John to Washington, where John John would remain on a base. Simon understood it was best that he not know where John John was and accepted this without comment, but it was difficult to see his cousin go.

Simon and John John had been inseparable as boys. They had fished together, gone bird shooting together, gone to school together, learned at their grandfather's knee together. They had chosen to attend the same university and had lived together throughout their school years in the United States. Their bond was strong and deep. It was tested when Simon decided to become a police officer and John John then had to explain to him what some of the family businesses had entailed. It had been an awkward conversation for both of them to have, but they had come out of it respecting each other, if not fully understanding why each had made the choices they had.

Ganja was a staple in Jamaica. Although it was not technically legal, everyone looked the other way. When the politicians realized it would be a gold mine for them personally, they circumvented America's war on drugs by sanctioning the export of ganja but working to help America, Canada and the UK with the odd drug bust of heroin, cocaine and opioids brought in by John John's competitors. This way, everyone was happy; they did not lose the aid packages that they relied on from these first world countries. Jamaican politicians became adept at walking a fine line between international politics and personal gains. Simon had made John John promise not to sell hard drugs in Jamaica and in exchange, he would look the other way when it came to the exporting of ganja and other hard drugs from Latin America. John John had even given the names of low-level drug dealers who tried to sell hard drugs in Jamaica to Simon, who had moved quickly to put these people in jail. It worked well for everyone. John John had his competitors locked up; the government could show the world they were partners in the war on drugs and Simon could feel secure in the knowledge that he was protecting the people of Jamaica as he had sworn to do.

They had found a way to work together without confronting each other—which both had admitted to themselves, was the hardest thing they had ever done but was necessary to preserve their relationship. They were cousins but as close as brothers and the prospect of not seeing each other again was a difficult cross to bear. Robert could see this and gave them some time alone as he briefed the protective detail on what had happened.

"You will take care…" John John was hesitant as he asked Simon to take care of his two children. In the Jamaican tradition, John John was not married to their mother, but both children lived with him and were provided for and protected by him.

"Aunt Julie has already moved them into my house," Simon answered. His wife, Pamela, was a good woman; she understood the family dynamics and knew what was expected of her. She and Simon genuinely loved each other and worked together as a team. When Simon had told her of his need to take in John John's children, she had not questioned him but set to work on getting their rooms ready and enrolling them in school. They would be raised with her children, with all the protections and privileges the family could provide.

John John nodded. He knew how much Simon loved his children and he knew they would want for nothing, including love and affection not only from Simon and Pam but from the extended family as well, but he would miss seeing them grow up. There was no price too high to pay for his family. His father had taught him that, his grandfather had taught him that and Simon had taught him that.

Simon and John John sat next to each other. They said nothing, but their thoughts were the same. Simon knew that Uncle John and, now his children had sacrificed the most in keeping the family safe and secure. Everything Simon had was due in no small part to the actions of Uncle John and John John. He could not express to John John how grateful he was to his cousin and how much he loved him and would miss him.

John John had done everything in his life, secure in the knowledge that he knew who he was, where he had come from and that his family loved him. His strength came from that knowledge and now, when he needed to be the strongest he had ever been, his source of strength would not be with him. The realization unbalanced him, but it did not break his resolve.

The two men stood up as Robert came over and announced it was time to say goodbye. They looked at each other and shook hands solemnly. Then Simon pulled John John into a long embrace. It seemed to give them the strength they needed to step away from each other.

"Don't worry about anything, John John. You have done your part; it is time for the rest of us to step up now. I *will* see you again, my brother." Simon's voice was filled with emotion.

John John nodded and patted Simon's shoulder. Words failed him. He stood there unmoving as Simon walked away. Robert gave him some space. Eventually, John John turned to Robert and said firmly, "Let's go."

CHAPTER 14

THE BASE

I nervously paced the confines of my room for over an hour. A call from Aunt Julie had assured me that both John John and Simon were safe, but it had not gone smoothly. One of the Americans had been shot in the melee. I was panicked to think it may have been Robert, but Aunt Julie had innocently informed me that it had not been Robert and the relief that I had felt made me take a seat. I managed to keep my emotions in check as I finished the conversation with her, but when the text had arrived from Robert saying they would be picking me up shortly, my nervous tension returned.

I told myself it was the anxiety of seeing John John under these circumstances and my nervousness about completing the mission at hand, but if I was candid, it was Robert. He completely unnerved me and I was at a loss to explain why. I jumped at the quiet knock on the door and ran to open it, my facing lighting up when I saw John John. I wrapped him in a hug but could not help looking over his shoulder to see if Robert was there. He was and our eyes met.

"Ready to go, cuz? Wait until you see our new digs! The decorator loves camouflage green." John John was speaking to me.

Dragging my eyes from Robert's, it was then I noticed the bruises on John John's face and the bloodied lip. "What the hell, John John?

What happened to your face?" Both John John and Robert refused to meet my eyes, so I assumed that John John had received these injuries at Robert's hands. I flew at Robert, fists raised.

"You son of a bitch! I told you no harm was to come to him. Look at him!" I managed to land one blow before John John dragged me off a shocked Robert.

"Down, girl. It was not Robert. I fell getting off the boat onto the dock. If you want to blame someone, blame Simon. He knows how much I hate boats and being that far out to sea." John John struggled to hold me. He had not realized how strong I was. The look of surprise on Robert's and my face at this revelation made John John laugh, and the tension was broken.

"Sorry. I should not have assumed it was you." My voice was quiet as I spoke in Robert's direction, not meeting his eyes.

"You both have one fucked-up set of family values," Robert commented as he grabbed my bag and led the way out of the hotel. John John and I followed. John John had not released his hold on me and his continued laughter annoyed both of us.

John John filled me in on how the extraction went as Robert drove them to the base. I was kept outside as Robert rushed in to tell the SEAL team the cover story that John John had concocted to explain injuries. He warned them all to stick to it as I had quite the right hook. They stood up as I walked in with John John and Robert made the introductions. They showed me around that barracks that would be John John's home for the foreseeable future. It looked like a large warehouse with individual cages set up with a cot, a small table with a lamp and a metal chest for their personal belongings. Tarpaulins covering the cage wires provided the only privacy. There were eight in all. At the end of these "rooms" was a bulletproof glass box with the same setup for John John. Behind all of that was an open space containing a kitchen, long dining table and couches with a TV and game box set up at one end. It was very manly; I found it depressing.

One of the SEAL members took my bags and showed me to a small room that was a closet that had been repurposed to furnish as my room. There was a private bathroom adjoining it that I would use. It did not take me long to settle in and I joined the men at the large dining room table. It was clear that the men were not comfortable with a woman in this setting. They were quiet and nervous. In true Jamaican fashion, it was John John who tried to bring everyone together by offering that I cook them a big Jamaican dinner.

"You can cook, can't you, Jo? I mean, you lived in the States for twenty-one years, you had to learn to cook, right?" It dawned on John John after he made the offer that he was not sure if I could cook anything at all, much less a complete Jamaican meal.

I was not amused. "Typical Jamaican man. Offer me up without even knowing if I can do what you want. See? Now you know why I married an American." Everyone around the table laughed at the exchange.

"Lucky for you, I can cook Jamaican food. I need to go to the supermarket and get what I need."

"Ah, that's my girl. Robert will take you, won't you, Robert?" John John was back to his playful self and enjoyed the panicked look Robert and I shot each other. He wished Simon was with him to enjoy the chaos he was creating.

Luckily for me, I managed to find a West Indian supermarket not far from the base. I could only cook Jamaican food with shortcuts that I had learned while living in the States. The time Jamaican food took to prepare and cook required more patience and cooking skill than I possessed. Jamaica had as many Jamaicans living outside of the island as on it and food prep had adapted to accommodate the lack of time and resources most Jamaicans residing abroad had to work with. These shortcuts were my saving grace. As I directed Robert where to go, I prepared a list of all the things I would need to get. Robert dutifully pushed the shopping cart, picked up the items I needed on shelves I could not reach and helped me to look for what I needed in an unfamiliar setting. We had not had time to address the awkwardness between us and honestly, did not want to, so we completed our errands in silence.

By six o'clock that evening, I had managed to produce a pot of rice and peas, curry chicken, jerk ribs and an island salad complete with a lemon vinaigrette. For the one vegan in the bunch, I had prepared curry chickpeas. John John had phoned while Robert and I were shopping to inform me that we had a vegan in the bunch. Again, typical of a Jamaican man to throw a last-minute wrench into the best-laid plans. The Jamaican phrase "Wheel and tun agin" came to mind as I went in search of canned chickpeas. How many times had I witnessed my mother, grandmother and aunts plan a dinner party on forty-five minutes' notice from their darling husbands? It was the Jamaican way.

"What? No crab back?" John John asked.

I was about to cheekily remind him that he would not be getting crab back for a long time, but I remembered that none of us were here by choice but brought together by the actions of others that we now had to work together to undo. The words died on my lips and I said nothing but smiled weakly as we all sat down to eat. As usual, I found Robert's eyes on me with a sympathetic look on his face. He always seemed to know what I was thinking. I was annoyed at the thought.

The conversation was animated as everyone bonded over the food. It was unanimously agreed that I was an excellent cook and could stay as long as I wanted. I added very little to the conversation but accepted the accolades graciously. After dinner, the men offered to clean up. John John and I decided to take a walk. There were still things we had to discuss, but our predicament was not what was on John John's mind.

We walked in silence until John John broke the silence. "You know I met Thomas, more than once. He came to domino parties at my house with Simon."

I was shocked to hear that. Thomas had never uttered a word of this to me, but he had usually come home drunk when he had a night out with Simon, which consisted of sloppy lovemaking and him falling into a deep sleep. "How would I know that, John John? Up until a month ago, I didn't know you existed. Now you tell me you knew my husband, even partied with him, but never took the time to know me? How am I supposed to react to that information?"

"I knew you, Jo. I knew everything about you. I was at your wedding and shared in your happiness and drank to a long and happy life together."

I stopped walking, looked at him and sat down. "You were at my wedding?"

"Yes, I was. The night before your wedding, Simon, Thomas and I were at Uncle Frank's. Your mother said he had to spend the night there, remember? I was with Simon when we picked him up. I saw the way he kissed you, the lingering look he gave you when he left you. We talked late into the night. Any doubts I may have had about how much he loved you...well, I did not have then anymore after that night."

John John took a deep breath. "He loved you more than anything, I never doubt that, but his idea of protecting you was not our way. He felt he could protect you by taking you away from all of us.

I warned him that it would be a mistake to do that. The only thing that can bring the women of this family to their knees is the loss of love, as you loved Thomas. I saw the loss of him bring you to your knees. It broke my heart; I was angry at him for a very long time."

John John's words set me on edge. If he knew how the women of this family reacted to the loss of their loves, why in God's name would he do that to his sister? I still could not wrap my head around the fact that he had killed Sally's husband. I had not had the time to discuss this with her before we left the island, but I was totally on her side and still held it against John John. Sometimes, the men in this family left a lot to be desired. While I listened to what John John had to say, it was hard to take it to heart.

He did not seem to notice. "Did you know your father offered him a job? Offered him one of the businesses to run? It would have belonged solely to the both of you if he lived in Jamaica with you. Did you know about that offer?" He looked at me then.

I was surprised. "Thomas never told me about it, but it doesn't surprise me. Thomas refused to take anything from my father. He did not like him very much and resented the way he had treated me growing up."

"It was more than that. Thomas did not trust your father; he did not trust any of us to protect you. He thought he could do a better job and wanted to get you as far away from us as possible. Who knows? Maybe he was right, but seeing the pain his death caused you, it was hard to understand his reasoning when it was his death that neither he nor us could protect you from." John John's words cut deep.

"Why are you telling me this, John John? It has no bearing on anything we are doing now and it is painful to hear."

"I'm telling you this for a reason. Should the time come again when you fall in love again, don't love blindly. Don't love as a young girl, but as a woman who has a lot to give, including the love and protection of her family."

I laughed bitterly. "You are advising me to fall in love with a man who will accept not only me but my family? That man does not exist, John John. I have no desire to fall in love or leave my family ever again. Losing Thomas almost killed me. I have no intention of ever giving a man that kind of power over me again. Not to mention that I would now have to worry about one of my cousins killing him on bad intel." I was angry and bitter at all the men in my family who thought they could live my life better than I could. Thomas had been party to keeping secrets from me, secrets that now affected the trajectory of my life. Now that I knew those secrets, I was forced to face the fact that the life I had with Thomas was over and it was never coming back, except in my dreams.

I shook my head. Thomas knew me better than anyone in the world. He loved me more than anyone in the world. He knew what the loss of his love would do to me. Maybe he thought the shock of who and what my family was would be the only thing that would get me up and fighting. That sounds like how he would rationalize the situation and he was right. My love for Thomas would never die, but living the reality that was my new life with my family was getting me out of bed every morning. Thomas was right about one thing: I would not subject anyone else to my family. I now understood why the man who loved me more than anything kept me away from them for as long as he could.

John John watched me as I worked through all of these feelings. It was a strange time to be taking stock, but that is what I was doing. I was not a young girl head over heels in love. I was a woman facing the realities of a life I did not know I had. A life not of my choosing but one I felt obligated to protect and nurture.

John John and I looked at each other. This was an awkward conversation for cousins to have, especially two cousins who hardly knew each other but had a difficult task to accomplish. It was best if we did not get distracted by conversations like this one and I said as much to John John as we walked back. The men had started drinking the bottles of rum I had managed to find when we walked into the barracks. They offered some to John John and me. John John happily accepted, but I decided to take my leave and go to bed. Robert offered to walk me to my room, but I declined, maybe a bit harshly, but I had had enough of men and their chivalry for one night. It took a long time for me to fall asleep, but when I did, my dreams were consumed with Thomas and the life we had shared together.

The next morning, several hungover men awoke to the smell of callaloo and saltfish, fried bammy, scrambled eggs and hot Blue Mountain coffee, which seemed to be appreciated even more than the food. The first words out of John John's mouth earned him a swat across the back of his head, which had to be painful, given the hangover he woke up with. I had woken up in a nasty mood.

"What? No ackee and saltfish?" he asked.

"You like tin ackee?" The face he made and the negative shake of his head confirmed why I had not purchased the tins at the store. "I didn't think so. Eat. We have a lot of work to do today."

The first part of dismantling the US operations was reasonably straightforward. It involved going after low-level customs agents and border patrol people who looked the other way when the drugs came in. Robert assured us that getting indictments and convictions for these people would be easy. They were all, more or less, already on the DEA's radar and now that they had proof of their illegal activities, it was easy to cut off the chain of supply. Going after the drug dealers and the complicated hierarchy that came with a drug distribution system would be more complicated and would require more direct involvement by John John, which made me nervous, but I knew Aunt Julie was busy working on a plan to get John John out of the United States.

The Jamaican side was proving more difficult. Simon had identified a successor for the current prime minister, a progressive politician named Alan Sullivan. He was born in a neighborhood controlled by Uncle John. He was known to both John John and Simon as an honest and upstanding man. He was a rising star in Jamaican politics and was respected by both sides of the political aisle. One of his teachers had come to Uncle John early on, saying he had a brilliant mind and deserved better than the circumstances of his birth. Uncle John had sent him to the same private school that John John and Simon attended, always on scholarships, so he never knew the identity of his benefactor, making sure there would never be a chance that he would influence Alan. Uncle John never met Alan but followed his progress from a distance. Alan had excelled and soon did not need Uncle John's help, earning scholarships to prestigious schools in the United States and England solely on his merit. He had left the neighborhood behind but had never forgotten where he was born and returned to Jamaica after finishing school, determined to make a difference and give every Jamaican child the opportunities he had received, firm in the belief that his island home had provided all the tools he used to succeed. His faith in Jamaica and what it could become was absolute and unwavering. While Aunt Julie worked hard in the dining rooms and verandas of Jamaica to promote him as the future of the island, Sally worked hard in the slums and downtrodden neighborhoods to do the same.

The one obstacle was the current prime minister. Simon had been able to find out that it was the PM who had patrols out on the waters surrounding Jamaica the night John John had fled. He did not know for sure that it was John John who had been on the boat that got away. His spies had told him that while John John was nowhere to be found, they could not say for sure if he had left the island. This lack of confirmation that his worst fears were upon him had emboldened the PM and he had made a fiery speech indicating he would not leave his post willingly. Simon's call to John John and me had us listening intently with heads down, wondering if good would eventually win over evil this entrenched.

Simon planned to meet with the PM, tell him that the US government had a dossier of information on him and was closing in fast. With or without John John's help, they had what they needed to put him behind bars and would soon be making a formal request for his extradition. Simon asked me to return to Jamaica with the dossier on the PM so he could present it as proof.

Robert, hearing this, stepped into the conversation. "Simon, this is Robert. You told me you had this handled."

"Yes, Robert. We do have this handled and frankly, this is none of your concern." Simon's voice had a dangerous edge to it.

"The deal you have with me makes me Josie's handler in getting the information we need from you to fulfill our part of the deal. Now you are putting her in harm's way. What is to stop this man from making you both disappear as he did with John John's father and tried to do with John John?"

"We know how to protect ourselves, Robert; your assistance is not needed." Simon was shouting at Robert. The fact that Robert called Jo "Josie" irked Simon. He also did not want to admit that he now had the same doubts but was not about to let this arrogant Yank know that.

"Well, based on our signed agreement, I do not agree with this." Robert had also started shouting.

"Just stand down, both of you!" John John was furiously trying to come up with a solution. "On second thought, I don't think a dossier will be convincing enough, Simon; I think it needs to be you and Robert who meet with him."

"No way, absolutely not. I am not running to the Yanks," Simon began, but John John interrupted him.

"Simon, he is not afraid of us yet. The best way to handle this is for you to meet with him because Robert now has enough information to put *him* in handcuffs and wants *him* extradited to the States. Honestly, Robert, you have no choice but to back this play because no one in his political party will ever extradite him. It is the only way to get rid of him. He can appoint Alan as his immediate successor. We don't even need to go through an election. No one is going to object to Alan taking over. It is the best immediate solution, Simon." John John was right and we all knew it.

"Jo, do you have the dossier on the PM?" I nodded yes, and John John continued, "Simon, let me talk to Jo and Robert. I will get back to you in a couple of hours."

Robert, John John and I retired to the dining table after I retrieved the dossier. Neither John John nor I had taken the time to read it in any great detail; we were more concerned about the American one. As before, we divided into three and each read our section. Once done, we reported our findings to each other.

John John started. "He was the contact person in the government when my father was alive. He worked with my father to open the drug channels, using his position to grease the wheels in setting up shipping and distribution connections for Dad and making sure he and his friends collected their share of the profits while doing it. He was also the one who received the extradition order for my father." John John paused here, overwhelmed by emotion.

"What is interesting is that he does not seem to know the connection Uncle John had to our grandfather. How is that possible?" I wondered.

"Because they were always discreet. At that time in Jamaica, it was not acceptable to have an outside child sit at the dining table. Our grandfather did it, but they were inconspicuous about it. Dad was never seen with his father or his brothers in public. Their meetings were always clandestine, at places no one would think to look," John John explained. "Even when Simon and I were at school, we never had roommates and always lived off-campus. No one realized that we knew each other, much less lived together. That was drilled into us as boys by both Dad and Grandpa."

"You're telling me that no one in Jamaica knows about John's connection to your family?" Robert asked incredulously. I shrugged my shoulders. How the hell would I know? The realization of how long this secret had survived on a small island where everyone seemed to know everyone's business was mind-boggling to both Robert and me.

"Of course, there were people who knew, but it became a case of not knowing what you knew," John John said absently. Now, that was a sentiment I understood.

Robert mulled this over before he responded, "Is that why you said the PM is not afraid of your family yet? You plan to confront him with what he did to your father and do what exactly? Kill him?" Robert had figured out exactly what we wanted to do with the PM.

Neither John John nor I answered him. John John was sitting on the table his back to us. I was leaning against the table, both hands gripping the edge of the table as I tried to wrap my head around this new predicament. Robert moved his hand to cover mine and I turned to look at him. "With the information in this dossier, I can tie him to crimes committed on American soil. Can you assure me that once this is over, I can have him so he can face justice for his crimes here?" Robert asked.

John John was slow to answer. "No, buddy, I can't. His fate will be in the hands of the Jamaican people, not yours. The crimes he has committed against the Jamaican people, including my father, far outweigh anything he has done in America."

Robert's hand was still covering mine on the table, "Crimes against the Jamaican people or your family?" Neither John John nor I could look at him. We certainly did not want to answer that question. "You want revenge? I get that, but how is revenge going to achieve the long-term goals you have for Jamaica?"

I looked at him then. He saw that I understood what he was saying. Revenge was clouding our judgment and jeopardizing Uncle John's dreams for a better Jamaica. As Robert squeezed my hand and let it go, I realized what we needed to do.

"Robert, you have the name recognition; the PM knows you are in charge of John John's case because you requested his extradition. With John John gone, it stands to reason that he would be your next target," I said.

"How do you know I requested John John's extradition?" The look on Robert's face when I said that was almost comical.

"Because the PM told me. That's how we knew who to contact with this plan," John John responded quietly.

Robert did not know what to think. I could see him weighing his options carefully before deciding what to do. "I will have to put up a fight about letting him resign instead of facing his crimes in the United States."

"It's the only way for him to live. Left to us, he will walk away with Simon to his death." As John John said this, I realized just how dangerous my family was.

Robert digested that for a moment, his eyes on me the entire time. Slowly, he turned to John John. "I can live with that; what do you want me to do?"

We called Simon back and the plan came together. Robert would fly into Kingston and meet with Simon. Together, they would meet with the PM. The best-case scenario was that faced with the magnitude of his crimes; he would step down and appoint Alan as his successor. It was up to Robert to make him see this scenario as the best option. The worst-case scenario was that the PM would leave Jamaica House in Simon's handcuffs, never to be seen or heard from again. It was up to Simon to make him see this as his worst option. Robert had floated the idea of offering the PM immunity from prosecution in the United States if he agreed to leave office willingly. We had all objected to that, but Robert had pointed out that it would be the path of least resistance for a smooth transition of power. He was right and I focused on the big picture. Reluctantly, I agreed and joined him in convincing Simon and John John that it was the right move to make for the greater good.

The only sticking point came when I said I was going with Robert. Robert objected strenuously but was overruled by Simon and John John, who realized that I needed to go home for a couple of days. John John could see the toll the day had taken on me. He realized I needed some time to adjust to my new normal. Besides, things were progressing quickly and I needed to collect the information for Robert to complete the next phase of the project, taking down the American drug dealers employed and empowered by Uncle John.

CHAPTER 15

REVENGE DENIED

I could tell that Robert was still not happy about having to take me along—not only because he didn't want to, but because it also provided a logistical nightmare for him. He did not want us flying to the island on the same flight, just in case anyone was watching. I was so lost in my thoughts; I didn't hear the knock at the door. I was standing at the small window in my tiny room, looking out. A storm had come in and the wind was whipping the rain into a frenzy of movement. Water fell in disarray, pounding everything it touched. The turmoil it created matched my mood. We had lost sight of Uncle John's dream today. Had it not been for Robert, we would have made a grave mistake and plunged Jamaica into political chaos, all in a quest for the instant gratification of revenge.

I was so engrossed in imagining what could have gone wrong that I wanted to believe the comforting hand on my shoulder belonged to Thomas. Unconsciously, I turned my head to rest my cheek against its warm comfort. It wasn't until I heard Robert say my name that I realized he was standing behind me. It was his hand on my shoulder. I could barely contain the sob of disappointment that escaped my throat as I tried to move away from him, but he would not let me go. His hand snaked around my waist and held me to him.

"I know today was hard for you," he started.

"Hard for me?" I asked harshly. "We nearly destroyed everything we had agreed to build, all for the sake of revenge."

I could feel Robert's breath on the back of my neck; his lips caressed my hair as he whispered, "But you didn't. You brought it all back to center."

I moved away from him then. "No, I didn't. You did." I could not bring myself to look at him.

Slowly he turned me around to face him. He lifted my chin, forcing me to look into his eyes. "Josie, today's decisions were made because you realized what the right course of action was and you pushed for it to happen. You and your family are trying to do something no one has ever done before and survive doing it. It is going to get a lot harder from here on out."

I understood; he was trying to warn me about what was to come. Robert searched my eyes for a reaction to his words. There was none, so his eyes lingered on my mouth. My breath sharpened and I could feel my stomach start to flutter. I was conflicted and he could sense it. He realized that I was not ready to take that step toward him, so he moved away from me, giving me the space I needed to collect myself.

"Is that what you came to tell me?" I asked as I moved past him to the door.

"No," he said. He was all business. "Have you heard of Little Goat Island?" he asked.

"Yes. It is a small island less than a mile off the coast of Jamaica, not far from Kingston, if I remember correctly."

"You do remember correctly. There is an old seaplane base there, constructed by us Yanks, as your cousins like to say to me. In 1940, we signed a lease with your colonial masters, which makes that little island a piece of US territory for ninety-nine years."

"Really?" I asked. "I did not know that." I was intrigued.

"I hope you don't have the same fear of boats your cousin has because you and I will fly to that island from Key West. Your Aunt has arranged for you to be picked up and delivered into her care while I am picked up by Simon and delivered into his." Robert did not sound happy about spending any time with Simon. I started to laugh at the look on his face. I saw him hide his smile as he waited for me to stop laughing.

"We leave tomorrow morning," he said.

I still had a smile on my face when I opened the door to my room. Robert followed me as I walked out of the room and into the kitchen. The men were voicing their objection to their cook leaving.

"Don't worry. It won't be for long, and if you don't hurt my cousin again,"—my gaze moved to their major—"I might just bring you each back a nice treat." The shock on their faces was amusing. All eyes shifted to Robert, who shook his head and raised his hands to indicate that it was not he who had spilled the beans.

"It was your idea to have John John tell me that lie?" I asked Robert. He did not move; he looked at John John, who looked away. John John was not crazy enough to admit that the lie had been his idea. Seeing no relief coming from John John, he just turned and retreated to his desk in silence.

All eyes were back on me. "You may not want to apologize to my cousin for hitting him while I am in earshot," I said to the major. I could tell he did not remember doing any such thing. "Furthermore, you may not want to do it while you are drunk and I could have split your skull without you even feeling it." The threat in my words, was unmistakable.

The major was embarrassed but still had a sense of humor. "Miss Josephine, please don't make my treat another bottle of rum." The room erupted in laughter and I could not hide my smile. I looked over at Robert; he was standing at his desk, watching me as usual.

The major made a peace offering to me that evening, asking me if I wanted to practice my kickboxing with him in the ring they had set up in the building. Thomas had introduced me to kickboxing and we had enjoyed working out together. With pride, he would say that he had found a way to work out his wife's famous temper without it getting him killed. I had become good at it, much to my family's dismay. The women in my family hated physical exercise or anything that required them to sweat. "Sweating is so unladylike," my mother had commented after watching me at one of the classes I took. As one of the other SEAL team members laced up my gloves, I noticed all the other team members gathered around the ring; they were excited to see the matchup. After that, my eyes were only on the major. He had skills and I found I had to concentrate on staying on my feet.

———

From his desk, Robert had notice Jo the minute she walked out of her room. Her body in the tight workout clothing was captivating. He could not take his eyes off her. She had twisted her long hair in a loose bun on top of her head and he watched as it slowly started to loosen and fall in unhurried cascades as the major pushed her harder and harder. Without fully realizing what he was doing, he got out of his seat and walked around to the front of the desk, leaning against it with his feet crossed in front of him, his hands gripping the sides of the desk every time the major landed a blow. It did not take her long to figure out his weaknesses and before long, they had a real fight on their hands. The SEAL team members were excited as the fighting got more intense. Robert was concentrating so hard on watching her; he did not notice John John until he leaned on the desk beside him.

"You going to break that desk down if you don't loosen your grip." John John said softly. It took a moment for John John's words to register, but as they did, Robert released his grip on the desk and folded his arms in front of him. "My money is on Jo. She has already figured out he is slow and cumbersome and will tire soon; she will use that to her advantage." John John's analysis was the same conclusion Robert had drawn, but he said nothing as he continued to watch her.

"Why is she here, John John? Why would you send her to fight your war?" Robert's voice was a growl.

John John's first instinct was to take offense. He did not need a woman to fight his battles, but he had seen the look in Robert's eyes before and felt sorry for him. "I've seen another man look at her the way you look at her. He married her and took her away from us. Then he died and she came back. She could have lived the rest of her life in the blissful ignorance her mother does, her aunts do, Simon's sisters, but our Jo found another path to walk and it has led her here, to you."

Robert looked at John John, his dilemma evident in his eyes. John John looked away and continued. "I killed my sister's husband. I thought he had betrayed me and didn't give him a chance to explain. I didn't give my sister a chance to defend him. I killed him in front of my sister and her children. I didn't even think twice about it. It went against everything I had been raised to believe, but I did not hesitate. This business does something to you. It takes away your humanity; it kills your empathy and turns you into a monster." John John's voice was quiet and trembled with emotion. "Jo is my way back. She found my sister, and in doing so, found a way to bring us back together for a cause that we had forgotten we were pledged to honor. I liked Thomas, but his death was the best thing that could have happened to our family. It brought her back to us." John John's voice trailed off; he could not continue.

"Why are you telling me this, John John?" Robert asked. John John had just confessed to committing crimes, including murder and drug trafficking, but none committed on American soil that he could prove.

John John cleared his throat and looked at Robert. "Because she deserves better. Thomas understood that; so did her father in letting her go. But our Jo, she's the noble knight of the family. She will fight to the death for what she believes in, what she loves. She will never walk away until the fight is over. For our family to survive, we need her." John John's meaning was clear, even though he had not put it into words and Robert nodded; he understood. Her family needed her and would never allow him to get in the way.

In silence, they turned to watch the end of the fight. The major was tiring and was ambling around the ring. Josie's body was covered with a thin layer of sweat, in the fading light, she seemed to glow. Her hair had come loose and was framing her face; it whirled around her as she moved in for the kill. She darted in for an uppercut, followed by a round kick that she put so much force into, it propelled her off the ground and she flew at the Major. Before he could react, he was on his back. She landed with the grace of a cat to the wild applause of the other SEAL team members. Somehow her eyes found Robert's and he desperately wanted to believe that the radiant smile on her face was just for him. He could not take his eyes off her. John John patted Robert's shoulder in unspoken sympathy and left to congratulate his cousin. It took several minutes before Robert could move. When he did, he went to sit behind his desk and turned his attention to the dossier he had been reading.

The fight had been exhilarating and I slept like a baby that night. The plan was for me to fly into Orlando the day before Robert left. I wanted to check on my house; then, I would drive to Key West to meet Robert for the flight to Goat Island. With everything that I had been through over the last six months, I thought I would be immune to the flood of crushing loss and hurt I felt as I drove up to the home Thomas and I had shared. It was the first time I had returned since his death and walking into the house was enough to stop me in my tracks as I entered. I allowed the familiarity to wash over me, but I was not prepared for the wave of pain that came with it. I walked into our bedroom, touched our bed and walked through the bathroom to the closet. His clothes were still there; I buried my face in his shirts. His shirts smelled like him and a new wave of pain washed over me. Maybe coming here was a mistake; I was not ready to face this house without Thomas. Even with everything I had been through, I was not strong enough to deal with the loss of Thomas and now was not the time for me to feel defeated and unsure of myself. I made myself get up and walk through our bedroom to the door that led out to our lanai. I sat outside and watched the wind make small waves in our pool.

The life that Thomas had provided for me was uncomplicated and drama free. Growing up in my overbearing and domineering family, I knew that the quiet he provided me had settled my soul. As I sat there on our lanai, I longed for the simple life we had created together. I realized that with my family, I always seemed to be holding my breath, waiting for the next shoe to drop. In this house, it was calm, but the overwhelming sense of loss and regret I now felt made me feel like I was drowning and I could not catch my breath. I had not wanted to leave my home after Thomas had died. I had wanted to stay here and get used to this new normal, my life without Thomas, but my mother and Aunt Julie would not hear of it and before I knew what had happened, I was on a plane back to Jamaica. I looked around the lanai and saw covers on all the furniture and noticed how everything had been put away and covered up as if it would never be used again. Anger bubbled up inside me. This was my house, my home and I did not want it to look dead and unused. I quickly removed the covers from the lanai furniture and started a fire in the firepit. I had always loved the juxtaposition of fire and water. Thomas loved the water and had fallen in love with this house solely because of the swimming pool.

Because I loved fire, I had asked Thomas for a fire feature to complement the flowing water. As I sat and watched the flames, I remembered the excitement on Thomas's face as he had presented me with the firepit for my birthday. The happiness of that day brought a smile to my lips and it reminded me that this house was once filled with so much happiness and joy. Thomas and I had been in love and blessed with our life together. Was my overwhelming sense of loss ungrateful? Was I dishonoring his memory and the life we had built together by not remembering and holding on to the beautiful existence we had created together? Yes, gone too soon but worth treasuring and cherishing. There were valuable lessons to be learned from our love — lessons of trust, respect, hope and happiness. We were made for each other and fate had kindly brought us together. I should be thankful for the time I had with Thomas, appreciative of the lessons he had taught me, the confidence in myself his love had given me. Wallowing in the loss of him was undoing all the benefits loving him had given me.

It had been Thomas's decision for us to live in the United States after we were married. I never questioned it. It was a decision John John had disagreed with, but given what I knew now and knowing Thomas as I did, I understood the reason behind his decision. If we had stayed in Jamaica under the influence of my family, would I have recognized and appreciated the gifts of confidence and strength of character he had given me? Would I have realized that the independence he afforded me would be the shield I needed to protect myself against the collective will of my family? Thomas loved me unconditionally; there was no question about that. His love for me was all that ever mattered to him and he had put no one above me, especially my family. Love in my family came with strings attached and a whole host of conditions; I saw that now. Would I have recognized that without Thomas's intervention? I was fire and the water I needed to keep me in check was gone. Thomas had spent twenty-one years keeping the firestorm at bay. I didn't know if I could contain it without him. Did it even matter if the fire consumed me now that Thomas was gone?

I thought about Sally. She had loved and lost, too, under the cruelest of circumstances. Yet she had not hesitated to jump in and do what was needed to protect the brother who had caused her loss and the family who had all but abandoned her. She was extraordinary in her dedication to our family and her focus on maintaining their status quo. I was drawn to Mother; I had felt compelled to seek her out and that had started me on this path I would never have taken without knowing her. Sally was blood of my blood; our connection had only deepened. She was strong, independent and had survived against odds I could not even imagine. We were members of the same family, but two completely different people and I was intrigued by her.

The sun had gone down and the wind had picked up. I could smell rain in the air. I had not been able to think this clearly in months and was grateful for the moments of clarity, but now I was hungry. The lady who took care of my house, cleaning it weekly and making sure everything was in working order, had been surprised to get my call but was glad that I was coming back and happy to stock the fridge with some groceries. As I made a chicken salad, I reveled in the freedom of taking care of my meal and cleaning up after myself and the peace that I found in being alone. The pain of Thomas's absence was still there, but the happiness and joy he and our home had brought me was quietly seeping into my soul and quieting the turmoil in my mind. I thought again of Sally's strength and willed some of it into my being. I suddenly missed her very much and promised myself my first stop in Jamaica would be to see her. My cell phone rang, startling me and breaking the silence surrounding me.

"Hello," I answered, slightly shaken.

"Josie, are you okay?" Robert's tone was questioning; I could tell that I had worried him with how I had answered the phone.

"I'm fine, Robert," I answered. My abrupt responsive stopped him from pressing me further.

"I wanted to let you know I've been delayed. I won't be getting into Key West until Friday." That was two days from now. I did not respond. "If it is hard for you to stay there, why don't you drive down to Key West? I can arrange for you to stay in a hotel."

I cut Robert off. I did not want Robert intruding in my home with Thomas. "I'm fine, Robert; this is my home. I have always been happy and comfortable here. Why would that change?" My tone was harsh, but he did not belong here. I still loved my husband, I always would and for now, my heart only had room for him.

Robert was silent. Even over the phone, he could sense a change in me, at least toward him. "I'll text you when I leave Washington so that we arrive in Key West at around the same time."

"That works for me. See you in a couple of days." My voice was light but firm. "Safe travels," I added as I hung up the phone. I was grateful for the respite; I wanted to be home by myself. I wanted to remember the confident woman who was quick to smile and completely loved. The woman Thomas had created.

There were two women in Sally, the mother figure I had been intrigued with and my cousin Sally, who was a force to be reckoned with. Being in this house, I realized there were two women in me: the one Thomas had created with his love and the one my family had created with their lies and deceit. I needed the time alone to reconcile them both and I could only do that in the place I felt the safest in.

The next two days went by in a whirl of emotion. I called Aunt Julie and Simon, and told them what was happening and that I was okay. The steel in my voice was enough to stop their offers of company. I assured them that all was well and the plans were still in motion. Then I shut my phone off. I shut out the world and felt everything I had denied myself to feel since Thomas's death. I let the pain of loss wash over me; then, I let the happiness he had brought me, make me smile. The confidence he had instilled in me seeped into my bones and made me strong. Thomas's love was the shield that I needed.

I was watching the fire again the night before I was to leave. I felt at peace. Love surrounded me now. I could feel Thomas; I could feel his love envelop me. I would always love him and miss his physical presence, but the gifts he had given me during our life together would always be with me. I was not weak or weepy anymore; I had a job to do; failure was not an option. Failure would see not only the demise of my family but would plunge the island of my birth into chaos.

Uncle John had always believed that faced with the consequences of their misdeeds, men would choose to atone for them instead of paying for them. I focused on this. Aunt Julie had brought us all together and she had put into motion this plan to save the family once again. She was devoted to Uncle John, no question there. She loved him above her brothers, as my grandfather seemed to as well. She was the keeper of all the family secrets. But that cave down at the beach house, the place my father valued more than anywhere else in the world, held Uncle John's secrets. It was time to confront my family's legacy and put the secrets to rest, once and for all. The secrets lived on my land, making them my responsibility, mine, and mine alone.

The drive to Key West was uneventful. I was ready to go. The best thing I could have done was come home. It was my home and always would be. Thomas would always be there and I wanted to be where he was. His spirit was strongest there. He gave me the strength I needed to move on without him. I was not moving toward Robert—of that, I was sure—but I needed to secure the survival of my family. I needed to correct the wrongs my family had committed. In my heart, I knew it was not only time to atone for them, but to face them. Now, I was prepared to do both.

Robert could see the change in me immediately. The smile on his face faded as soon as he saw I did not return it. We exchanged hellos and I asked if we were ready to go. I was anxious to get back to Jamaica. I could sense him stealing looks at me as we flew in silence, but I ignored him. I had a job to do, as did Robert; he was a means to an end for me and whatever feelings he had for me were no concern of mine. As soon as we landed and secured the plane, Simon arrived to pick up Robert. Following him in another boat was Benji to pick me up. Simon and I hugged each other quickly. He searched my face and I could tell he was relieved to see the resolve in my eyes. Robert and I did not have a chance to say goodbye. Even though I knew he wanted to, I did not and quickly followed Benji to the waiting boat. I glanced behind me and saw Robert standing next to Simon's boat, watching me. I turned my gaze back to the horizon, my island home outlined in front of me. Benji had strict instructions to bring me to Aunt Julie, but I had a stop to make first and asked Benji to take me to the offices of the Working Women of Jamaica. Benji was about to object, but I leveled a fierce gaze at him.

"Benji, I need to see my cousin Sally."

CHAPTER 16

COMING HOME

Sally looked up from the papers she was reading as I walked in. From the look on her face, she was surprised to see me and just for a moment, I thought, not happy to see me.

"Jo, what are you doing here? Is everything all right?"

I realized she was asking about our undertaking and not John John's welfare in the hands of the American authorities. I guess I should not have been surprised by her lack of interest in the well-being of the man who had killed her husband.

"Everything is going according to plan. Robert asked for some more information and I came down to collect it since he is with Simon confronting the PM." I'm not sure why I felt the need to lie to her, but I had been thinking a lot about Sally. While I felt a strong kinship with her, something about her story was not adding up. Instinct told me to tread carefully; Sally had as many secrets as my Aunt Julie did. She was more guarded with me than Aunt Julie was.

Sally looked relieved and sat down, pushing the papers she was reading out of view. I noticed but said nothing. My eyes were on her face as she turned to smile at me and I smiled back. She was a beautiful woman. Years on the streets had not hardened her like it had the other women. Her soft curves were evident under the tropical sundress she wore. Her face was smooth, her skin flawless and dewy. I noticed her subtle application of makeup. She had indeed come out of the darkness of Mother and into the light as the beautiful and powerful Sally Rollins Brown.

"I think I have missed you most of all," I said casually. I tried to keep my voice light. "If we had not found each other, do you think we would be where we are now?"

Sally smiled. "That was something I don't think anyone saw coming." She looked at me, curiously.

"Do you remember when Aunt Julie said she has known where you were all along and was waiting for you to reach out? Why didn't you, Sally? We were right there. Why did you hide from us? From Aunt Julie?"

The guarded look in her eyes was back. She did not look at me as she sat down, so I sat down across from her, making it clear that we were going to have this conversation. I needed to hear it.

Sally took a deep breath. "I know how you were treated by the men in your life, especially your father, our grandfather, but that was not my experience. My father taught me to think; he showed me that my opinions were valued by asking for them. He treated me as an equal and taught me not to expect anything less than equality from the men in my life. He gave me the confidence to stand up and demand what I wanted. He gave me a place at the table and I adored him for it. He was my hero, my teacher, my protector and my agitator, all in one. He was my everything; when I lost him, especially in the way I lost him, I was inconsolable. Not even Marvin could stop the tidal waves of grief and loss that washed over me." I could see the tears well up in her eyes and I felt her pain. The only man who had ever made me feel that way was Thomas and I know what the loss of him did to me. What was it John John had said? *Only the loss of true love could bring the women in this family to their knees.* And she had lost not only her father but her husband as well.

"I blamed everyone: Grandpa, Aunt Julie and especially our uncles. Every time I saw them, it was a bitter reminder that my father had died because of their secret. They were still living and prospering while he rotted in the ground. Then Marvin was killed." Her voice trailed off and I knew she was not going to say anymore.

"You decided to take your children and do what, Sally? Hide in plain sight?" I could tell the question unnerved her, but this is where things did not add up for me. Aunt Julie had said that she always knew where Sally was and was waiting for her to reach out. Sally was standing in front of me, explaining why she did not reach out; it still did not make sense, especially for her children. Why would she not put them under the care of our family, under the care of Aunt Julie? Her feelings for her father were genuine; I could see that. But the way she had jumped in when the family was threatened, that did not smack of the resentment she described to me now. I looked at Sally, really looked at her. To the outside world, she was a whore, living on the streets of one of the toughest cities in the Caribbean, but the woman standing in front of me was no whore. She bore no signs of the hard life she professed to live. She was beautiful, but also cunning and smart, much smarter than I. She had never reminded me more of Aunt Julie than she did right now.

She was saved by Benji, who arrived to say Aunt Julie was waiting for me. I nodded, not taking my eyes off Sally's face.

"Sally, why don't you join me? I would feel more comfortable having you with me when I see Aunt Julie." Sally was surprised by the invitation; the guarded look in her eyes was still there. "It is probably best if I tell you both, at the same time, what Robert wants from us.

Unless, of course, you want to hear it from Aunt Julie later?" I left the question hanging. Sally stood up to join me.

Aunt Julie had been anxiously awaiting my arrival. Simon and Robert were still with the PM and that meeting was also weighing heavily on her mind. She hid her surprise as Sally walked in behind me, greeting both of us with the customary kiss on the check and quick hug. She asked about John John and listened intently as I told her how he was faring in the custody of "the damned Yanks," as she called them.

"Robert's legal team has gone over all the documentation we gave them, and they have some questions," I explained when asked why I had come back to the island.

Aunt Julie and Sally sat across from each other, both turning to look at me as Aunt Julie asked, "What kind of questions?"

"The dossiers are very detailed and explain the where, what and how, but they want John John to identify all the voices on the recordings; they want him to start identifying the who." I watched closely and would have missed the look that Aunt Julie shot Sally if I had blinked. "This is causing me some concern; won't John John implicate himself if he can identify all these drug dealers?"

"He can't." It was Sally who spoke. Aunt Julie leveled her a look, the same look that had frightened me into submission as a child.

"He can't what?" I pressed.

"He does not need to identify them," Aunt Julie was quick to answer, not taking her eyes off Sally. When she noticed my intense stare, she turned to look at me and smiled. "We have pictures, video recordings of all the transactions—or at least these people's reactions to the transactions. John John does not have to identify anyone."

No, this was not strange at all, I thought to myself. *Why would anyone find it odd that the head of the largest drug cartel in the Caribbean could not identify the people he was making drug deals with? If all the movies were real, this was usually done in person.* I sat there, my gaze darting between Sally and Aunt Julie. "John John is the head of the drug operation? He is the one calling all the shots?" I asked.

Neither of them spoke. Sally looked down at the table, but Aunt Julie looked me, her gaze unwavering. "Your Uncle John is the head of this family. All orders come from him."

I nodded at her explanation. It was what I had expected to hear. Uncle John has put all these procedures in place. Even from the grave, his dedicated soldiers carried out his orders, never deviating from the roadmap he had laid out for them.

"Josephine, you have met my brother. He is a lot of things, but ruthless and calculating, he is not. He is good with people, especially Jamaican people and he runs the Jamaican side of the business very well." Sally stopped here and looked at Aunt Julie. It was almost as if she was asking permission to continue. "He was never the face of the foreign operations." Sally stopped talking.

Yes, I had met John John. He was fun to be around, commanding when he had to be, but much more suited to planning a fishing trip or bird shooting weekend than a drug distribution network. I looked between Aunt Julie and Sally, patiently waiting for the story I was going to be asked to present to Robert.

Aunt Julie pulled out a dossier, similar to the ones in the Cave and pushed it across the table to me. I looked at her; Sally would not meet my eyes. Slowly I opened it up and started reading. When I got to the first photograph, I began to see the big picture. "Peter? Peter is the one trusted with the family business abroad?" Peter Clark was a violent, uncontrollable drunk. Anyone who knew him would never believe he was the head of a drug cartel. He was a cartoon character and my cousin Beth's husband. "You want me to give Peter to Robert as the ringleader of the largest drug cartel in the Caribbean? Robert will spend five minutes with Peter and realize it is not true. We will never pull this off." I closed the dossier and looked at them both.

"It's the truth." Sally was insistent. "Peter is the one who handled all the deals abroad. John John appointed him as his lieutenant after Marvin died. It was a smart move on John John's part. If the authorities ever closed in on the business, Peter would take the fall because no one knew what John John looked like."

"This is how we get rid of Peter? By having him take the fall for John John? They have a voice recording of John John talking about drug deals and killing people. Robert will never accept it was Peter," I said. Therein lay the catch—it was John John's voice on Robert's recording, not Peter's.

Aunt Julie had had enough. "There is enough evidence in that dossier to bury Peter; there are pictures, recordings and travel documents that will match every stamp in Peter's passport. Furthermore, it was not John John's voice on that recording; it was Peter's. It was Peter discussing drug deals and killing people, not John John." I was in shock. Aunt Julie had choreographed this to perfection. She was right; the dossier had everything Robert needed to convict Peter and exonerate John John.

"And how do I explain how we got all this information? Am I to tell Robert that we were spying on our leader?" It was Sally who answered now.

"I took them." She answered softly. "I blamed Peter for Marvin's death. Now I take my revenge. Peter was the one who whispered in John John's ear that Marvin was the traitor, but it was never Marvin; it was always Peter." I looked at Sally, really looked at her. In her eyes, I recognized the steely resolve of Aunt Julie.

"How do you know it was Peter, Sally?" My voice was soft but firm.

"I always suspected it. Who else could it be? I thought long and hard; it could only have been him. That is why I decided to find out for sure." Sally's voice was steady but not entirely convincing enough.

"You, Sally? How? You have been hiding in the shadows for years. No passport, no money. How could you have possibly known when Peter was traveling and follow him to play detective?"

The answer was right there in front of me and I stopped asking questions as the realization hit me. Sally was my Aunt Julie's protégé. They had been together, planning the destruction of Uncle John's drug network, for years. That is why Sally was so close, just outside her window, night after night. Only Aunt Julie could have moved Sally in and out of the country without anyone knowing.

"Why are you sure now that it is Peter?" I asked.

Sally was quick to answer. "John John confirmed to me that it was Peter who told him to kill Marvin. He told me the same night he met you."

Again, my gaze moved from one to the other. They had an answer for every question. How long had Aunt Julie and Sally been planning this? They had mapped out every step, anticipated every pawn's move and were ready to checkmate—except for one thing.

"Peter is already working for Robert." I could see this was news to them and something I had just realized. "When we were in Robert's apartment, he told me that it was Aunt Julie who had given him the information about when I had found out about Uncle John and what the family business was; he knew a lot about my life with Thomas. Aunt Julie would have never told him, but only a family member could have."

Aunt Julie and Sally were trying to digest this as I continued. "If Peter thinks John John is going down, I am sure he had taken precautions to make sure he does not go with him. Peter is not as stupid as you give him credit for being."

"If Robert has been working with Peter, then he is not going to buy any of this," Sally said softly. Neither of them had anticipated Peter turning on the family.

"Peter was made the face of the drug operation for a reason. He is disposable, and we counted on his ego getting the better of him eventually. He was only too happy to take over from John John because he thought he would do a better job and he has, but only because he follows orders better than John John ever did. And the reason for that is that he wouldn't do a thing to mess up this opportunity for himself. Another thing we counted on. If he is Robert's informer, we have to figure out how to make that work in our best interest as well." Aunt Julie was thinking out loud.

"As Robert's informer, Robert will know he was at all of the meetings outlined in the dossier, right?" I asked softly. "All I have to do is convince Robert that Peter has been the one lying to him and not us. This dossier is very compelling. If Robert cannot prove that John John was the voice on that tape, that it was Peter's voice instead..." I let my voice trail off.

"You are going to have to be very convincing." Aunt Julie was looking at me again. She was trying to figure out if I could pull this off.

"I know." I looked at the two women across from me. They had set Peter up brilliantly. Knowing Peter as I did, he was only too happy to accept the promotion from John John, probably telling himself he was doing John John a favor. Aunt Julie and Sally had used all of Peter's insecurities against him and now he would pay the ultimate price. These women were devious, conniving, manipulative and dangerous. They were blood of my blood and had attacked and destroyed anything or anyone that threatened the people they loved. They were the lionesses who had protected the pride against all enemies from within and without. They were asking me to let go of the last vestiges of my life with Thomas and embrace my new role with the same single-mindedness they had. The protection and success of our family was the only thing that mattered to them and they were asking me to join them. I had known love; I had known happiness; I had known security. Could I give that up? Was I as strong as they were? Was I as unselfish as they were? Could I live and die for the cause?

I stood up, clutching the dossier to my chest. "I need some time to go over this dossier, to make sure there are no discrepancies that we cannot explain. I am going down to the beach house until Robert is ready to go back to the States. Our next step has to be very carefully planned out."

"I'll come with you." Sally stood as well, but I held up my hand to stop her.

"No, Sally. This is something I need to do myself."

Aunt Julie understood and motioned for Sally to sit down. "I'll get Benji to drive you down." She stood up and kissed me gently on the check. I did not look at either of them as I left.

Benji could sense my mood and we said nothing as we drove out of Kingston. After forty-five minutes of silence and me lost in my reverie, I noticed that Benji had decided to take the South Coast Road to the beach house instead of through the mountains, which would have been quicker.

"Benji, why are we going on the South Coast Road?" I asked.

"Your father always took the South Coast Road," he answered.

"My father?" I looked at Benji, confusion evident in my tone and look.

"He is on my mind today" was Benji's response.

As we traveled in silence, I stared out the window. The South Coast Road was one of the oldest roads in Jamaica, dating back to the British control of the island. It connected Kingston to the breadbasket of the island, so named because it grew the bulk of the food we consumed. It is the most desolate road in Jamaica, just two lanes with the mountains on one side and alternating views of marshlands or coastlines on the other. Still untouched by modernization, it was an absolutely beautiful drive. For the first time, I realized just how spectacular the lush vegetation and vistas we were driving through were. I wound down the window and breathed in deeply, letting the cleansing air course through me.

I heard Benji's soft laughter. "Your father used to do that too." I turned to look at him, puzzlement on my face. "He used to wind down the window and breathe in the air like that, every time I drove him down here. He told me he was cleaning his soul."

I said nothing and looked out the window again.

"You know I met your father and Uncle John on this very road." I could not hide my surprise and looked at him. His eyes never left the road.

"You knew my Uncle John?" I asked.

"I did. Your father was very close to John, more so than his other brothers and they spent a lot of time together down here. It was John that found that land your father bought. Together, they poured the foundation the house is built on." He looked at me as he said this. I could see he wanted my undivided attention. It was apparent Benji had something to say, so I settled in to listen.

"I was a young boy living not far from here. My parents were very poor. We had a little plot of land we grew pumpkin and watermelon on. It was my job to sit on the side of the road and sell them. One day, I was sitting there, minding my own business, when some bad men coming down from town stopped to get some watermelon. They asked me to cut it up for them and then tried to leave without paying. I tried to stop them with my cutlass, but they took it away from me and were going to chop me up when your father and Uncle drove by. They should have kept going—the men that stopped were used to killing and killed a man as easy as they did a bird in the bird bush—but your father and Uncle stopped. Neither one of them liked to see poor people taken advantage of." Benji stopped the car. The landscape had started to change and the lush greenery was giving way to the honeycombed coastline, where craggy limestone cliffs loomed above sandy coves hugging deserted beaches. I caught glimpses of the foaming waves as they crashed down on the dark sand, waiting to take the weight of the water and absorb it into itself.

Benji pointed to a sparse area of land clutching the side of the road. It was a small indentation; there was barely room for another car to pass by as we pulled to a stop.

"I was right over there." He pointed to the indentation. "They had me on my knees, ready to chop off my head. John and your father stopped the car, right in the middle of the road and pointed guns at the men. They told me to get into the car, which I did. Later that night, they dropped me off at home. The bad men had killed my parents and burned down my house. They stripped the plot of land bare of the pumpkin and watermelon and left my parents' bodies in front of the burned-down house. I had nothing left." Benji's voice quivered but never broke. I stared at him and then turned my gaze to the indentation of land, letting the scenario he described so vividly play out in my mind's eye. We got out of the car as Benji continued his story.

"Your father and John helped me to bury my parents. Then they took me to Kingston and I was with them ever since. When they poured the foundation for your father's house, they came to my land and poured the foundation for my house, saying it was time to re-build. I could not have done it without them. I did not want to do it without them; they were my brothers. When John died, I stayed with your father. It was like we had both lost an arm and only the other knew how that felt. Now I have lost both my brothers."

I had no idea what these men had meant to each other. Again, it dawned on me that I knew nothing about my family.

"We found that cave in the mountains behind your father's house together. It was the three of us who built everything in that cave, built it to protect the family and its secrets. All of its secrets." For the first time, Benji looked at me and I looked at him. Benji was not looking at me like the little girl that I had always been to him. He looked at me as he had looked at my father—with love and respect. Respect, he felt, I had earned. I said nothing.

"In the back of the cave, behind the very last bookshelf is a small opening. There is a safe in there; the combination is 11-25-78. Do you recognize the number?" he asked.

I nodded that I did; it was my birthday.

"What you find in that safe is part of your inheritance and part of your father's legacy. He is not the man you think he is, Jo. I wish you had the chance to know your father the way I knew him." I grabbed Benji's hand. The pain he was feeling was tangible and I felt it course through my body. There was so much I did not know.

"Benji, I had no idea about any of this. No one ever said anything and I am embarrassed that I never thought even to ask. I feel like someone else has been living my life and now I am stepping in half-way through. It is overwhelming," I said softly.

Benji nodded; he could not fully understand how I felt because he had the luxury of knowing all along. "It was a good thing that you were away for so long. Things need to change and you can see everything with new eyes. You will help to guide this new course and make sure it is right for all of us. You know I will do everything I can to help you."

I did know that, and I felt comforted by his declaration of loyalty. We got back in the car and continued on the drive. For the first time in my life, I realized that I had always loved this drive, not only for its beauty but also for the peacefulness, I felt as the miles melted behind us. The gentle roll of the turquoise waves came into view as they flowed gently up to the sandy beach that kissed the sea. Above that cove stood the home that my father, Uncle John and Benji had built. The house my father loved—and the home, I realized, I felt the most serenity in.

As we pulled in, darkness was settling in. I caught the last view of the cove as twilight dimmed the edges and blended the view into a muted landscape softened by the dwindling light. Benji said good night; I hugged him as we parted ways. I could tell he was exhausted; it could not have been easy for him to share his memories with me. I told him to drive back to Kingston as soon as he was up the next morning. He asked me how long I planned to stay.

"I am going to be here for a couple of days, Benji. Tomorrow I am going hiking and will probably be gone all day."

He nodded; he knew what I would be doing. "Before I go, I will ask Tecia to make dinner for you and leave it. You will probably want to be alone when you get back."

"Thank you, Benji." I did not know what else to say. "Benji, I can take care of myself. I want you to know that. I can take care of myself and the people I love."

"I know, Jo." He looked at me and I could see the trust in his eyes. "I would not have told you all these things if I did not know that."

CHAPTER 17

THE CAVE

I was up before Tecia arrived in the morning. I fixed myself a bite to eat and packed an avocado sandwich and two bottles of water in a small backpack and headed out. I did not feel the need to lock up as I left. My father had been well known in this area and well respected. No one would come into his home unless invited. Everyone down here knew if they needed something, my father would have given it happily. He did draw the line at taking without asking and folks knew that was the quickest way to lose his favor. I thought back to his funeral and the mourning that seemed to envelop the entire district upon his death. I had found myself comforting people I barely knew, but who knew my father better than I did. That was even more significant now, given Benji's reminiscing yesterday.

Before I knew it, I was at the cave entrance. As I moved inside the narrow walls, I made a mental checklist of all the documents and evidence I needed to collect for Robert. The second part of the project was to gather enough evidence to put all the major players in the US drug network away. I picked out the dossiers I needed and put them on a table close to the entrance of the cave. Then I turned my attention to the back of the cave and searched for the bookshelf. There were three bookshelves lined up like knights guarding long-forgotten secrets, but I knew what to look for and the last bookshelf yielded to my force, shifting to show me the hidden opening that held the safe. I punched in the numbers and leaned in for a closer look.

Inside were four notebooks and a ledger. The ledger contained detailed descriptions of "favors" my Uncle John had been asked to do. Most of the "favors" listed were illegal—at the very least, morally compromised. As I went down the list of names, I recognized many of them as friends of my father's or friends of friends that I knew as acquaintances. The ledger was as detailed as the dossiers were. As I scanned the list, my anger rose and an idea of what to do with this information popped into my head. I put the ledger aside and looked at the notebooks. Upon closer inspection, they were journals, Uncle John's journals. I inhaled sharply. Why would Uncle John's journals be my inheritance? Shouldn't they go to Sally and John John? I paused, contemplating this as I flipped through them. In the last journal, halfway through, I recognized my father's writing. I exhaled the breath I had been holding and settled in to find out about my father.

The first three journals were all about Uncle John; he had started writing them when he was in the army and his insights were ahead of his time. I read about his rationale for getting into the drug trade and my grandfather's and father's objection to it. My Uncle Henry, Beth's father and my Uncle Frank, Simon's father, had sided with Uncle John and an empire was born. My father had not wanted John's solution to the family's fortunes, it seemed to have caused a rift between them, but just for a short time. As I turned to the fourth journal, their disagreements were behind them and they were not only brothers but best friends. The fourth journal started with Uncle John's account of his first run-in with the PM, who at the time was minister of foreign affairs. Uncle John detailed his disgust for the man and his greed. He realized he was only interested in enriching himself and his friends and was perfectly happy to have the people of Jamaica survive on the scraps from his table. "Keep them hungry, tired and poor, and you control them," he had told Uncle John one night. John was determined to bring him down and went to his father and brothers with a new plan to legitimize the businesses and bring the PM down once and for all.

Uncle John found an ally in my father and grandfather, but Henry and Frank did not want to change the status quo. They lived well off of Uncle John's dealings and did not see the change as anything more than rocking the boat. It came to a head one night when they visited John to ask a favor.

"John, we're having a problem with a union organizer." Uncle Henry started the conversation as they sat in John's home, having a late dinner. "The man wants to unionize our cane cutters; can you believe that? We give them good pay and this man wants to take their money." Uncle Henry scoffed as Uncle Frank nodded vigorously in agreement.

Uncle John put down his fork and looked at his brothers. "From what I understand from Jack, this man also wants to give them health insurance, benefits and a forty-hour work week, which Jack agrees with."

"Jack does not understand how much that will cut into our profits." Henry was angry that John and Jack had spoken about his side of the family business.

"Really?" John asked. "Jack has worked the numbers; this would cost us ten percent of the overall profits every year and give us the benefit of a solid workforce who knew what they were doing and would make the whole operation more efficient. Jack feels we would make up the ten percent and more by not having to train new people every season as well as the savings on accidents in the fields."

"This is not Jack's business, John. It is mine and Frank's! We disagree with Jack's assessment." Henry was beginning to lose his temper, which never ended well for anyone.

"What do you want from me then? If this is your and Frank's business, why you talking to me?" John was getting tired of this conversation and wanted it to end.

"We want you to talk with the man, explain to him why he needs to leave our people alone." Henry was in control now, confidently telling John what he needed from him.

John stopped dead. The fork that was close to his mouth dropped to the plate. He leaned in, face to face with Henry. "You want me to kill this man?"

Frank jumped in. "We want him to go away, John. However, you make that happen is your business."

"I don't suppose you have discussed this with Dad or with Jack?" John asked.

Frank and Henry exchanged nervous looks. Henry cleared his throat before he spoke. "This is our business, John; we don't need them to make this decision. Frank and I are asking you to help us. Isn't this what you do, John? And we need you to do it."

My father walked in just as John threw the first punch that landed squarely on Henry's jaw, knocking over the chair he was sitting on. The blow was so hard, it pushed Henry into Frank and they both tumbled to the floor. As a stunned Henry and Frank tried to untangle themselves, John explained to Jack what his brothers had just asked him to do. Angry, Jack went over and kicked Henry.

"You come into our brother's home and ask him to commit murder because you don't want to work a day longer and an hour harder? What is wrong with you?" Jack was shouting.

"Get out, both of you! If anything happens to that man, I will make sure you both pay for it. You lucky I don't tell Dad about this." John's voice was quiet. He sounded defeated and wanted it to end.

Henry and Frank scrambled up from the floor and hastily left. In shock, Jack turned to John, who had sat back down to finish his dinner.

"What you mean, don't tell Dad?" Jack looked at John, "They have no right to ask that of you, John."

"Don't they?" John did not look up from his plate. "It won't be the first time I have killed to protect this family, protect our money."

Jack straightened the chair Henry had been sitting on and sat down. He understood what John was saying. The weight of the family's sins was bearing down on John. It was a load that would crush him.

"John, the businesses are doing well. We don't need the drug money anymore; we can come out of that now." Jack's voice was earnest.

"This is not a business you retire from, Jack. Besides, all the money we make now is going to the communities. It is equipping schools, hospitals; it is providing food, clothing, scholarships to the people that need it most. Even if I wanted to stop, I couldn't let those people down." Jack understood what John was saying. The legitimate family businesses could never provide for the poor of Jamaica like the drug business was.

"There are no coincidences in life, Jack; everything happens for a reason. When men are confronted with the consequences of their misdeeds, they will choose to atone for them instead of facing them. We are atoning." The melancholy in John's voice broke Jack's heart.

"Whatever happens, Brother, we will face it together," Jack reassured his brother, but this proved not to be true.

I took a breath and closed the notebook. I could not believe what I was reading. It sounded like an intriguing novel instead of my family's history. Tears welled up in my eyes as I felt the pain Uncle John was in at that moment. I turned back to the notebook and noticed that Uncle John was no longer the narrator. I turned the page and recognized my father's writing immediately.

John has been arrested! I know Henry and Frank are behind it. The cane cutters were unionized. I backed it myself. Henry and Frank were livid, especially Henry, who accused John of making it happen. I assured him it had nothing to do with John, that I was the one that gave the union my support, but I know they don't believe me. I can't tell Father what Henry and Frank have done; it will kill him. But I will never forgive them.

The last entry was the most chilling.

John is going to be killed! Members of the corrupt government think that John will turn them over to the United States authorities and they will lose everything. I know Henry is behind it, whispering his poison in their ears; Benji confirmed that tonight. I have asked Benji to find out what they plan to do. Thank God, no one knows about the cave. If they knew what was up there, John would be dead by now. John wanted it kept between Benji and the two of us; I am so glad now that I agreed. I pray that Benji can find out what they plan to do so we can stop it. I have to tell Dad, but I cannot tell him that Henry and Frank are behind this betrayal. That will kill him. I honestly don't know what to do.

John is dead! Dad and I arrived too late. I had to see the charred remains of my brother in a prison cell. Dad broke down. I have never seen him grieve like that. He has aged overnight. He has disappeared with John's children and won't tell me where he is. I had Benji claim John's remains and we buried him on the mountain by the cave. My heart is broken. I will never forgive Henry and Frank. I saw them today, Frank would not meet my eyes, but Henry shows no remorse. They know I know what they have done; they also know I will not do anything about it for our father's sake. That knowledge protects them, but it eats away at me, piece by piece. I am angry and bitter. My heart has turned to stone.

I closed the notebook; my entire body was numb. I put the note-books back in the safe and carefully arranged the bookshelf so no one, but I would know where they were hidden. The ledger, I took with me and added them to the dossiers I had picked up, putting them all in my backpack. I moved on autopilot as I left. I noticed the sun was low in the sky; I had been in that cave all day. I could not think as I carefully picked my way down the trail and arrived at the house. Thankfully no one was there. I put my backpack down and sat on the verandah, watching the sunset. My father, the old pirate,

Simon had always called him, loved to watch for the flash of green just as the sun set into the Caribbean Sea. He had excitedly pointed at the setting sun and urged me to look for it. In all those years, all those sunsets, I had never seen the green flash, even as my father exclaimed in joy, "There it is! Did you see it, Jo?"

I saw it now and the dam broke. I had no idea I could cry like this. I cried for the father who had been betrayed and no longer had enough love in his heart for me. I cried for Uncle John; whose good intentions had led to his death. I cried for my grandfather, who had died from the loss of the ones he had truly loved, but mostly I cried for myself. I cried as I let Thomas go. I would always love him, but he could no longer be my excuse for not moving on. I had to pay for the sins of my family and there was no room for anything that made me weak in my resolve.

I felt strong arms lift me; I felt the hard body I was pressed against. I did not look at who was holding me. I didn't need to. I knew it was Robert who held me. I did nothing but cry as I let go of the only life I had ever known. He said no words of comfort; he just held me. My entire body enveloped in his as he tried to soak in my pain. I don't know how long I cried for, but when I awoke, he was still holding me. It was dark outside, the full moon high in the sky. We were lying on the wicker sectional. I turned my head to look at him. Even in sleep, his protective grip on me had not loosened and his body was wrapped around mine. I felt safe and calm and reveled in that feeling for a moment, but Robert was a threat to my family, I had to let him go too.

I moved out of his arms and he woke up. For a moment, we just looked at each other. Neither of us knew what to say. In his eyes, I saw questions. In my eyes, he found no answers. He let me go and I stood up. I turned and walked out to the veranda, watching the moon cast diamonds down to the sea below. They danced on the dark waves. Robert came to stand behind me, not touching me, but close enough so I could still feel the warmth his body radiated.

"Do you want to tell me what that was about?" His tone was gentle.

I shook my head, indicating no. The electricity between us was magnetic and I could not be sure he wanted to put his arms around me as much as I wanted him to.

I cleared my throat. "What are you doing here?" It suddenly occurred to me that I did not want Robert this close to the cave that held all our secrets.

"I finished my meeting with the PM and you had disappeared. No one in Kingston knew where you were, so I figured you must be here." That was enough for me to step away from him. He was not even supposed to know about this place.

I was finding my North Star. "How did it go with the PM?"

Robert sensed the change in me immediately. "Simon and I confronted him with the dossier. Simon revealed John's relationship to your family and explained that he was there to arrest him and that he would never see the inside of a Jamaican jail, or he could be turned over to me. Simon's threat was obvious and it got his attention. He agreed to resign and name Alan Sullivan as the next prime minister of Jamaica. He seemed more afraid of Simon than me after the family ties were revealed. The option of a jail in the United States for the rest of his life seemed more appealing to him than the consequence of facing your family. We will offer him a deal to tell us all he knows and he will probably live very comfortably in the States for the rest of his life. He knows he will never be able to return to Jamaica."

I nodded. The irony of this man living comfortably for the rest of his life made me angry. Both Uncle John and my father were dead and would never have that option. I was sure it was not as easily accomplished as Robert was making it out to be. However, they had achieved the outcome we wanted, so I did not need the details of how it had been completed. There was still a lot left to do. "Why are you here?" I asked him again.

"Well, we are supposed to go back to the States together, remember? You are in Jamaica to pick up something we need?" It sounded like a question and my eyes quickly turned to the backpack lying two feet away from him.

"It's in Kingston," I answered quickly. "I have to make a stop in Kingston before we leave." That part was real. I planned to visit my uncles, Henry and Frank before I left Jamaica. I needed to call Aunt Julie and ask her to be there as well.

He nodded. I was not sure he believed me, but hell, what choice did he have? "I guess we should get some sleep and head out early in the morning." He was circling me again.

"You can sleep in that room." I pointed to a door directly behind him and turned to head to my room, making sure to pick up the backpack and take it with me. As I moved toward my door, I stopped and turned around. He had moved to his door and opened it. My voice stopped him.

"Robert?" He looked at me. "Thank you." He looked at me for a long second and nodded.

"You're welcome, Josie." He turned to go into his room as I went into mine.

CHAPTER 18

THE BEACH HOUSE

I was up early the next morning and called Aunt Julie. I asked her if I could have lunch at her house and if she would invite Uncle Henry and Uncle Frank. I wanted it to be just the four of us. She was silent for a moment but agreed to make the arrangements. She called me back just as I stepped out of the shower and confirmed everyone was able to meet for lunch. I agreed to meet her at 1:00 p.m. I then called Benji and asked him to pick me up at 2:00 p.m., from Aunt Julie's and take me to Goat Island. He agreed without question. I picked up the backpack and headed out to the dining room. Robert was already there, having breakfast and chatting with Tecia as if he had known her all his life. The ease with which Robert seemed to be in my home unnerved me. I sat down as Tecia brought me a cup of tea.

"Thank you, Tecia." I acknowledged her with a smile. I turned to look at Robert, who watched me with guarded eyes. He had seen so many of my moods; I am sure he was waiting to see which one greeted him this morning. That softened me and I smiled as I addressed him.

"If you are ready, we can leave in an hour or so." He nodded in agreement. "I need to stop at Aunt Julie's for about an hour, then I will meet you at Goat Island. We should be able to leave by 3:30 p.m. if that works for you?" I looked at him.

"That works. I have to stop at the embassy to arrange the PM's extradition to the States." I nodded as we ate. "This is a beautiful piece of heaven you have here," Robert said, breaking the silence.

I started to correct him by saying it was my father's piece of heaven but stopped myself as I realized it was now mine. I had never thought of it as heaven on earth, but maybe it was. I know Robert was watching the emotions that were playing out across my face as I tried to work through this new realization. Honestly, nothing in my life was the same again, not even my feelings for this place.

Robert cleared his throat to get my attention. "I thought I might go for a swim before we leave. Would you like to join me?"

My eyes turned back to him and I thought about it for a moment. *Would I?* "Sure," I answered and smiled. I would very much like to go for a swim.

As we walked down the steep steps that led to the beach, Robert tried to take my hand to help me, but I pulled it back. I had been going down these steps all my life; I knew better than he did how to navigate them. I jumped in front of him and scurried down the remaining steps as he followed, picking his way. The water was warm and soothing. I took my time and enjoyed the sensation of weight-lessness as I floated on my back, admiring the blue sky above me. It was a brief moment of respite and I enjoyed the peace it brought me. It took me a moment to realize that Robert was tugging at my arm. I looked at him, the irritation clear on my face.

He pointed behind me and I realized I was about to drift onto the reef. I laughed at my lack of attention and turned to look at him, a contrite smile still on my face. Before I knew it, I was in his arms and he was kissing me. Against my better judgment, I folded into his arms and into his kiss. After the emotions of yesterday, it was as comforting and soothing as the warm waters I was floating in. As his kiss changed to one of passion and I felt his arousal against my leg, I pulled away.

"Why not?" I could hear the frustration in his voice as he asked that question. His forehead rested against mine; I knew it was time to answer.

"Because I have already had my happily ever after," I said quietly.

"But I haven't. Not yet," he responded as his eyes bore into mine. The emotion in his voice and the sorrow I was causing him was evident. I could fall in love with any other man on the planet except Robert.

So, I pulled away from him. I walked out of the sea without a backward glance, picked up my towel and walked up those treacherous steps, each one taking me farther and farther away from him. I had an important meeting to prepare for and Robert was the last thing I needed to be thinking about.

I could hear him moving around as I dressed in my room. He would not meet my eyes as I came out and closed the door. I had hurt him; I knew that, but there was nothing I could do about it. I knew I could not lead him on, but the tension between us was not helping and I had to do something to defuse it. We did not talk to each other as he drove us back to Kingston; what was there to say? He was angry. His hand between us clinched in a fist; the other one gripped the steering wheel so tightly that his knuckles were white. Without a word, I took the fist and smoothed it out, interlocking my fingers with his. He turned to look at me, but I looked out the window and would not meet his gaze. Slowly he released the pressure and his hand relaxed into mine. Not one word was said between us for the entire drive to Kingston, but he didn't release my hand until we pulled into

Aunt Julie's driveway. I grabbed the backpack and opened the passenger door before he could get out and do it for me. I did not want to see his eyes; I did not want to know what he was thinking. I jumped out without a backward glance, reminding him I would meet him at 3:30 p.m. Aunt Julie was already at the door, waiting to greet me and I needed to be ready for the battle ahead.

Aunt Julie was in hostess mode and chatted away, seeming not to notice my silence. She did get my attention when she looked out the window and remarked that Henry and Frank were pulling into the driveway. I took a deep breath and settled my nerves as she greeted them at the door and showed them into the drawing-room. After drinks were served, it was Henry who indicated that the pleasantries were over.

"What is so important, Julie, that Frank and I have to drop what we are doing in the middle of the day to come and have lunch with you?" He said this to his sister, but his eyes were squarely on me. As I had asked, Julie had not told either of them that I would be there.

"I have no idea, Henry. Josephine asked for this meeting, not me," Aunt Julie answered as all eyes turned to me.

There was no point in beating around the bush. "Uncle Henry, did you know that Uncle John kept a diary? I expect not, but Daddy did and he picked up where Uncle John left off, the night Uncle John was killed. A murder arranged by you and Uncle Frank because he would not commit murder for you, isn't that right?" You could hear a pin drop.

Uncle Frank looked like I had punched him. Neither of them had realized that I knew about John, who he was, or the connection to our family. Uncle Henry's realization had turned to anger that was beginning to mount, but the look of shock and disbelief on Aunt

Julie's face stopped me dead. She was doubled over and gasping for breath.

"What is happening? What the hell is happening?" she kept asking. Uncle Frank collapsed into the seat next to her as Uncle Henry lunged at me. The hard slap across my face mobilized me as I turned and put all my weight into a round kick that launched Henry across the room, landing him on the floor before anyone could move. The shocked silence soon turned to screams of agony from Henry as Frank rushed to his side and Aunt Julie started to cry.

"You have no proof," Henry managed to gasp. But I was ready for that. On cue, Uncle John's voice filled the room, followed by Henry's and Frank's, as they asked him to kill the union organizer. Uncle John had taped the entire conversation on a tiny voice recorder that I now held in my hand. Henry and Frank froze in shock as Aunt Julie listened to the conversation, her distress growing with every word.

"Was it you, Uncle Henry, or Uncle Frank who went to the PM and warned him that Uncle John's extradition would result in his testifying against them all?" I asked.

Uncle Frank turning to look at Uncle Henry, was all the answer I needed. "It was you, Henry! But, Frank, you did nothing to stop it. You are equally responsible for Uncle John's death and your father's death." Aunt Julie had stopped crying as I finished speaking. Uncle Frank was back in his chair, sucking down his drink as Uncle Henry sat up, still on the ground, looking like he wanted to kill me too. My cheek was throbbing from where he had hit me and I briefly thought of Robert and what he would do when he saw the bruise.

"What do you want?" Uncle Henry's voice was low and dangerous. He had never liked me; I now knew why and today would do nothing to endear me to him.

"I want what Uncle John wanted: to get our family out of the drug trade and to provide for the people of Jamaica as we always have." I took a deep breath and plunged in. "Both of you will pay half of your company's profits into an account set up by the Working Women of Jamaica. Sally and Aunt Julie will administer this account and make sure it goes to the people whom Uncle John wanted to help. You will deposit these funds monthly and should your profits suddenly decline, you will be personally liable for the shortfall."

"I'm not doing that." Uncle Henry was not going down without a fight.

"Yes, you will, Henry. Or this tape and Uncle John's journal will be handed over to the authorities. Uncle Frank will take the fall for Uncle John's death, but you—you, I will turn over to the DEA as the head of the family drug cartel and you will die in a Yankee prison."

I had Uncle Frank's attention. Simon, as head of the police, was his son. He loved his son and would do nothing to hurt him or damage their relationship. "I agree. I will do it." He sounded almost relieved.

"Frank!" Henry shouted.

"What, Henry? What can you possibly have to say now? We did it! We killed our brother. His death killed our father. Did you think there would never be a time when we would not have to answer for it?" Frank was pleading with Henry. But it was Aunt Julie who sealed the deal.

"Henry, for the rest of your life, you are going to have to look behind you to make sure I am not there with the bullet that will end your life. I will never forgive you for this. Miss one payment, pay one penny short and I will make your wife a widow, and Beth will never see another penny from me or any member of this family, including you." Aunt Julie's voice was low but dripping with hate. Any love she had for her brother was now buried with her beloved father and favorite brother. Without another word, Henry picked himself up from the floor and left, slamming the door behind him. Aunt Julie collapsed beside Frank and drained her drink. I refilled both their glasses.

"How could you let this happen, Frank?" Aunt Julie would not look at him or touch him as they sat side by side.

He started to cry. "I got caught up in it all, Julie. Henry said it was the only way to save ourselves. After what I saw it do to Dad and then to Jack...I didn't know how to undo any of it." His voice trailed off.

"Jack knew all of this?" Aunt Julie looked at me sharply and I nodded, not breaking her gaze. She dissolved again into tears. Uncle Frank cried silently, neither of them looking at each other. Uncle Frank understood what Aunt Julie was going through and quietly supported her by just sitting there.

"It explains so much," she was finally able to say as memories of past tensions between Henry, Frank and Jack came back to her. In this new context, she understood what the cause was. Beside her, Frank just nodded.

Out of the corner of my eye, I saw Benji coming out of the kitchen. Expecting to see us all at the dining table, he would be moving toward this room, looking for us.

"Aunt Julie, there is more. Uncle Henry and Uncle Frank were not the only people Uncle John did 'favors' for. In this ledger are records of other requests. I want you to use them to get money from all of these people to fund Uncle John's dream. Do you think you can do that for him?"

"I want to help!" Uncle Frank sat up and leaned forward. "When men are confronted with the consequences of their misdeeds, they will choose to atone for them instead of facing them. I need to atone,

LYNDA R. EDWARDS

Jo." Uncle Frank's voice was pleading. The fact that he had said those exact words gave me some comfort, but the new Josie could not fully trust Frank or his motives.

"This is Aunt Julie and Sally's project, Frank; I am not sure your help will be welcome." I hesitantly answered as I looked at Aunt Julie for guidance. None was forthcoming, her mouth set in a thin line.

"No, not with the disbursement of the funds. I want to help in acquiring them. I want to be the one to call in the favors. I think I am in a pretty good position to know what to say that will be the most effective." His voice was firm, but he understood he was not trusted. I looked at Aunt Julie as I handed her the ledger.

"Fine. Aunt Julie, here is the ledger. It is to stay in your possession. Give Uncle Frank what he needs to do to get the job done, one at a time," I emphasized. Could we trust Uncle Frank? The question nagged at me. I knew I could not trust Uncle Henry and his control over Frank was also concerning. Aunt Julie took the ledger with shaking hands; she had yet to look at Uncle Frank or say a word to him. Benji was at the door. Silently he took in Frank's anguished face, Aunt Julie sobbing as she clutched the ledger to her chest and the big bruise on the side of my face. He said nothing as he exited just as quickly as he entered. I knew he would be waiting for me away from whatever was happening in this room. Benji would want none of what had occurred here today.

"Aunt Julie, I have to go," I said as I knelt to hug her. "Are you going to be okay?" I was nervous, leaving her with Frank and he knew it.

"I'm truly sorry, Jo." He turned to me as he said this. I looked at him but did not say a word. What could I say?

"How could you be a part of this, Frank? It goes against everything we were raised to believe. John was our brother." Aunt Julie had

182

finally turned to look at Frank. I realized I had been dismissed. They had a lot to talk about and I knew Aunt Julie was strong enough to handle this situation, no matter how much it hurt her. I kissed her gently and left the two of them to talk as I went to find Benji, backpack in hand. To it, I had added the fake dossier that had been created to implicate Peter. Aunt Julie had handed it to me as soon as I had walked through the door.

I found Benji in the kitchen with ice wrapped in a kitchen towel. Silently he pressed it against my bruised check and winced with me as I winced at the pain it caused. I smiled at his reaction. He did not smile in response to me.

"Benji, as soon as you take me to Goat Island, I need you to go to the beach house, get the contents of that safe and bury them with Uncle John. Then seal up the hole the safe is in. I don't want anyone ever to find that there was something back there. Erase any evidence of anything ever being there." Benji nodded silently, not taking his eyes off of me. He knew what I wanted to be done and why.

Any evidence of Henry and Frank's treachery would die with them. Their children would never know what they had done to this family and more importantly, Sally and John John would never be able to hold it against their cousins. Family unity was the only way forward and the dead would keep their secrets.

We silently left Aunt Julie's house and drove along the coastline. I kept the ice on my cheek. I dreaded Robert's reaction when he saw it, but I could not dwell on it. I had a lot to do and the next step was freeing John John and implicating Peter. I knew this would not be easy; Robert was no fool; I had to get him off his game to have a chance of selling this to him. The only thing that got Robert off his game was his burgeoning feelings for me.

Upon seeing me, Robert grabbed my face, turning the bruised check so he could see it better. He looked at Benji, still holding my face. Benji gave nothing away and handed me my backpack as I pulled away from Robert.

"What the hell happened to your face?" Robert asked, anger evident in his voice.

"I walked into a door," I answered.

Robert said nothing as he prepared the seaplane for takeoff. He was angry and I needed him to stay that way. We landed in Key West without incident, but he changed his plane ticket to fly with me, contrary to the original plan. I did not question him as we boarded and sat side by side on the flight to Washington. His only acknowledgment of my injury was asking the stewardess for an ice pack, explaining to her that I had had a run-in with an oxygen tank while diving on vacation. She nodded at this explanation. It seemed to be a common injury.

Once we had landed in Washington and collected his car, I turned to him. "Robert, would you mind if we went to your apartment?" I asked innocently.

"What? Why?" He was distracted and then realized what I had asked.

"Before we go back to the base, I think it is time we both put our cards on the table and it is probably best if we do it in private." He turned to look at me before starting the car. I was trying to figure out if he was accepting my explanation or looking for the motive behind my request. Finally, he nodded and turned on the ignition of the car, put it in gear and backed out of the parking spot. I breathed a silent sigh of relief.

CHAPTER 19

A RECKONING

We drove in silence. The distrust that had sprung up between us was counterproductive to the completion of our plan. I did not know what to do about it. I had never experienced this with Thomas. We were a team, from the very first day we decided to be together. Trust was never an issue for us and I was at a loss as to how to repair the damage. I toyed with the idea of using Robert's feelings for me against him, but in my heart of hearts, I couldn't do it. It would be dishonoring the love I had shared with Thomas. Tears came to my eyes as I realized that, for the first time, I had thought of Thomas and our love in the past tense. I turned my head to look out the window. I did not want Robert to see me cry ever again.

"Are you hungry?" Robert asked me. We were in his apartment. I had grabbed my backpack as soon as he had stopped the car. As he had opened the door, I went straight to the window and looked out as he brought our bags in. He could tell I was upset but did not ask why. He was giving me time to collect myself and my heart softened even more.

"No, thank you. Are you?" I turned to look at him. He shook his head no and I moved to his small dining table with the backpack.

"Here are the dossiers you need to go after all the leaders of Uncle John's American operation. You will also find photographs and recordings of drug deals and the money laundering operation. Everything you need to get a conviction is in each one." I put all but one dossier on the table in front of him.

"We will still need a corroborating witness who can tie everything together." He sat down as he said this and started going through the dossiers. I knew what he meant.

I took a deep breath, "I know, but it is not going to be John John." He stopped reading as I said that and looked at me. His eyes were hard and his mouth was set in a thin line.

"John John won't be able to pick any of these people out in a lineup and he won't be able to corroborate anything you find in any of these dossiers," I said quietly.

Robert put down the dossier and looked at me. We were eye to eye, each of us absolute in our resolve.

"Why not?" He asked. His voice was as hard as steel.

"Because John John is not the head of the snake," I responded. He looked away from me. I could tell his mind was racing as he processed this unexpected information.

"That is why you never asked for immunity for John John. You knew I wouldn't find anything to charge him with—or is it that you will not provide me with the evidence I need to convict him?"

I had forgotten what a man of integrity looked like. He now realized I had been manipulating him from the start and I could tell from the look of hurt in his eyes that he was wondering if all my actions had been part of the manipulation. If he was a man of conviction, then John John would be spending the rest of his life in an American prison.

I held the final dossier in front of me, like a shield of armor. I handed it to him. I could not meet his eyes. Wordlessly, he took the dossier from me and opened it. I heard him let out a deep sigh and his hand went to his brow. He turned the pages silently.

"You know who that is, don't you?" I asked quietly.

He nodded slowly, his eyes still on the pages as he turned them. He stopped turning as he got to the page with the transcribing of the conversation that had led him to John John. He looked at me sharply.

"Are you are telling me that the voice on the tape I built my entire case on is not John John's?" He did not believe this for a minute because he knew who had given him the tape.

"It is not John John's voice, Robert; it is Peter Clark's voice." My voice did not waver in its conviction. He understood exactly what I was asking him to do.

"Would you have asked Thomas to do something like this for you?" The anger and hurt in his voice nearly crushed me.

"Thomas made sure I would never be in a position to ask any of this of him." He nodded in agreement as I said this. "Everything you need to convict Peter is in that dossier, pictures, airline tickets, pictures of passport stamps and recordings. You and I both know that Peter can identify everyone in the dossiers because he was there at every meeting."

"Yes, I do know that. What I don't know is why you think I would do this for you and your family?" The look in his eyes was piercing. I was hurting him to the core, but I could do nothing to stop it.

I could not answer him. I shrugged my shoulders, indicating I did not know and a single tear escaped my eyes and ran down my cheek. I didn't know if it was genuine or contrived and that stabbed at my heart. I could tell that Robert was wondering the same thing.

Suddenly I could not breathe. My heart was breaking; I desperately needed some air.

"You know, I am pretty hungry." I was talking fast, trying to hide my feelings as I headed for the door. "I think I will run down to the deli on the corner and pick up a sandwich. Do you want something?" I was out the door and gone before he could answer. Robert did not follow me.

What was I doing? How had it come to this? Was I always this person? The questions tumbled through my mind as I ran out of his building. I had asked Robert to lie for me, lie for my family. I had asked a good man to go against everything he believed in to protect my family, not even me, but my family. Unknowingly, I had asked another good man to do the same thing twenty years ago; his response had been to take me away from my family. But he was gone, his protection was gone and I was navigating the minefield that was my family on my own. I had wrapped myself in good intentions, justified the means to achieve a noble end, but would the means ever justify this end? Robert had made me question everything. That's what I was thinking just before everything went black. I did not feel the blow to the back of my head, so deep in my thoughts, I had not realized I was being followed.

I woke up in an alley. I had no idea where I was or how I had ended up there, but I did know I could not take a full breath. Then I realized it was because someone was on top of me. It took me a moment to focus on the head above mine. I turned my face to breathe in and saw the hand with the gun to my head. The man on top of me raised his head. I turned my face to look at the man trying to kill me. He was using his body weight to hold me down as his free hand tried to loosen the button on my jeans.

"You awake now? Your uncle told me to make sure you see and feel everything I am going to do to you." His words barely registered as I started to struggle, arching my hips to throw him off me. My hands were trapped behind me and I fought to free them.

"Henry said you were a fighter. Good, I like it when a woman fights back." He used his foot to kick my legs open and slammed my head against the concrete, disorienting me even more, so it took me a moment longer to realize he was pulling my jeans down.

This animal was going to rape me before he killed me. That realization mobilized me and I arched up, freeing one of my arms pinned behind me. I grabbed the hand that was holding the gun. The beast was stronger than anyone I had ever encountered before and his intent to hurt me focused his strength on subduing me. He tried to wrench his arm away, but I held on for dear life. My hand was now gripping the gun. He kicked my jeans away and was now trying to rip my panties off with one hand, but it was slow going because I held on fast to the hand holding the gun wedged between us. I couldn't tell which way the gun was facing, but my hand had moved down the barrel. As he struggled to maintain his hold on the weapon, I maneuvered my finger to the trigger. I paused for a split second. If I pulled the trigger, I did not know who I would be shooting, but I could not let this man rape me and either way, he was going to kill me. I pulled the trigger and felt the vibration of the shot go through me as I passed out again.

I don't know how long I was out, but when I woke up, I couldn't breathe again. Something was crushing the life out of me. With a jolt, I realized that there was a dead man on top of me. My head hurt so badly, but the need to get air into my lungs propelled me into motion and I pushed the body off me, taking in a deep breath as I did so. I struggled to get to my feet. The pain was unbearable and the skin on my stomach burned terribly. I looked down and saw the scorch marks on my flesh from the hot gun barrel. I was wearing my blouse and panties only. My sandals and jeans were nearby, so I forced myself to put them on. I had to get to the street before I passed out again. I stumbled forward, using the brick wall to support me as I pushed myself forward. *I need to get to the street*; I kept telling myself. My head was clearing, but I knew it wouldn't be for long because the pounding in my head was getting louder. I put my head down, letting my hair fall into my face, hiding it so anyone looking at me would think I was just another homeless soul and stay away from me. I wrapped my arms around my wounded stomach and hunched forward to protect it from the wind and the debris it was kicking up. Slowly, I made my way back to Robert's apartment. The walk seemed to take forever. Finally, I made it to his door; I could feel my strength seeping away as I knocked at the door. I looked up as Robert opened it.

"We have to leave now! He knows where I am," I said as I fainted.

I woke up slowly. I was so thirsty, but couldn't find the strength to ask for water. My throat was parched; I had no idea where I was. As if coming out of a long, dark tunnel, I fought my way back to consciousness. I opened my eyes and took in my surroundings. I was on a couch in a room I did not recognize. I could sense someone close by and suddenly remembered what had happened to me. In terror, I sat up, frantically looking around me. Powerful arms took hold of me and I screamed as loud as my parched throat would allow me.

"Josie! It's me, Robert. Stop fighting! You are going to hurt yourself even more." I stopped moving as soon as I heard Robert's voice.

"Water, water!" I begged and he held a glass to my lips as I drank deeply. "Oh God, he was waiting for me!" I was terrified. "Where are we?"

"We are in a hotel, nowhere near my place," he answered, watching me.

He saw the fear in my eyes and the unspoken question they asked. "We use this place as a safe house. We have our separate entrances and exits. No one saw me carry you to my car or bring you up here. You are safe, Josie." He could see fear pushing me toward hysteria.

"I had to kill him, Robert! He was going to rape me and then kill me!" He gathered me in his arms and held me close as he rocked me back and forth, trying to soothe me.

"I am so sorry I put you in danger." Was Robert blaming himself? I was confused as to why. What did he have to do with my Uncle Henry? "Peter must have had you followed. He is the only one who could have arranged such a brutal hit on you; I am so sorry."

I raised my head from his shoulder and looked at him. Robert looked away from me as he answered. "I met with Peter before I left Jamaica. Josie, he told me where to find you. He gave me directions to the beach house. I don't know how he knew what you were doing, but somehow, he must have realized you were going to implicate him. You said he..." His voice trailed off.

My head was pounding. I knew it was not Peter who had done this. It was my Uncle Henry, but something stopped me from saying anything to Robert. I could not think clearly. The horror of what had just happened to me and the realization of who was behind it was more than I could process. Robert moved away from me.

"Take these." He handed me two tablets, and I took them automatically. The fear was leaving my body, but the pain was setting in. My stomach ached and I reached down to feel the thick bandage covering it.

"Robert, the body? The gun! My fingerprints are on the gun!" If the police got involved, it would be all over. I was sure my uncle had not reached out to this man directly. That is not how my family operated. There were always layers of separation, but my Uncle had made sure I knew who wanted me dead. That scared me more than anything else. Henry had confidence in the man he sent to kill me. He would be infuriated to hear of the failure and that would make his ensuing wrath an even more significant threat to me.

"It's all been taken care of. I called a friend in the police department. He found the body and the gun; there is no trace of you. As far as anyone knows, it's just a drug deal gone bad. No one knows about you, Josie and no one ever will." He was shaken, I could tell from the tone of his voice. He had crossed a line helping me cover this up, we both understood that.

"I need a shower." I felt so dirty. I did not want Robert touching me. I did not want anyone touching me.

"Let me help you," Robert offered.

"No, I...no," I said as I pushed him away. I could see the door to the bathroom open across from me. I got up and walked through the door, not even bothering to close it as I stripped my clothes off and stepped into the shower. No matter how hard I scrubbed, I could not wipe away the feel of that killer's hands as he followed my uncle's orders. A man I had known all my life just tried to kill me—not only kill me but wanted me to suffer before I died. The realization that this was my family buckled my knees and I fell to the floor. I heard the shower door open.

"All I can feel is that man's hands all over me," I whispered in despair.

Robert pulled me to my feet; his arms encircled me. "You don't have to do this alone, Josie. I'm right here with you!" Robert's voice was full of love. I allowed him to touch me, to hold me. His hands moved to push away the demons haunting me. I turned in his arms to face him so that I could look into his eyes. Slowly I moved my lips to his, kissing him tentatively. My urgency grew as I realized how much I needed him. How much I needed to be held by him, loved by him. He understood what I needed from him and gave willingly.

I tore at his wet clothes until we were both naked, pulling him close as our kisses became more ardent. He lifted me and I wrapped my legs around his waist. His arms braced me against the shower wall as he entered me. We both cried out as long-awaited passion and emotion collided with each other. We shuddered together, holding tight as our lips locked in a never-ending kiss. We sank to the shower floor, water cascading down on us as he held me tightly in his arms. Our hunger for each other satiated, but our need was too intense for either of us to let go. We stayed there until the water began to lose its heat and I shivered.

Robert stood up, cradling me in his arms. He stepped out of the shower, grabbed a towel and sat me down on the edge of the bathtub. He dried me off, his touch gentle and caring. I did not let go of him. He understood that I could not, not yet. Still naked and damp, he carried me to the bedroom and laid me on the bed. Never releasing his hold on me, he lay down beside me. He dragged the blankets over both of us, his lips hovering by mine and held me as we both fell asleep.

The nightmares came, disturbing my rest. I must have cried out because Robert shifted to cover me with his body, protecting me from the dreams, wanting to drive them away. I opened my legs as he moved against me and let him in. He moved slowly and deliberately, forcing the nightmares away and holding me as I feel back into a deep sleep.

I awoke gradually. I felt groggy and opened my eyes to see Robert watching me closely. His eyes never left my face and I focused my eyes on his intent stare, at least until the first wave of pain hit. That is what he had been waiting for and sprang into action. The pain took my breath away. I was gasping as he put two pills to my lips and encouraged me to swallow. I did, still trying to catch my breath as I fell back into his arms.

"Oh, God! The pain!" I moaned.

"You took quite a beating yesterday, not to mention the burns on your stomach," he tried to explain. "I was able to bandage it again while you were sleeping."

"I have never felt pain like this; my whole body feels like it is on fire!" I gasped, waiting for the painkillers to take effect.

"I know, I know." His voice was angry as he held me tightly. The muscles in his arms bulged with the effort he was making to control his fury. "I called the base and told John John that we are working through the dossiers together and will be back there in a couple of days. I allowed him to call Simon and fill him in."

I did not look at him. "All the dossiers?" I asked.

He turned my face to him so that I could see the wrath in his eyes. "All the dossiers! Peter will pay for what he did to you." Another line crossed, but we had done it together and I moved into his arms. He had given us two days together. Two days to forget what had brought us together and what had the power to tear us apart. I understood this, but Robert did not and right now, I needed him too much to think about it. I just wanted to be loved unconditionally; he wanted to love me unconditionally, so we made the most of it.

We spent the time as lovers do, getting to know each other. We made love when we weren't talking. He gave me time for my body to heal and nursed me zealously. He gave me time for my mind to heal and the nightmares went away as I slept in his arms. We did not talk about love. I knew he loved me and he knew I allowed him to make love to me; that is all we could offer each other at this moment. The forces that would drive us apart were just outside the door that neither of us wanted to open, so we cherished the time we had together. He hoped it would be enough to keep me by his side. I hoped it was enough to help me save my family.

The night before we were to leave, Robert had opened the door. He had asked the major to pick up the dossiers from his apartment and bring them to the hotel. I huddled under the covers in the bedroom and refused to listen to the conversation he was having. I heard muted voices talking and realized Robert was telling him about the attack on me and arranging for a security detail to pick us up in the morning and take us to the base. I didn't want the morning to come, but I knew it would and I would have to finish all that I had started, including Robert. Naked, I climbed out of bed and stood at the window, looking at the city lights below me. I heard Robert come in and felt his arms slip around me, holding me close. He could feel the tension in my body and moved his hands slowly to try and release it. I turned suddenly, surprising him, and kissed him with a passion I didn't know I had. I tried to push him back toward the bed, but he stopped to look at me. He had tasted the tears that were falling.

"What is it?" he asked.

I could not answer; I did not want to answer. What was I going to say? I had deceived him yet again. I wanted him but could not have him. There were no words, so I shook my head and kissed him again, using the passion he felt for me to stop his questions.

Tomorrow, I would deal with my responsibilities, but tonight it was just Robert and me. That's all I wanted to focus on. Tomorrow would come soon enough and it did.

We awoke together, not saying a word, just holding each other as we watched the sunrise. There was no more time to make love or get to know each other. Our time together was up and we had to get back to the base and start dismantling what my family had spent decades putting together. I had to get back to Jamaica with John John. I had been confronted with the consequences of my family's misdeeds, and as a family, we had chosen to atone for them instead of paying the price others would have to pay. It was my job to make sure that happened, but I now realized that not all of us would be able to atone; some of us would have to pay. Uncle Henry would, Peter would, Beth would and her son, Timmy, might as well. I certainly would. These thoughts distracted me as I showered and dressed.

Robert asked if I wanted breakfast and I shook my head no. I did not trust myself to speak. I just went to him, and we held each other close until the knock at the door came to separate us. With a lingering kiss, Robert let me go and opened the door.

CHAPTER 20

DOLLY HOUSE MASH UP

We left the hotel through back doors and dark tunnels. Robert was taking no chances. His body shielded me as we walked and as he ushered me into the back seat of a large SUV, where darkness enveloped me. The windows were tinted black; no one could see inside the vehicle. Robert and I sat in the back with a driver and an armed soldier in the front. As soon as we started moving, Robert raised the privacy window between us, explaining that it was bulletproof, just like the entire car. As soon as it was up, he pulled me close, but I grunted in pain. The burns on my stomach objected strongly to my sitting position, Robert shifted so I could lean against him and ease the pressure on the wound. His hands stroked my hair and rubbed my stomach in small, comforting circles.

"How are we going to explain this to John John?" I asked him.

"I had the major tell him you took a tumble off the seaplane. He will believe that." Robert responded absently as he continued to watch the street for hidden dangers. I wanted to ask him how he was so sure John John would believe it; then I remembered the story I was told about how John John had been hurt. I wanted to caution Robert about doing that but decided to leave it alone.

"And the burns on my stomach?"

Robert looked at me, raising a questioning eyebrow. "Why would you have a reason to show him your stomach?" he asked.

I shrugged; he had a point there. Besides, as soon as John John realized I was fine, he would not give me another thought. That's how the men in my family operated and I was used to it.

"As soon as we get to the base, I will have the medic take a look at it," he said, again looking out the window. I settled in against him. The drive to the base would take at least an hour, maybe longer with the traffic, we were driving in. The heavy traffic was concerning to Robert, but for me, it delayed the inevitable. Besides, there was a question that had been nagging at me and now was as good a time as any to get an answer.

"Robert, how did you get Peter to start spying for you?" I asked. Robert turned his full attention toward me.

"What's his deal anyway? How does a lowlife like that marry into your family? He does not seem like the type of person that would fit in well. He is an addict with very particular tastes," Robert said.

"Yes, he is." I proceeded to tell Robert about my last run-in with Peter, where I put him on his back. I felt Robert's arm tighten protectively around me, but that was his only reaction to my words. "He met my cousin Beth when they were teenagers, it was love at first sight, at least for her. To him, he saw an easy meal ticket. Against all our warnings, she married him and they had Timmy, whom I am very fond of. Thomas and I love him like a son." My voice trailed off as I thought of Timmy. He had just lost his uncle and now I was about to take his father away from him. I felt a pang of guilt about that, but somehow, I would find a way to make it up to him.

"We picked him up at a brothel in Miami known for trafficking young girls. He had one tied to the bed and was beating the shit out of her when he wasn't raping her. He was out of his mind on God knows what. When he came to his senses and realized how much trouble he was in, he begged me to let him go and in exchange, he would give me information about an international drug ring. I was not sure if he was telling the truth; he was a sniveling, pathetic weasel of a man, but his intel led me to John John." Robert's voice dripped venom as he spoke about Peter. "Josie, I can't let you go back to Jamaica until he is in US custody, where I can shut him down."

"How are you going to do that, Robert?" I asked.

"I have been thinking about that. The information you have given me shows me who all the players are. If I can start surveillance on them and build individual cases against each of these people, then I don't need to involve John John or you any further. What I need is a way to get Peter stateside and I am hoping John John can help with that."

"Your team thinks John John is the key. How are you going to convince them he is not?" I asked.

"You said John John couldn't identify anyone in the photos, right?" He looked at me for confirmation. I nodded yes. "I am going to show him a lineup. If he can't pick out any faces and put names to them, then my team is convinced he can't help. He then becomes Simon's problem, not mine. But he will tell me how to get Peter stateside and how to get him to meet with one of the men we are surveilling. That is how I get Peter." Robert's voice was as hard and slightly terrifying.

"Wow, I guess I was not as much of a distraction as I thought I was," I said lightly, hoping to change his dark mood. He smiled ruefully at me.

"No, you were." His smile was so beautiful. "A beautiful, enticing and incredibly sexy distraction." He kissed me deeply and I returned his kiss.

"Then John John and I go back to Jamaica?" It hurt even to ask the question.

"Do you have to go back?" His voice was deep with feeling. "I don't know if I can let you go now." His arms wrapped around me possessively.

"I do, Robert. I have unfinished business in Jamaica and I have to find closure for a lot of problems I didn't even know I had to face." That was all I was willing to say. We finished the drive, in silence, just holding each other.

John John was waiting for us as we drove up to the barracks. He helped me out of the car. "Damn, girl, with that round kick of yours, I thought you would be more graceful getting out of a seaplane." I smiled at him as he gingerly led me up the steps. We were in Robert's house now and he took charge. He led me to my room, ordering me to lie down, advising me that the medic would soon come in to look at my wounds. With a quick kiss, he settled me on the bed and left. I waited for the medic to arrive. I could hear Robert barking orders, putting together a war room that would take my family down once and for all. John John, seeing that I was fine, had left me at the door of the barracks to join the deliberations. I could tell he was ready for this to be over and wanted to go home. The medic came in, changed my bandages and cleaned the wound. Robert had asked him to give me something to sleep and I took it without question. I awoke to find a sandwich next to my bed. I ate that quickly and fell right back to sleep. The light was beginning to fade when I woke up and walked outside to find John John and the Major in a heated discussion. Robert had just revealed that John John could not help them and Peter was now their target. The Major, remembering the soldier who was wounded while getting John John out of Jamaica, was pissed.

"Are you telling me we've been babysitting the wrong drug dealer?" The major asked Robert the question, but his eyes were on John John. I went to stand beside John John.

"You saw it for yourself; he can't identify any of the dealers. Like it or not, he was not his father's heir apparent." Robert spoke off-handedly, and I could tell his last remark, irked John John. I put a hand on his arm to stop him from reacting.

"We stick to the plan, keep surveillance on these guys and take them down one by one. It will take more time, but we can build an airtight case against each one. They will all be in prison for the rest of their lives. This information is valuable, but we need more," he said as he pointed to the dossiers. Whatever goodwill had existed when I left John John with these men had eroded in my absence. Even knowing John John as little as I did, I'm sure he did nothing to stop it. John John was fun to be around to a point, but I had been quick to realize he was a massive pain in the ass when he wanted to be.

Muttering a slew of profanities under his breath, the Major stomped out of the room. Everyone else waited to be dismissed by Robert, glowering at John John as they waited. With a nod, Robert indicated they could leave and I let out the breath I was holding.

"I see you are still making friends and influencing people, John John," I said sarcastically.

"They don't know how to have any fun, Jo. This has been a real hardship for me," John John complained. Robert's hard look told me he objected to John John's characterization of his living conditions.

"Things are fine in Jamaica, in case you were wondering." I was irritated with John John too.

"I know. Simon told me everything," John said sulkily. Now I was annoyed. He had heard from Simon, so what I had to say did not matter? The men in my family had no appreciation for what we, their women, did for them.

"John John, how do we get Peter stateside and how do we get him caught in our surveillance?" Robert asked, now that it was the three of us left in the barracks.

"Fuck if I know," was John John's response. "Now that you have made him the head of a drug cartel, how am I supposed to answer that question?" John John was obstinate and now I was pissed.

"Look, John John; Peter is your ticket home. Now I need to know how to get this asshole out of our lives and I need your help. I suggest you start cooperating." John John understood what I was saying. Aunt Julie had offered Peter up to get John John home; he knew what he had to do.

He walked over to the dossiers and started going through them, looking at names instead of pictures, something both Robert and I picked up on as we exchanged knowing glances between us. If Robert had thought that John John was faking not being able to put faces to names, this was proof that John John was telling the truth. I silently applauded my cousin for thinking to do that. Then it occurred to me that he may well not know any of these people by face, but only by name. After getting to know John John and watching how he operated, he was just an order taker like Peter. If Peter had implicated John John as the head of the drug ring, then he could not know who was giving him his orders. The head of the family drug operation was still in hiding. John John picked up a dossier and handed it to Robert.

"This is Peter's hookup in Miami. He meets with him and everything flows out from there. Intercept one of the drug shipments and Peter will be on the next plane to Miami. Let me talk to Simon. I will make the arrangements and let you know when and where." Robert took the dossier and started leafing through it. John John and

I exchanged looks; I nodded slightly to let him know he had made the right move. John John would not be talking to Simon but to the unknown person who would tell Simon when and where to intercept the shipment. Peter would be given the task of going to Miami to solve this latest problem. Peter would jump at the chance. Power and respect were both drugs to Peter and he would not pass up the opportunity to grab both and to prove himself worthy by handling the crisis himself.

John John smiled and laughed. "I'm out. There is a nice Jamaican gal that cooks in the mess hall. I will get my dinner and stay the night with her. See you tomorrow!" He was out the door before Robert or I could say anything. I shook my head. *Damn Jamaican men*, I thought.

"He works fast," Robert commented.

"Jamaican men are opportunists, Robert; nothing goes to waste with them," I said as I started to walk away. Robert grabbed my hand, drawing me to him and kissing me deeply.

"I am going to miss sleeping next to you tonight," he said.

I smiled at him sadly. I would miss him too, but I said nothing. It was time to start cutting the ties to Robert. The smile left his face as he watched me. He knew I was retreating from him.

"Aren't you hungry? You haven't eaten much today." I ignored him as I walked toward my small room; he did not need to see the sadness in my eyes. I did not need him anymore, or at least that is what I needed him to think.

Sleep would not come as I mulled over the problem of Uncle Henry. I was at a loss as to what to do about him. I still did now know who had taken over the running of the drug operation from Uncle John. I had my suspicions, but I couldn't figure out how it all worked. I could not put all the pieces together and it was irritating me to no end.

When I eventually fell asleep, the nightmares came. Robert was not with me to keep them at bay and the full onslaught of them had me drowning in night terrors. I woke up screaming to find men with guns surrounding me as Robert knelt beside me, shaking me awake. I threw myself at Robert as he ordered everyone out of the room.

"She's bleeding," the major pointed out as he left. Robert looked at him and he pointed to my stomach, where a bright-red patch of blood had appeared on my T-shirt. I was trembling, frightened by the vivid nightmares and would not let go of Robert.

"Honey, lie back," Robert said after everyone had left. "I have to look at your stomach." We both looked down as Robert lifted the shirt. I had torn at the bandages in my panic. Robert replaced the bandage and climbed into the small bed, picking me up and laying me down in the comfort of his arms. He was wedged against the wall with his head and shoulders against the hard concrete.

"Robert, you can't sleep in here; you can't sleep like that. You have to go." I knew as I said the words that they had no conviction.

"It's just for tonight; tomorrow, I will move us to one of the apartments on the base," he said as he settled in.

"What? No, you can't!" Everything would be lost if Robert got kicked off the case for consorting with me.

"Josie, as far as anyone knows, you are a facilitator; you are helping me keep John John in line. You are not involved in this case and have no bearing on its outcome. *And* I don't care what anyone thinks. I'm here to stay, Josie." He held me tightly. "I'm here to stay."

I did not know what to say. Honestly, I didn't want to say anything that would make him leave. As soon as I went back to Jamaica, it would be over, but until then...

"John John is going to throw a fit," I said.

Robert's laugh was not kind. "I hope so." It seems he had had enough of John John too.

As luck would have it, John John was not an issue. I woke up with a tearing headache and a raging fever. Both Robert and I were soaked in my sweat. The burns on my stomach were bleeding and infected. I saw John John standing at the bedroom door as the medic and Robert worked to bring the bleeding under control. When I looked back, he was gone. Robert carried me out of the tiny room to a waiting car and we drove the short distance to the apartment he had secured. The medic was with us. After giving me a shot of antibiotics, he left Robert with fresh bandages and instructions on how to bring the fever down. Robert apologized just before he plunged me into a bathtub full of cold water and ice cubes. I screamed in agony but was too weak to put up much of a fight. The water loosened the crust of dried blood and pus on my stomach, but I still cried out in pain as Robert cleaned it off, applied antibiotics and put on fresh bandages. Exhausted, I turned my back to him as he lay me on the bed but melted against him when he lay down beside me, taking me in his arms. Together we fell asleep.

I woke up before Robert did. I was on my back, he on his stomach with his arm thrown protectively across me and his face toward me. I watched him as he slept, reminding myself that he was the last man on earth I could fall in love with. I felt a deep sadness as I had the thought. He was exhausted, I could tell, so I gently moved his arm and crawled to the end of the bed, closing the door quietly behind me. The fever had broken, but I was weak and very thirsty. I drank two glasses of water, made myself a cup of tea and sat down at the kitchen table to get my bearings. Uncle Henry had to be dealt with. There was no atoning for his sins. He had to pay, but it had to be done in such a way that it did not impact Beth or Timmy. I knew Simon and John John would step in and help with Timmy. I wanted him to be surrounded by strong men with integrity and honor. Maybe I needed to take John John off that list, but John John was fun-loving and knew how to enjoy himself. I knew Timmy would need that kind of influence in his life. He was too serious for a child his age. It crossed my mind that Robert would be the perfect mentor for Timmy. *But that was not possible*; I reminded myself. I tried not to get distracted by thoughts of Robert, but he was now as much of a dilemma as Henry was proving to be. Whatever I decided to do about Henry would be my responsibility and mine alone. I could not involve my cousins in determining his fate or in meting out his punishment.

I heard movement in the bedroom and got up to make coffee. I knew Robert would need it. I smiled at the thought, ever the dutiful Jamaican woman, anticipating her man's needs. But to be fair, no one had ever needed to take care of me the way Robert had been required to.

"You look beautiful," Robert commented as he saw me. I looked drawn and pale; my hair was wild and uncombed as it fell in heavy waves below my shoulders and down my back.

I responded with a weak smile. Robert returned the smile. My words gave him hope and that was something I did not want to do. "Robert, I—" but I was interrupted by a knock at the door. As Robert answered the door, I went to put on some shorts; I was just in a T-shirt and panties. I came out of the bedroom to find the medic helping himself to coffee as Robert and John John sat uncomfortably at the table.

"Well, you are looking much better. Robert must be taking good care of you," the medic commented cheerfully. Robert continued to look uncomfortable as John John scowled at him. He did not seem to notice the tension in the room as he gave me another shot of antibiotics, checked my stomach, decided that I was on the mend and just needed oral antibiotics. Robert thanked him and held the door open as he left. John John stayed.

"Want to explain to me why you have gunshot burns on your stomach?" he asked. Robert started to answer, but I put my hand on his arm to stop him. It was time Robert understood the family dynamics.

"No, I don't," I responded. I could see John John begin to simmer with rage. "Understand something, John John. You are my responsibility; I am not yours."

"What's the plan? You just going to stay here and play dolly house wid the Yank?"

"Don't talk to me about dolly house, John John. You have a woman and children in Jamaica; my husband is in a grave six fit under. Anyone know 'bout mashing up dolly house, it is you." I could tell that Robert was desperately trying to follow the conversation we were having. One wrong word, he would be at John John's throat and that would not help matters.

"As soon as Peter is in a Yankee jail and they don't need you anymore, you and I are on a plane back to Jamaica. We have to clean up our mess there, remember?" Robert could understand that and I saw the hurt in his eyes as he walked past me into the bedroom to get dressed. When he was gone, I turned on John John.

"It would help if you would not piss off everyone you meet. We need these people; we need Robert, more than they need us and you are not helping." I was angry and took it out on John John.

"Looks to me like Robert needs you more than he needs me," he muttered, not ready to concede.

"Not helping, John John." My voice was low and dangerous; he got the hint. Robert had come out of the bedroom. He handed me a phone.

"This is an encrypted satellite phone; I thought you could use it to call your mother or Aunt or whomever you want to stay in touch with." He did not look at me. I was angry and needed to prove a point, so I grabbed Robert and kissed him as John John looked on. Robert did not return the kiss.

"John John, let's go. Josie, I will see you later." With that, he was gone. He was angry and rightly so, but he had to understand that, at some point, he would have no place in my life. John John was correct; this dolly house would eventually mash up.

Dinner was ready when Robert came back that evening. The pantry and fridge were fully stocked, so I decided to cook dinner. I opened a bottle of wine, poured myself a glass and waited for Robert's return. I could tell he was surprised when he opened the door and saw the table set and dinner waiting on the stove. He moved to the table and stood watching me. I turned to him, and it became a test of wills. Slowly he bent down and kissed me. I kissed him back. Our dinner conversation was forced.

Robert helped me clean up. As he put away the last dish, he swept me up in his arms and took me into the bedroom. Our lovemaking was frenzied, almost angry. We both had an agenda. His was to keep me with him and mine was to let him go. Our passion spent, we retreated to opposite sides of the beds, facing each other, not touching, just staring at each other until we fell asleep. Robert was gone when I opened my eyes the next morning. It was then I realized that I had slept through the night without a nightmare.

That was the pattern for the next two weeks. He was gone before I awoke in the morning, back for dinner and the same frenetic lovemaking. He was working feverishly to get surveillance in place all over the country as well as to get Peter out of Jamaica. The pressure he was under was immense. The test of wills each night between us was not helping either of us. I had confided in Aunt Julie and after a long silence I took for disapproval, she told me I had to put an end to the tension between Robert and me. He had a long road ahead and so did I. It was not likely our paths would ever cross again and it was time to go home. There was nothing left for me to do in the States and I was needed back in Jamaica. I knew she was right. It was time for me to leave.

I could see the exhaustion in his face and the strength of will he had pulled together to do battle with me as he walked through the door that night. It broke my heart. After we ate, I cleaned up and went to sit on his lap. He tried to lift me, but I stopped him.

"No, Robert, I don't want our last night together to be like this." He sagged against me; the fight left him as he understood my words.

"I love you," he said simply.

"I know, but you have to let me go." My voice was cold and hard. I kissed him gently. Slowly, I stood up, took his hand and led him to the bedroom. We both understood that this was the end and wanted it to be slow and caring, full of the love I could not admit I felt for him. I undressed him and lay him on the bed. He watched me with burning eyes as I undressed and climbed on top of him, moving slowly, allowing the passion to build. When he could take it no longer, he rolled me over onto my back, both of us coming to a trembling end as he fell on top of me, drained and emotionally spent. I held him tightly as his breath slowed and he relaxed against me. I tried to comfort him as he had comforted me, but I knew I was hurting him deeply and as much as I wanted to, I could not take that pain away from him. He was looking at me and I steeled myself to look at him, ignoring the pain I saw in his eyes.

"Where will you go?" he asked.

"Orlando," I responded. "You can send John John to me when he has completed what you need him to do." He nodded and turned away from me. He fell asleep then and I watched him for the longest time. When he awoke the next morning, it was me who was gone.

One week later, my doorbell rang, and I opened the door to see a smiling John John, pushing his way in as I looked behind him to see if he was alone. He was.

CHAPTER 21

HOME AGAIN

John John was talking a mile a minute and my disappointment in not seeing Robert at the door was distracting.

"John John, slow down! I have had nothing but peace and quiet for the last week, so give me a break, please."

"I said I am hungry. What do you have to eat?" He drew out each word in an irritating drawl. I swatted his head to let him know I was not amused. I knew he was arriving today and had prepared food for him. We were scheduled to fly back to Kingston in the morning, and my bag was packed and waiting at the door. He continued talking as I fixed a plate for him.

"Man, Robert is on a mission. Everyone is dropping like flies and no one knows what is hitting them. More importantly, they can't figure out how it is happening. *And* that is good for us, little Jo." He was almost giddy with delight. This was all a game to John John. He did not see the danger behind every corner like I did, but it sounded like Robert was taking every precaution to protect John John as the informant, thus protecting me.

"Word on the street is that Peter is singing like a bird. Anything he has to say will only incriminate him, but I am sure he is too terrified and desperate to figure that out." John John scoffed. "He won't last one night in prison." Somehow John John was playing both sides. I had no idea how he was managing to stay in the loop and frankly did not care. The fact that all their focus was now on Peter could only work in our favor. It finally dawned on John John that I was not participating much in the conversation.

"Robert drove me to the airport himself." John John put down his fork and was watching my reaction. I looked up but did not say anything and returned to eating, although all I was doing was moving food around on the plate with my fork.

"I told him that when this is all over, I hope you guys find your way back to each other," John John said quietly.

"Now, why would you tell him something like that, John John? It's never going to happen and that was just cruel of you." My words caught in my throat.

"He's a good man Jo. He is completing the mission *you* gave him like a man possessed and protecting us while doing it. That is a good man in my book," he said.

"He is a man who I have lied to repeatedly, deceived and manipulated at every turn. I used his feelings for me to compromise his integrity, as he, in turn, has lied for me! As soon as he realizes that, he won't even want to hear my name again." I was on the verge of tears.

John John put down his fork and pushed back from the table, tipping his chair back balancing it on its hind legs as he examined me with arms folded across his chest.

"Is that the excuse you are using to push him away?" John John asked and my hands balled into fists as I sat across from him. "Thomas knew as much about your family as Robert does. Thomas loved you until the day he died. But his answer was to run away and take you with him. Robert is facing all we can throw at him head-on and fighting for your survival, for our family's survival. Even when you found out what Thomas decided to do, without consulting you, you still loved him—but for the man who has gone into hell to fight for you, nothing? You can't see the hypocrisy in that?" he asked.

"Fuck you, John John," was my response.

"Fuck me? Okay, fuck me then. I'm done talking. It's your mistake to make, not mine," he said as he turned back to his plate. We finished eating in silence. I had not spoken to Robert since I left him in Washington. My days had been filled with talking to Aunt Julie and Sally, making plans. Hurricane Beth had erupted when she found out that Peter had been arrested. She was going to every member of the family, begging for help to free Peter. On Aunt Julie's instructions, no one was offering to help financially or otherwise, including her father. She was hysterical, shooting her mouth off about things Peter had told her, things she had no right to know and things that could get her hurt. Aunt Julie had moved Timmy in with my mother and Paulette. The plan was for me to go straight from the airport tomorrow to a family meeting with Beth. I was not looking forward to it. Peter suspected, with help from Henry, no doubt, that I was behind his arrest and had shared this suspicion with Beth. She was out for my blood.

The nights in Orlando had been long and lonely, the nightmares were back and sleep was nearly impossible. I missed Robert and, in this house, I missed Thomas. He was everywhere I turned and I ached for him. But it was not Thomas I wanted to talk to. I wanted Robert's advice on how to handle Beth, how to handle Henry, how to move on with my life. It was Robert's touch and counsel that I wanted to turn to, but that meant I would have to be honest with him and knowing that I could not, should not, was torturous. I had picked up the sat phone a hundred times over the last week to call him, even dialed the number, but I could not bring myself to do it.

I was haunted by the pain in his eyes, pain that I had caused. I had no right to ask him for anything or to rely on him in any way. I had walked away from him when he needed me most; what right did I have to need him now?

John John disappeared as soon as we landed in Jamaica. I had no idea how he got out of the airport or where he went, but Benji was waiting for me when I exited the customs hall. His eyes took in my tired smile as he grabbed my bag and led me to the waiting car. I was quiet as I prepared myself to face Beth. It was not going to be pleasant and I needed all my strength to deal with her. It wasn't until Benji pulled off the main road onto a back road leading to an area in Kingston that I was not sure I wanted to venture into, that I started to pay attention to where I was going. The Gardens were notorious for gang activity and drug violence. Not even the police came into this area willingly and I knew a lily-white princess like myself had no business being here. I was about to question Benji as to where we were going when we pulled into a nondescript driveway, where Sally waited to greet me. I took a moment to gape at her. Mother was gone entirely. The frumpy, aging caterpillar had turned into a sleek, beautiful and chic butterfly. She had certainly come out of the shadows and into the light. Suddenly I remembered a picture of Aunt Julie that I had seen when she was around Sally's age; the resemblance was uncanny. We greeted each other with a kiss on the cheek and a quick hug. She invited me to come in.

"Whose house is this, Sally?" I asked as we moved to the door at the side of the house.

"My father's," she answered quietly.

We walked inside to find Aunt Julie sitting at a long dining table that looked vaguely familiar, but I could not place it. I greeted her with a kiss and sat down to her left, wincing as I bent to sit down. Aunt Julie noticed the wince.

"I hear you ran into some trouble in Washington," she said, her voice hard. I had not mentioned my injuries to her in our conversations, but I was pretty sure I knew who her informant was. I nodded but said nothing as I sat down. I ran my hands along the dining table, trying to remember where I had seen it. I knew I had never been to this house before.

"You recognize the table?" she asked as Sally sat down on her right-hand side.

"I do, but I can't remember where I know it from," I said.

"It was your grandfather's table. I had it brought here after he died. It is the only table all his children ever sat at together. I wanted it to be here," she said, her voice trailing off.

Now I recognized it. I agreed that it should be here and sat back, partly to ease the pressure on my stomach and also to take in this scenario. Aunt Julie and Sally looked very comfortable in this setting; it occurred to me that this was not the first time they had been at this table together.

"Do you know who ordered the attack on you?" Sally asked.

I looked at Aunt Julie for guidance before I answered her. Her eyes urged caution. "Robert seems to think it was Peter. He met with Peter before we left and Peter knew I was in Washington. I told you it was dangerous to underestimate him." I looked at Aunt Julie's downcast eyes and realized she did not believe my attack had been Peter's doing.

"That bastard won't last a day in prison," Sally spat.

"That's what John John said too," I said as I looked at her. If she and John John were going to have Peter killed, I wanted no part of it.

"So how does this work? I figured that Aunt Julie had taken over from Uncle John, but for the life of me, I can't figure out how a white, uptown Kingston socialite pulled off being a badass drug don or how and when Sally came into play. The dossiers completely threw me off." Aunt Julie and Sally looked at each other, not saying anything. "Oh, come on! I think I have earned my spot at this table; the least you can do is tell me the truth. I am so tired of all the secrets and deceptions."

"Your Uncle John thought of everything, planned for every eventuality. I was by his side from the beginning and learned everything I needed to know from him. Even death couldn't stop him. The legend of John Rollins is alive and well; invoking his name still commands respect. There are a trusted few allowed at this table, much less in this house," Aunt Julie said. "You are right. I would never have earned the respect of hardened criminals, but sending out a small cadre of lieutenants and enforcing strict discipline made me a ghost, but one to be feared and that is how your Uncle John and I made it work. John John helped immensely in his way, but he followed orders, just like the others. I was grooming Sally to take over when John John killed Marvin; it was then we saw an opportunity to start fulfilling John's dream. Sally is an excellent spy. I will admit, you were a wild card we did not see coming, but what you have been able to accomplish has earned you a seat at this table."

"I'm honored," I said sarcastically. "Now what?"

"Now we finish what we have started. We get out of the illegal drug business; the money we make from legal drug sales will be used to build schools, urgent care centers and homes in communities like these. The money you have been able to get from your blackmail idea will help to generate jobs so we can pull these communities out of the cycle of poverty they have been caught up in. Michael joining the board of the Working Women's Association has been beneficial," Aunt Julie explained.

"Michael?" I asked. "How did you get him to join the board? He turned me down flat," I said.

"Let's just say that Sally can be very convincing," Aunt Julie answered with a smile.

"I'm happy for Michael; he needs love in his life," I said as I understood her meaning.

"Love? Who said anything about love? We needed something from him and I found a way to get it from him," Sally answered.

"Sally, Michael is a good man. He has been hurt so many times; it's not fair to use him like this." I looked at her. I was angry.

"Give me a break. He's not complaining. As long as he does what he's told to do, I'll make sure he is happy," Sally responded.

"Sally, that's cold." I could not condone what she was doing to a friend of mine, of Thomas's.

"Do you love Robert Manning? You did what you needed to do to get him to do what we needed him to do," Sally shot back. I could not meet her eyes. What she was doing to Michael was no different than what I had done to Robert.

"As I was saying, Michael, making the WWA a not-for-profit has allowed these bastards to get tax write-offs for their 'contributions.' We will disburse the money more efficiently than the government would anyway. If the government changes, it does not affect the WWA and its funding. Our 'donors' may soon forget they are being blackmailed when they see the financial benefits of their donations to *their* bottom line. It was a stroke of genius on his part," Aunt Julie continued.

"Speaking of which, I am late for a board meeting and I know you guys have somewhere to be. I will see you later," Sally announced as she got up and walked out of the room.

I was silent. The turn the conversation had taken had soured my mood considerably. Aunt Julie watched me for a long time before she spoke. "What do you want to do about Henry?"

"What?" I asked as her question dragged me out of my reverie.

"I know it was Henry who ordered you killed—raped first if I am not mistaken. What do you want to do about him?" I sat quietly as I contemplated her question. My aunt was a very dangerous woman. There was no line she would not cross. "We could have him killed; it is the very least he deserves," she continued.

"Help me to understand something. You are ready and willing to break the cycle of poverty in Jamaica, but not the cycle of violence our own family has perpetrated? Do you have any idea how fucked up that is?" I asked.

She shrugged. "If you want to maintain peace, you must always be prepared for war," was her answer.

"I am amazed at how you rationalize everything." I was shaking my head as I spoke.

"Beth is shooting off her mouth, talking about things she should not be. First and foremost, we have to put a stop to that. She is looking for blood—your blood, Jo—and that does not work for me." She was trying to get me back on topic and she was right. Beth had to be neutralized and if I did nothing about Henry, he would only try to kill me again.

This dilemma was not something I knew how to handle. I got up and walked to the window, looking out at the little garden beyond. The easiest thing would be to kill him, then threaten Beth with the same fate if she did not get back in line. I had no doubt self-preservation would shut her up, but I could not bring myself to do it. I desperately wanted to know what Robert would do in this situation and my mind ran through all the problems I had watched him handle. I tried to find the answer in the lessons I had learned from him.

"We could take away his businesses and give them to Beth. Maybe if she had something to focus on, she would find some purpose in her life. As much as she hates losing Peter, she would hate losing the lifestyle money has afforded her even more," I reasoned.

"We could, but I don't think it would get rid of their bloodlust for you." Aunt Julie shot back.

I had nothing. To date, nothing in my life had prepared me to make a decision about a situation like this one. As much as I dreaded what she would do, I would have to defer to Aunt Julie on how to handle this situation. The thought terrified me. She hated Henry for what he had done to Uncle John and her revenge would be vicious. In giving her permission to do this, I would also be guilty. I thought of Robert and how this decision would take me even further away from him.

"What do you suggest, Aunt Julie?" I asked.

"I won't kill him and he can thank his grandson, Timmy, for that, but I will make the rest of his life miserable. You have a good idea where Beth is concerned. Maybe some responsibility will make her grow up." It was clear Aunt Julie knew precisely what she was going to do.

"We should leave," she said as she rose from her seat at the head of the table. As she passed by me, she gave me a little pat on the shoulder and kissed the air by my cheek. "Brace yourself for what is about to happen," she advised. "It won't be pretty, but it will be effective." And so it was decided. As I followed her out of my uncle's house, I said a silent prayer of forgiveness for whatever was about to happen.

We arrived at Aunt Julie's house first. I heard her tell Benji to stay in the kitchen and make sure no one came into the living room, no matter what they heard. Benji understood what he was being asked to do and did not meet my gaze. I heard Beth before I saw her; she was screaming like a banshee, wanting to know where the "bitch" was. I took that to mean me. I stood by the entrance to the drawing-room and waited.

Hurricane Beth blew in. "You vindictive bitch! How could you do this to me? To Timmy? The child you say you love so much. What have I ever done to you to deserve this?" She was in full force.

Are you kidding me? I thought but said nothing. My eyes were now on the man following her: Uncle Henry.

"Hi, Uncle Henry." My voice was low. "Are you happy to see me?" I asked. The moment I saw him, a rage I had never felt before came over me. I saw the face of the man he had sent to kill me in his face and it was all I could do to stop myself from going over to him and clawing his eyes out. Beth's caterwauling was the only thing that brought me out of that hate-filled fog.

He said nothing as he moved to sit in the chair next to where Aunt Julie sat. Beth still wanted to be heard. "Peter has done nothing to deserve the charges against him, *nothing!* You are going to call whomever you called to pin this on Peter and tell them to let him go now, or I swear I am going to kill you!" Her shrill voice was rattling around in my head.

"Seriously, Beth? He was caught in a Miami whorehouse, drugged out of his mind, beating the shit out of young girl he was raping. Doesn't that sound familiar to you?" I asked.

"Bitch!" she shrieked as she launched herself at me. That was a mistake. I grabbed her raised hand and twisted it behind her back. Snatching her hair with the other hand, I threw her against the wall, using the full force of my weight to slam her into it, stunning her. It was then I heard Uncle Henry scream in pain. Keeping Beth pinned to the wall and her back to the scene, I turned around to see Uncle Henry's face beginning to twitch. His whole body was shaking. Then I noticed the syringe plunged into his thigh. I don't know what Aunt Julie was injecting him with, but it was inducing a massive stroke.

"The only reason you are not dead is because of your daughter and grandson. Jo, turn Beth around; she needs to hear this." Aunt Julie's voice was harsh and unforgiving. I turned a shocked and silent Beth around but took the precaution of holding her arms behind her.

"Daddy?" she whimpered.

"This is what is going to happen. Henry, you now have a disability and I hope your wife loves you enough to take care of you because no one else in this family will. Beth, you are now in charge of your father's businesses; you better make sure they generate enough for you and your father to live off. Timmy is now my responsibility. I will cover his education and all his needs. Henry, Beth, you both better agree to this quickly. Beth, your father, needs a doctor." Aunt Julie spoke matter-of-factly, never raising her voice.

"Daddy?' Beth was still whimpering. Henry was blinking furiously. He could not speak; the right side of his face looked like it had melted. "Yes, yes, we agree." Beth finally found her voice.

"Fine. One more thing. Peter Clark's name will never be mentioned by any member of the family again."

Beth looked frantically from her father to her Aunt and back again. She nodded in agreement as I let her go to her father. It was then I heard the ambulance siren in the distance. Aunt Julie removed the syringe from Uncle Henry's thigh and went to the door to meet them. Within seconds, she turned from a stone-cold killer to the crying and worried sister. I had not said a word and I had not moved, but I was just as terrified as Beth was.

I stood in the corner and watched the pantomime play out. Aunt Julie called Henry's wife and told her to meet them at the hospital. Benji appeared and said he had called Simon. Everyone was leaving for the hospital, but I stood unnoticed in the corner of the drawing-room. I had yet to move. Before I knew it, I was alone in the house and all I wanted to do was get the hell out. I called John John and asked him to pick me up. In a halting voice, I explained what had just happened, only telling him that Henry had had a massive stroke. I stood there in the dark until I heard his car pull up; then I ran like hell out of the house.

"Where do you want to go? To the hospital?" he asked.

"No!" I said, "Take me to your father's house." He looked at me quizzically but said nothing and put the car into gear. I was still trying to wrap my head around what I just witnessed, what I had just sanctioned.

I entered the house by the same door I had before. Instinctively I knew it would be unlocked. Everyone was welcome in Uncle John's home. It was dark inside and I made my way to the dining room table. I was shaking uncontrollably, and it was all I could do to dial the satellite phone. Robert answered on the first ring.

"Josie?" His voice was hopeful.

"Oh, God, Robert! I can't do this. I am not strong enough; I can't! I can't." I was sobbing.

"Where are you, honey? Please let me come to you," he implored.

"No, you can't. It is still too dangerous for both of us. You are all over the news down here; you would be recognized in a second."

I could not put Robert in danger. Everyone knew who he was now. The new government was touting his success in bringing down drug networks all over the United States and Latin America. To some in Jamaica, he was a hero, but to most of the people around me, he was the enemy and would be until they realized how much better their lives would be without the illegal drug trade.

"Then come to me, Josie. Please come to me." He was pleading.

"I can't, Robert." The reality of what I had just done in calling him was sinking in. My weakness could get him killed. "I'm so sorry!" There was a genuine anguish in my voice.

"Don't be. The best thing I have ever done was to fall in love with you." His voice was full of feeling. He knew we could not be together. He wanted to keep me safe as much as I wanted to keep him safe. "Please tell me you are okay that you are just feeling sad and needed to hear my voice." I could tell he wanted me to reassure myself; he knew none of that was true.

I took a deep breath and let it out slowly, "I'm fine, Robert. I am just feeling sad and needed to hear your voice," I answered.

"I'll stay with you on the phone for as long as you need me to, honey. I will find a way to get back to you; I promise I will." I could hear hope in his voice, hope I never wanted him to have. Hope, I realized, I needed him to have.

"I love you, Robert. I'm sorry I never had the courage to say that to you before," I said softly. I heard his quick intake of breath as I hung up the phone.

I was in my seat, ready to go the next morning when Aunt Julie and Sally walked in. I smiled at her nod of approval and waited as they sat down—Aunt Julie at the head of the table, Sally on her right, and me on her left.

"All righty, then, we have a lot to do, ladies. Let's get started," she announced as she opened the thick binder she had brought with her.

CHAPTER 22

UNCLE JOHN'S HOUSE

I had decided to move into Uncle John's house. I felt comfortable and secure there. For some reason, the nightmares went away as I slept in my Uncle's house. Whatever benevolent ghost was watching over me in that house was making my new life easier to adjust to and I clung to it. My neighbors were kind; word had gotten out that John Rollins's niece was now living in the house and I had nightly visitors bearing gifts of all kinds. To my face, no one showed any surprise at the color of my skin and they accepted without question that I was his niece. I suspected that had something to do with Lenny.

Lenny came with the house. He had been with my Uncle John since they were both young men and he took care of Uncle John and his home. I don't know how he found out, but I loved steamed callaloo with fresh lime juice and Lenny made sure I had it with every meal. Callaloo is a cross between collard greens and spinach and is found only in the Caribbean. It is steamed with tomatoes, onions, scallions and Scotch bonnet peppers. I had loved it as a child. As an adult, a friend had introduced me to adding a little lime juice to it and I was hooked. Every meal prepared for me by Lenny included some island delicacy that he had discovered I loved. After one week of eating by myself, I took my plate out to the kitchen step where Lenny ate and joined him for dinner. I finally convinced him that eating at the kitchen table would be far more comfortable for me than balancing the plate on my knee and he agreed to join me for dinner from that night onward. After dinner, he would go back to the step, light up a spliff and wait to introduce another neighbor who had shown up to welcome me to the neighborhood. Lenny knew everyone and everyone knew Lenny. I now lived in an area the police would not venture into, but I could walk out of my uncle's house at any hour of the day or night, sleep with the door open and feel safer than I had ever felt at any other time in my life. I credited this newfound security to my benevolent ghost who still watched over me.

On the second weekend of my being in the house, Timmy asked if he could come and spend the weekend with me. His mother had told him where I was living and he wanted to see for himself why his favorite aunt had decided to live in the notorious Gardens. I picked him up at school and drove to the house, waving at my neighbors as I passed the ones I recognized and making sure to wave to the ones I did not know. Timmy took this all in silently.

He went off to explore the house and then came back to find me as I sat at the dining table, looking over some plans for the new vocational center we were building in the community.

"Aunty Jo, whose house is this?" he finally asked. I sat back and looked at him. I had debated for days about how to answer this question. He was too smart not to ask it and I had gone back and forth about telling him the truth. I had decided to go with the truth.

"This house belongs to my Uncle John, your granduncle," I answered, waiting to see what he would ask next.

"Why would your uncle live in this neighborhood?" he asked.

"Because this is where he felt most comfortable. He helped the people in this community and they loved him and took care of him until he died," I responded.

"Is he black?" Timmy asked. He had seen the pictures around the house and was holding one of John John in his hands, looking at it. I could tell he recognized the face, but could not remember how he knew the face.

"Your great-grandfather was his father, but his mother was black, yes," I said.

He suddenly remembered where he had seen John John's face and his eyes grew wide. "This is the man that was on TV! He is a drug dealer. Why is his picture in this house?"

I took a deep breath. "Because he is Uncle John's son, so he is my cousin and your cousin."

"*What?*" Timmy exclaimed, his eyes as wide as saucers.

"Timmy, Uncle John loved Jamaica and he loved the people of Jamaica. He worked every day to help them have a better life. The way he found to do that may not have been the right way, but it was the best way he found to help people and do what he thought he had to do. His son—we call him John John—also tried to do the same thing." I was getting in over my head.

"By selling drugs?" Timmy asked.

"You see all the people waving at us when we drove in? They all knew Uncle John; they all know John John. They came to them when they needed help, like getting food, or money for school, or finding somewhere to live. Uncle John and then John John used the money they made from selling drugs to make the lives of poor Jamaicans better. It was a bad way to make money, but it served the greater good." I was at a loss as to how to explain this to a young boy.

"Like the Godfather, Aunty Jo?" Thomas had introduced him to the *Godfather* movies and they had watched them endlessly together. Timmy could recite complete scenes from each movie.

Thank you, Thomas, I thought. "Yes, Timmy. Like the Godfather," I answered.

"I guess you can't make an omelet without cracking a few eggs," he said. I laughed at his analogy.

"Was that something Uncle Thomas taught you?" I asked. It sounded like Thomas.

"Yes! Granny was mad at me because I used to make recipes in the bathtub. Uncle Thomas slipped and fell because the bathtub was slippery. She was going to spank me, but Uncle Thomas told her no. I was creative and you could not make an omelet without cracking a few eggs," he said, ready to move on to the next topic.

I remembered that day. Timmy liked to take shampoo, conditioner, soap, anything he could find in the shower and mix them all in what he called recipes. It made the shower as slippery as an ice rink and Thomas had cracked his head on the side of the tub. My mother was mad as hell, but Thomas had defused the situation and took Timmy out for ice cream because he was so upset that his uncle had been hurt.

"Timmy, are you okay, staying in this house with me?" I asked. I was not sure what his reaction would be to this new information.

"It's awesome that my uncle is a Godfather who helps people. I can't wait to meet my cousin John John!" I laughed at his reaction. *If only it were that simple*, I thought to myself. It was then I noticed Lenny standing at the door to the dining room.

"Hey, likkle ninja, want to go to the rum shop and get a sweetie wid me?" he asked Timmy.

"Yes, please!" Timmy jumped at the chance to check out the neighborhood. I thanked Lenny with my eyes and watched them go.

"Your uncle used to love paradise plum and busta manty back-bone. Do you like those too?" Lenny asked him.

"Paradise plum is my favorite," Timmy answered him.

"Den it mus run inna de family," Lenny said, looking back at me and smiling. I had never seen Lenny smile before.

From that week forward, every Friday morning started with a call from Timmy, reminding me to pick him up after school. Lenny taught him about his granduncle, who he now proclaimed was his favorite granduncle; he made friends in the neighborhood who invariably ended up back at the house to collect money to go to the rum shop for sweets. The backyard was littered with cricket bats and footballs that I dutifully collected each Sunday night and put away until they were dragged out the following weekend. Timmy started hanging out with Simon, John John and their kids. It was with some trepidation that I saw Timmy and John John bonding over Uncle John. Lenny told Timmy the history of his granduncle, while John John tended to glamorize the One Don reputation. Simon brought him back down to earth and between the three of them, Timmy learned the truth about his family in a way I wish I had.

Simon and John John had just arrived back with Timmy one Sunday afternoon about four months after I had moved into the house. Simon had offered to take Timmy back to Beth's house, for which I was grateful. Beth and I had an uneasy truce built on a tinderbox and I did not want to give her any reason to blow it up. It was usually Benji or Lenny who took Timmy back to her late Sunday afternoon. Timmy was used to the tension between us and seemed to take it in stride. As we waited for Timmy to get his things, they asked if they could speak with me. I led them into the dining room and we all sat down.

Simon started. "John John and I had an idea we wanted to run by you." I looked at him and nodded for him to go on. "About the vocational center. We wanted to ask you about its name."

Thomas loved to say that the first thing he fell in love with was my Jamaican accent. Many of his friends agreed, one, in particular, used to call me when he was having a bad day because he said the sound of my voice reminded him of a sweet tropical breeze and calmed him instantly. He was a good friend to both Thomas and me, so when an idea popped into my head at two o'clock in the morning, I called him the following day to discuss it with him.

"Hey Bri, Bri; it's your favorite island girl," I announced when he took my call. It had been nearly two years since I had spoken to Brian.

"My beautiful island princess! How are you, darlin'?" he said in a southern drawl.

"Hanging in there, Bri, hanging in there," I replied.

"Aw, man, it is so good to hear your voice. Take me away, island girl, take me away! I swear if someone asked me for anything right now, they would get it." I hoped he meant it and after a few more minutes of chitchat that included reminiscing about Thomas, I got to the point of the call.

"Hey, Bri, are you still trying to find a location for your call center?" I asked. Brian ran a paper company and they wanted a call center to help process orders for their business products, which included business cards, postcards and anything related to marketing a small business.

"We just had a meeting about that today. Why?" He asked.

I took a deep breath. "Would you consider putting the call center in Jamaica? Specifically, Kingston. We could set up a training center and you could hire Jamaican staff. They would all speak like me." I tried to entice him with that, but I was nervous. Not all Jamaicans spoke like me, but they could be taught to.

"Hmmm, never even considered Jamaica as an option. Why do you think that would work?" he asked.

"Well, it is closer to the States than India or Asia, so the hours of operation would be closer to your time zone. It would be an amazing opportunity for a struggling island and I think it is a cost-effective option worth exploring." I had no idea how to pitch this to him. Hell, the idea had come to me in a damn dream.

"It's worth looking into. Put some ideas together and I'll take a trip down there with my team and see what we can put together." This was not the answer I had expected to get from him.

———

I had no clue how to put any ideas together, so I took some pictures of available land to build on, paid an architect to put together some drawings as well as building costs and sent them to Brian along with stats from the Jamaican government on standards of education in Jamaica and underground fiber optics, which was an education in itself.

Within two months, Brian and his team were on their way to Jamaica and I was in a panic. Simon and John John came to my rescue, armed with Jamaican charm and a sales pitch I had no idea how they came up with, but included a vocational center and several bottles of rum; they took Brian and his team on an epic tour of Jamaica. Three days later, we had a signed contract with money to open an international call center and vocational training center down the street from Uncle John's house. People in the neighborhood would be given jobs there, after several weeks of training at the vocational center. Prime Minister Alan Sullivan granted the land free-zone status so that taxes would be minimal and Brian agreed to pay the staff twice the minimum wage and include benefits. Alan Sullivan also promised that he would personally be there to cut the ribbon on opening day.

Brian visited Jamaica regularly to oversee, but I had taken this project on and it was slated for completion in nine months. In truth, Brian's "visits" were to go off with Simon and John John, so I did not see much of him, but he always arrived with a check and for that, I was happy to see him. It was the hardest thing I had ever done on my own. My drive to make it successful was overwhelming and I fell into my bed every night exhausted but with my mind teeming with ideas to make it better than it was the day before. I was hoping that it would be the first of many vocational training centers for the many new job opportunities we were planning to bring to communities, like the Gardens, all over the island.

———

"Its name?" I asked. "It's a vocational center; what do you want to name it?" I didn't understand what they wanted to do.

"We wanted to ask you if you would name it the Thomas Bradley Vocational Center," John John said.

That caught me off guard and I took a large breath to steady my emotions, letting it out before I looked at them.

Simon continued. "If it weren't for Thomas's contacts, the call center wouldn't be happening. John John and I think he deserves the recognition. Not only for his contribution but also as your husband." I had not heard Timmy come in.

"That is a great idea, Uncle Simon. Aunty, I think you should do it," Timmy said excitedly.

"No one down here knows who Thomas was; it would not have any meaning to them. It should be named after Uncle John," I said quietly.

To my surprise, it was Lenny who spoke next. "Everybody knows who Mr. Thomas is, Jo. We know he was your husband and he took you to America. We thank Mr. Thomas every day! For giving you back to us with all dese wonderful gifts, you bring back wid' you."

I was overwhelmed and did not trust myself to speak. I just nodded my agreement to the idea. Timmy yelped in excitement and high-fived a smiling Lenny. Only Simon and John John understood what this honor meant to me. They quietly kissed me on the cheek and left with Timmy. Lenny walked out with them and I was left alone with my thoughts.

Thomas would always be with me. He deserved to be; he had worked hard at being my husband. It could not have been easy to marry into this family, not easy to go up against the force that was my father and aunt and stand his ground. He had given me a great life, with twenty years of peace, twenty years to find myself, to cultivate the strength I needed to come back and face a family that could crush you with a flick of a finger. Thomas's love and the life he built for us had given me the armor I needed to find my place in a world without him. I would love him until the day I died and I would spend the rest of my life being grateful for the many gifts he had given me. Now I was even more motivated to make a success of this project.

I noticed Lenny standing at the entrance to the dining room. For some reason, he never entered this room and I wanted to ask him why this room was off-limits to him. "Lenny, please come and join me." I motioned for him to come and sit at the dining table with me and got up to give him the seat I was sitting in. The sudden movement made me wince. The burns on my stomach had healed, but the skin was tight. When I moved a certain way, the stretched skin ached in protest. Lenny noticed and asked me to come into the kitchen. I followed him without question and leaned against the kitchen counter, pulling up my shirt as he instructed so that he could apply cocoa butter.

"This will help the skin to soften," he said.

I watched him as he bent to apply the cream. His hands were rough from years of hard work, but his touch was gentle. "Lenny, why don't you ever come into the dining room?" I asked softly.

He waited a long time to answer and did not look at me when he did. "I'm sorry dis happen to you, dat your uncle mek dis happen to you. I could not stop it in time, but if you had not killed dat man who hurt you, know that he would be dead by my hand or Benji's."

That was not the answer I was expecting, but it made sense that they knew everything that went on around us. Lenny was Uncle John's right hand, as Benji was my father's. Aunt Julie would want them close to her, giving her the advice and counsel, her brothers would have. But the guilt was not their burden to bear. "Lenny, I threatened Uncle Henry and he took the path of least resistance to try and stop the threat. He has always been a coward and a lazy one at that, or he would have killed me himself. You don't need to feel responsible for his actions."

"I have been with your family since your Uncle John was a young man. I watch how he grow with Henry. Henry was always jealous of how your grandfather and Julie love John. As they got older, your father and John were both cut from the same cloth and Henry envied their closeness. His resentment grew from there. Benji and I knew that one day, it would cause big trouble for everybody. I don't go into dat dining room because I am just a foot soldier inna dis war. I could not protect John from what happen to him and I live with that failure every day." He refused to look at me as he said this.

"Lenny, no one could have stopped what happened to Uncle John; it was out of everyone's control because the conspiracy was bigger than anyone could have imagined. You and Benji are not foot soldiers; you are much more than that. Aunt Julie trusts you both, as does Sally. I could not have made it through the last year without your protection or Benji's counsel, both of which I value beyond measure." I wanted him to understand he was not responsible for anything that had happened to the family. Every success and failure were a direct result of decisions we had made as a family and now we would have to walk the path to redemption together.

Lenny smiled sadly at my words. "You nearly kill Benji more dan one time when you start to find out about your family. Him and Sally try to run you off, but you don't back down. You have a lot of your Uncle John in you. Sally have a lot of your Aunt Julie in her and life has made dem two hard and tough women. I don't want dat to happen to you, Jo; I want you to stay like your Uncle John and always find love. Love for his family and love for his country push John; I need love to push you if you gwen sit at dat deh table." Lenny spoke quietly but earnestly.

I understood what he was saying; Aunt Julie and Sally would always see things through the lens of injury and betrayal. I needed to be the voice of compassion and be a counterbalance to them. I needed to bring my Uncle John and my father's perspective back to the table.

"You are a very wise man, Lenny. I am lucky to have you and Benji in my life. Know that I will always listen to what you and Benji have to say. I will always ask for your advice. You are the only true link I have to my family's past and I know I can count on you both to tell me the truth. I will need that truthfulness to guide me."

He looked at me then. I saw the same respect in his eyes as I had seen in Benji's. They would always have my back, as I would always have theirs. In me, they had found their way back to Uncle John and my father and we understood how important that would be in fulfilling Uncle John's dream not only for Jamaica but for our family as well.

CHAPTER 23

IT ALL COMES TOGETHER

I had been working nonstop. Brian was delighted with the outcome. He had met with all the staff and given a very inspirational welcome speech.

"I am truly honored to be a part of something that has my good friend Thomas Bradley's name on it. Thomas came to this island because he fell madly in love with an island girl, one he loved deeply until the day he died. He loved everything about her, but most of all, he loved her dedication, her dedication to him and her island home. He would be so proud of what she has done today. I know I am and I promise you, give me the same dedication that she did to this project and we can only succeed together." His speech was met with loud applause. He took my hand and kissed it. "That kiss is from Thomas," he said.

This time I did not feel the overwhelming sadness that I usually did when I heard his name. The grand opening was tomorrow and I was busy in the vocation center, getting it decorated and ready for the dignitaries who would descend on it tomorrow. Prime Minister Alan Sullivan was keeping his promise of cutting the ribbon along with Brian. Aunt Julie had cautioned me that it was now time to blend into the background. News coverage was extensive and she did not want my face plastered all over the world.

"We thrive by staying in the shadows, Jo," she had said as she declined the invitation to attend the grand opening. Lenny seemed to understand this and without being asked, he had arranged for a group of men to follow me everywhere, creating a human shield and protecting me from prying eyes. As annoying as I found it, I did understand the need for it. So, as the festivities got underway, I was at the back of the crowd watching like everyone else. Just as the prime minister was coming up to speak, John John and Simon joined me and my security melted into the background.

"Today, I am honored to be here and honored to be a small part of helping this community to grow. All of you working in this call center will help Jamaica to grow. You will show the world that the days of garrison politics are over. The days of violence and dependency on 'One Don' are past. We are our brother's keeper and our little island will show the world how we work together to lift us all. I am pleased to ask another friend of Jamaica to join me on this stage. He has worked hard to rid us of the scourge that is the illegal drug trade; he has put himself in harm's way to create a better life for more people than he will ever know. Today, he brings with him a contract signed by the US government for us to legally export ganja to the United States. Ganja will be used to help sick people, used for medical research. The United States government has also agreed to fund a medical wing at the University of the West Indies for the sole purpose of exploring all the medicinal uses of ganja. Jamaica will be among the leaders in pioneering the ganja medical field. Please help me to welcome Robert Manning to our island."

I watched as Robert took the stage. He shook Alan's hand. He shook Brian's hand, and then he turned to look at the crowd in front of him. Simon and John John were applauding raucously, attracting his attention and his eyes found mine in seconds. It was all I could do to remain standing. Robert said a few words I could not hear and handed the document to Alan with a flourish. Then he stepped back from the podium, applauding as he disappeared from my view.

"Surprise!" John John said. I turned to look at him, my eyes wide and uncomprehending.

"It was Aunt Julie's idea. If we introduce him as Jamaica's savior instead of her enemy..." Simon's voice trailed off as I understood his meaning. Aunt Julie had made sure that Robert would be safe and that I would be safe with him. I felt John John move beside me and a familiar hand grasped mine. Following Lenny, Robert held my hand in a firm grip as he led me out of the crowd to Uncle John's house. Neither of us said a word. Lenny opened the door, motioning for Robert to go in. He closed the door behind us and I heard the lock engage for the first time. Robert and I just stood there, hand in hand, staring at each other. Neither one could believe we were finally together.

"I've missed you," he said. I flew into his arms and our lips met and held. He picked me up; I pointed to the stairs, directing him to my room. He was gentle and I recognized his touch. As much as our bodies want to rush, our hearts wanted to take our time rediscovering each other and it was magical. When we were done, I lay in his arms, reveling in the familiar feel of his body against mine. We watched our hands entwine with each other.

"I heard you had moved into this house. I spent most of my nights imagining you here, moving through the rooms." His voice was deep and it seemed to reverberate through me as he spoke. I turned questioning eyes up to him. "We knew about this house, but we could never get anyone close enough to install surveillance equipment. We had it mapped out from aerial photographs, so I memorized every inch of the house. Every night I was away from you, I wished we had been able to put cameras in here so I could see you, microphones so I could hear your voice." His words brought me back to reality. As much as I wanted Robert here and I realized I did, I needed it to be free of the lies and deception that hung over us. I climbed out of bed and went to the window. The party at the vocational center was in full swing and I could hear the music in the distance. Robert came to stand behind me, wrapping his arms around me. I laid my head on his shoulder as I looked out at the street below me. I had worried him by getting out of bed.

"Robert, I want to take you somewhere and I need to tell you things. Will you come with me?" I asked, turning to him. I could see the concern in his eyes, but he slowly nodded yes. We quickly showered and dressed. His suitcase was in the house. I told him to pack an overnight bag, enough for a couple of days. We got into the car; I was driving and headed southwest out of the city. It did not take long for him to realize where we were going and he settled in for the long drive. Neither of us wanted to talk. I knew that the next few days would either bring us together or tear us apart for good and I did not want to rush it. He held my hand as I drove and we just enjoyed being together.

It was after midnight when we arrived at my father's beach house. I grabbed some flashlights and took his hand, leading him into the darkness that would take us to the cave. He followed me in silence. It was treacherous going in the dark, so we concentrated on getting there without hurting ourselves. Once inside, I turned on the lamps and turned to see his reaction.

"What is this place, Josie?" He looked around. It was empty now that all its secrets had been purged, but I could tell he felt its significance.

"This is the cave that hid our family secrets. All the dossiers were on those shelves, rows and rows of evidence of my family's criminal activity. Behind that bookshelf is where I learned that my uncles Henry and Frank killed my Uncle John and how his death fractured my family in a way that we never recovered from. Uncle John's death killed my grandfather and helped to kill my father," I said.

"The night I found you crying? That was when you found that out?" he asked as it all made sense to him now. I nodded, yes.

He looked around and then turned back to me, his eyes tender. "This room is empty now, honey. None of that has anything to do with how we feel about each other."

I took a deep breath and plunged into the darkness. I told him everything: how I had misled him into making the deal to save John John, knowing I was not giving Robert the person behind our family's drug empire. How I had given him Peter to set John John free by deceiving him into thinking it was Peter who had ordered the attack on me and how I had sanctioned the punishment of Uncle Henry for what he had done to me. For good measure, I also included my blackmail scheme, which was how we funded most of the upliftment projects we were now doing. "My family is everything you thought and more, Robert. My uncle believed that when men were confronted with the consequences of their misdeeds, they would choose to atone for them instead of facing them. We chose to atone instead of paying the price for our crimes and I deceived you into doing it."

Without a word, he turned around and walked out of the cave, leaving me standing there. My body went numb and I don't know how long I stood motionless before I could put one foot in front of the other and pick my way down the hill and back to the house. Robert was nowhere to be found. The door to the room he had slept in was closed. I stood outside for the longest time, but the door did not open. I knew there would be no atoning for my sins and the price I would pay would be Robert's love.

CHAPTER 24

REDEMPTION

The door was still closed to me the next morning. I hadn't called Tecia to tell her I was coming, so we were alone in the house. I made myself a cup of tea and waited for Robert to open the door. He did not, so I left him a pot of coffee and went down to the beach. My sadness was overwhelming, but I had survived the loss of love before and I knew how to handle it. It would hurt, but I would stand up eventually, brush myself off and go back to my family. There were still things to accomplish and I would learn to live with this loss as well.

I walked into the sea and allowed the salt water to wash over me. I floated on my back as the gentle waves wrapped me in their comfort. Forcing myself to focus on the moving shapes in the clouds, I stopped thinking. A firm hand grabbed my wrist and I turned to see Robert. He motioned with his head to look behind me and I realized I was again drifting onto the rugged reef. I found my footing and we stood, the water cresting between us. I looked into eyes flooded with pain — hurt I had caused. I waited for him to speak.

"I love you," he said quietly. I nodded; it was love for me that was causing his pain.

"But you can't trust me. You are a good man, Robert, a man of honesty and integrity. I can't offer you either."

"Would you leave your family to be with me?" he asked.

I shook my head, no. I would never leave my family again. If he wanted me, he had to accept that my family would always be a part of my life. He nodded and looked toward the sky. The anguish he was feeling was playing out on his face, there was nothing I could do to ease it.

"Would you tell me who the head of the drug operation is?" he asked.

"Was, Robert, was. I will tell you if you want to know but only because you can't prosecute them. There is no more drug cartel and you will never find evidence to use against them."

"Them?" he asked.

"Yes, my Aunt Julie and my cousin Sally. I now sit at that table," I answered.

He allowed this admission to sink in for a minute. He had never even considered the possibility that such an organization of brutality could come from women, come from me.

"We found love in a place where it was never supposed to bring us together. It took me a long time to accept your love for the gift that it is." Robert looked at me as I said this. "But I can't ask you to be less than the man I fell in love with, and you can't ask me to be less than the woman you fell in love with. You promised to find a way back to me and you did, but can you stay and still be the man I fell in love with? I need you to be that man, to stop me from drifting onto the jagged reef that is my family. I have deceived and manipulated you. Is it enough to vow that I will never do that to you again? Then I will make that vow! I promise to put our love above all else and never lie to you ever again, but *you* have to accept my family and the fact that I am one of them." Thomas had refused to do what I was asking Robert to do. I understood that now. Thomas must have realized what my family would eventually ask of me and had wanted no part of it.

He continued to look at me, his eyes unreadable. I was beginning to lose hope. For him to walk away was nothing less than I deserved, but I could not abandon my family now. I could not look at him anymore; I understood the pain I had caused him. I was feeling it too. I started to walk past him, he caught my arm, pulling me to him. "I can't watch you walk away from me again. I will share you with your family, but our love must always come first. Can you promise me that? Will you promise me that?"

I thought long and hard before I answered, searching my mind, my memories for the answer. I would never lie to him again. He deserved the respect that Thomas's love had taught me. John John was right; Robert had walked into hell for me and then walked right back out to love me. "I promise you: our love will always come first."

Our challenges were not over yet, but it was a start. Now that he had accepted what I had done, I wanted to tell him why I had done it. As we sat on my father's beach, I told him about the love my grandfather had for Uncle John's mother; the love between Aunt Julie, Uncle John and my father. The love Uncle John had not only for his family but also for the tiny island he came from and the realization that it could be so much more. I told him about Uncle John's dream for a better Jamaica and how committed we were to make it happen in his memory, one that I now held sacred. I made Robert realize that everything my family had done came from a place of love. I needed him to understand that this little piece of heaven, as he had called my father's home, came with a history and from that history, I had to make my future.

He had a million questions and I answered as best I could. What I did not have answers to, I promised him we would find them together.

We talked throughout the day and into the night. We were not planning our future; we were reconciling the past for the chance to move forward together. As we were getting ready for bed, my phone rang. I recognized Aunt Julie's number and told Robert who it was before I answered it.

The conversation was short; she wanted us back in Kingston to meet with her at Uncle John's house. I said we would drive in first thing in the morning and hung up the phone. "What do you think that's about?" Robert asked as he climbed into bed. I was silent as I settled into his arms.

"According to John John, my father offered Thomas a business to run if he stayed in Jamaica. As you know, Thomas declined the offer. I suspect you will be made a similar offer," I said. He was quiet as his hand caressed the area on my stomach where I had been wounded. I could see his mind working on this new dilemma. There were still so many things that could take him away from me. I was just about to drift off to sleep when he kissed me. His hands were moving over my body and it responded to his touch immediately. We retreated to the one thing that could always bring us back together—our passion for each other.

Robert took the wheel and drove us back to Kingston. We did not say much. We had said everything we needed to say at the moment. We had decided to face whatever waited for us together. We drove to the house in the Gardens. Lenny was waiting for us in the driveway. He took our bags as we walked into the house. I led Robert to the dining room and greeted all the people sitting at my grandfather's table. Aunt Julie at the head, Sally to her right, John John next to Sally and Simon, seated next to John John. The left-hand side of the table was vacant and I took my seat next to Aunt Julie motioning for

Robert to sit next to me. He took my hand under the table the minute we sat down.

"Robert, it is good to meet you finally. I am Julie Myers; this is my niece Sally Rollins, and you know John John and Simon." Aunt Julie made the introductions. Robert nodded at each person in recognition but said nothing. He resented being summoned, but for my sake, he would see how this all played out.

"I trust you and Jo had enough time to discuss the things you needed to?" she asked and Robert nodded that we had. She continued, "I want to thank you for what you have done for this family. I know we may not have been completely candid with you, but you kept your side of the deal and you will always have our gratitude for that." Sally, John John, and Simon nodded in agreement.

"With your help, our involvement in the illegal drug trade has ended, you have dismantled all the international connections and we are moving forward as a legitimate enterprise, intending to fulfill John's dream of breaking the cycle of poverty that has held Jamaica in its grip. You are a hero to the people of Jamaica and your government. I suspect you can ask for any diplomatic position and get it, especially with the support of the Jamaican government behind you," Aunt Julie said.

There it was. She was offering him a diplomatic post with the US Embassy in Jamaica. She would make sure it happened.

"With this posting, would my loyalties be to my government or your family?" Robert asked. "I want to make sure I understand exactly what my obligations would be if you needed any more 'favors' from me." Robert's tone was hard and I could see Aunt Julie's surprise at his reaction. She thought he would have jumped at the chance. I could see her face grow dark and she took her time before responding.

"Did Jo tell how my brother John got into the drug trade?" she asked and waited for Robert to shake his head no. "He was a soldier in your army. Special Ops, I believe you call it. Your government sent him to Panama to disable Manuel Noriega. Now, when I say 'disable,' they did not want him dead, they wanted him out of the way. They gave John a syringe with anticoagulants and told him to inject it into Noriega. It was not the first time they had asked him to do something like this. He understood that the US government would do anything to protect their own interests, even if it meant plunging other countries into chaos." Robert looked away as she paused for effect. I now understood what she had done to Uncle Henry to induce his stroke and who had taught her how to do it.

"He took the knowledge and expertise your government gave him and built the largest drug operation in the Western Hemisphere, but instead of keeping the profits for himself, he used it to help his countrymen. When your government perceived him to be a threat, they killed him, too, by getting the people of this island to turn on themselves. You have been involved in your government long enough to recognize this modus operandi, haven't you, Robert?" I watched as Robert nodded tersely in agreement.

"That is not what happened with your family, Ms. Myers. You came to me with a proposal that I accepted, which included honoring your island's sovereignty. We worked together to benefit both our countries," Robert countered.

"Ah, but would you have done that if we had not threatened to withhold the information you needed to benefit your country? Would you have done that if you had not fallen in love with my niece and recognized the need to protect her from your government?" She had him there and Robert looked down at the table.

"I also protected her from her own family," Robert said softly.

"Peter was never a member of this family," Simon spat as Sally and John John nodded in agreement.

Robert did not look at me; he looked at Aunt Julie. I hadn't told him that no one was to know about Uncle Henry's attack on me, but somehow, he understood that he could not correct my cousins, that they had to believe the attack on me had come from Peter and Peter alone. I could see Aunt Julie watching him and waiting to see what he would do. As Robert remained silent, she continued. "You do protect her, and that is why you are sitting at my father's table now in my brother's home," Aunt Julie said. "I know she has told you she is not leaving her family again. We have just started down a long road and no one at this table is prepared to walk away from it. We all did what we needed to do to get to this table. The question is, do we find a way to move forward together from here, or do we go our separate ways?" Aunt Julie was making it clear; this was her final offer.

My heart ached for Robert. His grip on my hand had tightened and I tried to transmit my love and support to him through our touch, but I knew he had to make this decision for himself. If it were only for me, it would one day turn to resentment. He had to make this decision based on whether or not he could live with the consequences of it.

Finally, he spoke, his eyes on Aunt Julie and no one else. "I will never compromise the United States! If the situation arises, I ask that we be open with each other and come to an arrangement that will be mutually beneficial to both our countries and honor the love that Josie and I have for each other."

Aunt Julie watched him; a small smile played around her lips. She admired Robert, I could tell. He had earned her respect. No easy feat and it would be her respect for Robert that would make her honor their agreement. "My brother John would have liked you and my brother Jack would have appreciated your commitment to his daughter. You and *Josie* have my word." She emphasized Robert's nickname for me as she said this. It was her way of signaling his acceptance into the family circle, not only to me but to everyone else who was listening.

There was still one more thing that I needed to settle. Robert and I had discussed it and we were in agreement. Our relationship was still new, there were a lot of details to work out, but I was adamant. I wanted to stay in Uncle John's house. Robert had agreed when I told him it was the only place I did not have nightmares when he was not with me.

"Sally, John John, I have a favor to ask." All eyes turned to me and I looked at Robert for one final confirmation. His smile said, "Go for it."

"I was wondering if I could stay in this house? I love it here and feel so comfortable," I said.

They looked at each other and Sally turned to me. "It's all yours, cuz. Enjoy!"

"Be careful of Lenny, Robert. When I was a child, the worst beating I ever get was from Lenny. I know Lenny love Josie, but you is a different story," John John cautioned.

———

After everyone left, I ran out to do some errands. The cleanup from the party at the vocational center was nearly complete and the call center was going to open the next day as the vocational center welcomed a new batch of students. I picked up the groceries Lenny had asked for and headed back to my new home. I was happy, the happiest I had been since Thomas died. I had kissed his picture as I had left the vocational center and sent a prayer up to heaven, hoping that he would know that I was content and had found my place in the world without him. I suddenly realized that thinking of Thomas now brought me joy and gratitude; the pain of his loss was no longer my constant companion.

I walked into the house with the grocery bags and headed into the kitchen. Robert was sitting on the step with Lenny. Lenny was smoking a spliff as Robert enjoyed a Red Stripe beer. He listened as Lenny told him about Uncle John and my father. He wanted to know them and Lenny had been happy to oblige. Robert jumped up to take the bags as I walked in and I noticed Lenny's eyes on us as Robert kissed me gently.

"Robert, I gwen grill two lobster fe you dinna tonight. You neva taste lobsta like how I cook dem," Lenny promised.

"I see you are making friends," I whispered, laughing softly.

"When a member of your family warns me about someone, I tend to take it seriously," he said. I knew he was only joking, but the smile faded from my face and he noticed. "I didn't mean anything; I was joking." He was quick to reassure me.

"I know, Robert. I know." We still had a long way to go in this relationship. We loved each other, but trust would take time.

———

Several months later, we were down at the beach house and Robert held my wrist as I floated in the gentle waves, staring at the clouds. True to his word, he would never let me drift onto the dangerous reef. He had been appointed the ranking chargé d'affaires, which was a permanent position in the US Embassy in Jamaica. One of his responsibilities was to make sure Jamaica never returned to the illegal drug trade and that the position of being a transshipment port would never begin again. Working together, we had been able to partner on several projects to bring jobs and educational opportunities to Jamaica and his popularity on the island continued to grow.

Michael had invited him to join the board of the Working Women of Jamaica Association, and Robert had accepted. Sally and Michael were now an item and had moved in together. Sally had confided that most of the board meetings resulted in her going into her office to work while the boys drank rum, swapping "fishing' stories, as she called them. I believed her when I had to put Robert to bed one night after one of these board meetings, with two aspirin and a glass of water on his bedside table. He had awoken the next morning grateful for the aspirin but not so thankful for the taunting he was receiving from John John and Simon, who had come over for breakfast after hearing about his night with Michael. They were tormenting him with the sausage, bacon and runny eggs that Lenny had prepared for them. Robert sat in agony as he tried not to run to the bathroom to throw up. Lenny had finally come to his rescue with a concoction that Robert had swallowed with some apprehension. To his surprise, it worked quickly to relieve his discomfort. He was able to enjoy the big breakfast, much to the chagrin of Simon and John John.

We were finding our rhythm and taking things slowly. John John, Simon and Lenny had all tried to help Timmy adjust to Robert being in my life. Robert and I had sat him down and given him a condensed version of Robert's role in seeing Uncle John's dream for Jamaica come to fruition. It was still important to me for Timmy to know the truth about his family, what we had done and what we were now doing. I had taught him Uncle John's credo when it came to righting the wrongs we had done and Robert was adding depth and dimension to it with his dedication to honor and justice. While

Timmy appreciated Robert's role in saving our family, he was still mourning the loss of his Uncle Thomas and the loss of his father, who had not lasted one night in prison, as John John and Sally had predicted. His full acceptance of Robert was taking time, but Robert continued to work at it and each week, the tension between them lessened.

My father's beach house was where we felt the most comfortable and where we went to be together. On Robert's suggestion, we had cleaned out the cave, removing all the filing cabinets and shelves. We had managed to turn a situation that was both dangerous and treacherous into a beautiful love story and it was in my father's home that we nurtured and helped it to grow.

Robert pulled me to him and I wrapped myself around him as he kissed me passionately. The waves moved in tempo with us. As we found completion, he whispered, "I love you, Josie! I will love only you until the day I die and for three days after that."

I believed him.

THE END

ACKNOWLEDGMENTS

This book practically wrote itself: it poured out of me from the minute I sat down at the computer and started to write after a nightmare that shook me to my core. Putting pen to paper would not have been possible without help from the following people.

Early on in the process, I enlisted the help of my uncle, Howard Finlason and my brother, Andrew Finlason, to research boats and international watermarks for me. I also relied heavily on their love of the South Coast of Jamaica to inspire Josephine's appreciation for her father's favorite place on earth. I sent the first draft to two people whom I knew I could trust to be brutally honest. Howard Finlason was one of them.

My cousin, Anna Henriques, was the second. For too many years, she has listened to my stories, always commenting with her Tinkerbell laugh, "You *really* need to write these down." Our late-night conversations about this book brought us together across the miles that separate us.

My father, who bequeathed his love of reading to me by telling me I would never be alone while reading a book.

To my "editing team" of Aurora and Joel Ehrman, whose attention to detail and dedication to making this book the best it could be inspired and humbled me.

CPSIA information can be obtained
at www.ICGtesting.com
Printed in the USA
LVHW081118180420
653957LV00028B/983